SOMETHING
THAT
LASTS

SOMETHING
THAT
LASTS

JAMES DAVID JORDAN

INTEGRITY®
PUBLISHERS
Nashville

To my wife, Sue, the woman who changed my life.

Acknowledgments

Writing a book is harder than it looks. Fortunately, I wasn't smart enough to figure that out eight years ago when I started *Something That Lasts*. I was, however, blessed to have a number of people in my life who cared enough about me to help me finish what I'd so naively begun. I want to thank some of them here: My wife, Sue, who gets me through everything with love, patience, and humor; my kids, Allie and Johnathan, who always act interested when I talk about my writing, even when they couldn't possibly be; my sister, Carla, who never falters and never lets anyone else falter; Dinah Myers, whose enthusiasm and faith have helped tremendously; my long-time secretary, Christine Davis, without whom I couldn't write books *or* practice law; Sally Kemp and Barbara Wedgwood, of SMU, who taught me how to write a novel; my agent and publicist, Tina Jacobson, without whom *Something That Lasts* would never have made it beyond Dallas-Fort Worth; author, Payne Harrison, who taught me the industry ropes; and the many family members and friends, too numerous to mention, who patiently read drafts and gave valuable feedback. I am greatly indebted to all of you.

part I

chapter 1

The Reverend David Parst sat in the long, narrow boardroom of the O'Fallon Bible Church and studied a finger-sized tear in the wallpaper at the opposite end of the mahogany table. He would have to get Maintenance on that first thing Monday morning. It made the church's signature conference room look cheap, like one of those rent-a-meeting hotel spaces.

Just in front of the offending gash, Tom Dickerson waggled a wooden pointer at a chart cluttered with financial details of the Sunday school building project. The members of the Building Committee slumped lower in their seats with each reference to interest-rate triggers and depreciation schedules. Although David was as numb as anyone from Dickerson's statistical flogging, his lack of focus at the moment resulted from something else. He was thinking about the far more intriguing meeting he was to attend when this one adjourned—the meeting with Erika Balik.

He glanced at his watch. It was already twelve thirty.

"Am I running over, David?" Dickerson was looking right at him.

"No, not at all, Tom." David straightened up in his chair. "I would like to tell you, though, how impressed I am with your command of this information." A smile lit his dark, angular features as he spoke. He made eye contact with each of the faces around the table. "I want you all to know that Tom makes a presentation like this seem easy, but it doesn't just happen overnight. He has put hours and hours into it. Please, go ahead."

Dickerson hitched his powder-blue polyester pants beneath the fold of his belly and referred the committee to a mimeographed sheet in their color-coded information booklets. David put his hand to his mouth to conceal a yawn and stretched one long leg out under the table. Within a few minutes he had again tuned out the presentation. Though he recognized the importance of sound business practices, he did not see his job as pulling the handle on an adding machine. His father had often told him that when you're building something that lasts, you shouldn't expect it to come cheap. That had certainly proved true in David's career.

During the first few years after he and his wife, Sarah, arrived in the tiny St. Louis suburb of O'Fallon in 1962, David had sometimes gone a full month without a paycheck. Always a gifted preacher, over the years he had developed an equal talent for marketing. His innovations had taken the religious community by storm. It had been a long struggle, but eventually he had led his fledgling flock from the evangelical backwaters to regional prominence. The *Post-Dispatch* had recently named him one of the fifty most influential leaders in the metropolitan area—no small achievement for a man of forty-two. Now, despite the moribund economy of the early '70s, when funds were needed, he always delivered—an emotional sermon here, a few phone calls there. His church had the finest facilities in the western suburbs and that was not about to change.

David ran a hand through his thick black hair and steered his thoughts back to Erika. "I'm sorry, but I can't make the Building Committee meeting Saturday morning," she had said over the telephone. "My regional managers are coming in for a strategy meeting. I'll be done around noon. Could you be a doll and brief me over a cup of coffee at around one fifteen?" It had not been so much a request as an instruction. Under the circumstances, though, he could not say that she was being unreasonable. He wondered if it would be awkward but concluded that there was no reason it should be. After all, they were both professionals.

At the front of the room, Dickerson lifted a pastel pie chart to the easel. He removed his aviator glasses and wiped his forehead with a handkerchief. David leaned forward, resting his forearms on the table. He tried to concentrate. His mind quickly reverted, though, to a mental snapshot of Erika's sardonic smile flashing out from a frame of shoulder-length blonde hair. He cleared his throat and scattered the image. *For heaven's sake, this is business; that's all. In her line of work she probably has private meetings with men all the time. Get used to it. This is what community leaders do.*

At the breakfast table that morning he had peeked over the sports section and, with a practiced nonchalance, mentioned the upcoming meeting with Erika. Sarah had sipped her tea and frowned but said nothing. With all the arguing they'd done lately, he realized that the timing hadn't been great. Nevertheless, he commended himself for telling her at all. If he had wanted to keep it a secret, he certainly could have manufactured an excuse. *And what is the big deal anyway? Erika is one of the largest contributors to the church. If God gives you access to people with resources, you have to court them. That's just common sense.* He looked at his watch again.

Dickerson set his pointer on the easel and took a deep, rasping breath. All eyes turned hopefully toward him. "So, in conclusion," he said, "I think the decision to go forward is an obvious one, both spiritually and financially. God willing—and if the unions don't strike—we should be in the new building by Easter 1975." He looked triumphantly at David. A relieved sigh of shuffling papers and shifting bodies drifted across the room.

"I don't know how the rest of you feel, but I couldn't agree more," David said. He smiled and once more moved his dark green eyes from face to face. "Thank you again, Tom, for your good work. I know that all of you have many other things to do on a Saturday, and I deeply appreciate your taking the time to meet. Why don't we all digest this information tonight and get together again for a few minutes after church tomorrow morning? We'll have a brief question-and-answer session. Then if everyone is ready to vote, we'll do it. If that's okay, we're adjourned."

"Pastor, do you think we should close with a prayer?" Margie Bolen said.

David gave himself a mental kick. "Oh, of course. Would you close for us, Margie?"

After Margie finished her prayer, David worked his way around the conference table as the committee members gathered their things. He found something to say to each person but was careful not to linger too long with anyone. Occasionally he bent over to whisper in an ear, pat an arm, and chuckle.

When they had all filed out, he stopped in his office and sat in the brown leather chair behind the desk. Swiveling to his right, he rolled a carbon onto the cylinder of the electric typewriter that sat on his credenza. After tapping out a four-sentence resolution for the committee to approve the next day, he reached across the desk and dropped the finished document into the metal in-box. His elbow bumped a plastic picture frame, knocking it flat.

He picked up the picture and studied it. It was a cartoon that his twelve-year-old son, Jack, had drawn on New Year's Day when David resolved to lose ten pounds. A Bible-toting preacher sweated guiltily as he stretched his hand toward a plate that held a single slice of chocolate cake. Above one ear, a tiny red devil smiled mischievously and pointed at the cake with his pitchfork. On a pillowy cloud behind the preacher's head sat a miniature angel surrounded by dozens of cakes of all sizes and types. The caption read: *Remember, it's all about getting to heaven.* David smiled and placed the frame back on the desk. He got up and grabbed his sport coat off the hook on the office door.

After leaving the church, he crossed the parking lot to the garage behind the parsonage. As he walked past the living room window, Sarah's slender figure appeared behind the sheer drapes. She was bending over Jack, her hand resting on his head.

Recently a troubling thought had flickered persistently in David's mind—the idea that perhaps he had aimed too low in marrying Sarah, that he had settled too young. Despite his efforts to banish the notion, it had persisted. Seeing her now in silhouette, though, reminded him of her gentleness, her grace, the traits that had captivated him from the beginning.

When he reached the garage, he turned and looked again. Sarah raised her hand, then moved it down and tousled Jack's hair, causing him to bound away from her. David took an involuntary step toward the scene. Then he caught himself, turned, and pulled open the garage door.

chapter 2

In the house, Sarah wiped her wet hands on her red pedal pushers. "Jack, please come back here. How can I anoint your head with oil if you keep running away?"

"It's not oil, it's water, and it's cold! Can't you make me a king without freezing me?" Jack said, shaking his head.

"All right. But when you do it in the skit tomorrow at church, they're going to use water, so you had better be prepared for it. Let's practice it again. Please come over here and kneel down—and try to say your lines properly."

Jack wandered back and knelt on the carpet in front of Sarah with his head bowed. She placed her hand on his unruly black hair. Nothing happened. She nudged him with her knee.

"The Lord doesn't look at the outward appearance, he looks at the heart," Jack said loudly. He thumped his fist against his chest but kept his head down and perfectly still. "Although I am young, my heart is devoted to God. I will serve him faithfully as king."

Sarah stifled a laugh. She put her hand under his chin and lifted his face toward hers. "I am quite impressed. You have a dramatic flair. In fact, you're almost Shakespearean. Now, do it just like that tomorrow and everything will be fine."

Outside, David's car engine ground to life and settled into a muffled grumble. Glancing at the window, Sarah caught her reflection. The morning light through the glass sparkled off her brown hair in a bronze halo. She tilted her head from side to side, enjoying the effect. Sarah considered herself plain. In reality, though, her delicate skin, high cheekbones, and wide chestnut eyes gave her a soft, subtle prettiness, the kind that grew on a person over time.

As she looked lower, her expression darkened. The bent light exaggerated the puffy rolls that had gradually risen on the outsides of her thighs over the past few years. She smoothed them with her hands, but they sprang back insistently. David laughed when he called them saddlebags. She knew he wasn't joking. Recently she had been waking up early to do calisthenics with an exercise program on TV.

"Mom, do you ever think you'd rather not have God looking at your heart?" Jack stood up and picked at the carpet fuzz that clung to his bell-bottom jeans.

Sarah turned toward him. "Nearly all the time."

"Dad says if your thoughts are clean, your soul will never need dusting."

"Yes, your father has always been able to turn a phrase."

Jack looked at her out of the corner of his eye.

She quickly added, "It's a gift of his, don't you think?"

He returned to picking fuzz.

"Is something bothering you, honey? Why are you worried about God looking at your heart?"

"It reminds me of X-ray vision. That freaks me out."

"I had never thought of it that way, but I see your point. By the way, I really don't like that expression."

"What?"

"Freaks me out."

"All of the kids say it. It doesn't mean anything."

"If it doesn't mean anything, then you needn't say it. People will think you're a hippie."

He rolled his eyes. "C'mon, Mom. It's not like I'm smoking reefer or something."

She put her hands on her hips.

He smiled.

"Listen, Jack, people are always watching the preacher's family. It might not be fair, but that's the way it is. Now promise me: no more 'freaks me out'—and no more 'reefer' either."

"Okay, okay. It's no big deal."

She bent over and kissed his cheek.

"Mom!" He twisted away from her and swiped his hand across his face.

"What's wrong? Can't a mother give her little boy a kiss anymore? Here, let me give you another one." Crouching, she moved toward him with her lips pulled into an exaggerated pucker.

He laughed and dodged her. "I think you're losing your mind."

"A distinct possibility."

"Hey, when's Dad going to be back, anyway?"

She straightened up abruptly and looked out the window. "I don't know—in a couple of hours, I suppose." The brake lights of David's car blinked in the sun and disappeared around the corner.

chapter 3

As he passed through the door of the Hardin Street Diner, David stopped and inhaled. Though a younger crowd seemed to be taking over lately, the restaurant's warm smell of eggs, toast, and coffee still reminded him of his grandmother's kitchen. From the jukebox, Carly Simon vented "You're So Vain." Two teenagers with shoulder-length hair and matching red bandanas were making out in one of the front booths.

He warily scanned the place. Other than the kids in front, it was nearly empty. A lucky thing; people were always looking for something to talk about. Spotting Erika in the back booth, he finger-combed his hair and started down the aisle, carrying his six-foot frame with the easy confidence of a natural athlete.

"Hi, Erika. Sorry I'm later than we planned. Once old Tom got revved up with his numbers, it was tough to turn him off." As he slid into the seat opposite her, he lowered his gaze to her silk blouse. It was unbuttoned to diaphragm level, revealing a milky curve. He looked away.

"It's okay. I appreciate your coming. I just couldn't get loose in time for the meeting. To tell you the truth, I've been sitting here for the past fifteen minutes enjoying the peace and quiet and a good cup of coffee. It's nice to have some time to myself. The entertainment's pretty racy, though." She nodded toward the teenagers, still clenching near the entrance.

David looked over his shoulder and scowled. "Don't parents teach their kids anything anymore?"

"Maybe they *are* teaching them." Erika looked at him matter-of-factly.

He smiled. "Frightening, isn't it?"

She shrugged.

He studied her eyes and noticed that, though usually deep blue, they appeared almost gray in the uneven light. "Anyway," he said, "I'm happy I could liberate you from your work for a while. Where's Ted today?"

She looked at her watch. "Right now he's settling in on the couch to watch the Cardinals game. Another productive afternoon for hubby."

David raised an eyebrow. "I take it baseball's not your thing," he said tentatively.

"Don't jump to conclusions. I love baseball."

He decided he'd better move on. "Well, it is a nice change of pace to go out for a cup of coffee on a Saturday afternoon."

"I'll bet you're not accustomed to weekend rendezvous with women in coffee shops."

"Actually, I rendezvous with women all the time. Most of them use walkers and can remove their teeth, but nevertheless . . ."

She laughed. "Hey, I can remove one of mine too. It got knocked out when I was a kid. Want to see?" She moved her fingers up to her mouth and opened wide.

"I'll take your word for it, thanks. How'd it get knocked out?"

"Playing hockey with my older brother and his friends when I was eleven. I looked like Bobby Hull through half of the fifth grade."

"Hockey?"

"I was a bit of a tomboy."

"You sure don't look like Bobby Hull to me, or a tomboy." His face warmed. He looked down and studied a purplish stain on the menu that blotted out part of the daily special.

"I'll assume that was a compliment. Thank you. You're not so bad yourself."

He studied the blotch even harder. A skinny, teenaged waitress appeared, slapped a glass of ice water onto the table in front of him, cracked her gum, and walked away without a word. David latched on to the glass and took a drink. After setting the glass down, he rapped his fingers on the edge of the table. "Well, I guess we'd better get down to business. I'm really excited about the new Sunday school complex. It's going to allow us to do great things for the church." He fished in the pocket of his sport coat and pulled out some folded papers. "I brought you a copy of the statistical summary that Tom passed out at the meeting."

"What's wrong, David? You can give a compliment but you can't take one?" She reached across the table and brushed her manicured nails lightly down the back of his hand as she took the papers. "Actually, it's kind of interesting to see you squirm. You always seem so sure of yourself. Now, let's look at that summary."

As he drove home, David rehashed the scene from the diner. Erika certainly seemed to have been flirting. On the other hand, *he* was the one who had commented on *her* looks. He could imagine the impression she must have gotten from that. *So she thinks I seem sure of myself? Well, I am senior pastor of one of the biggest churches in St. Louis.*

Despite a guilty feeling, he found himself comparing Erika to Sarah. Sarah was quiet, shy—so shy that David knew that some church members wrongly considered her a snob. Rigidly self-disciplined, she acknowledged no middle ground in her views of right and wrong. Nevertheless, she had a quirky wit that he still found fascinating. Early in their relationship he had thought she was odd because she occasionally laughed softly for no apparent reason. When he finally asked her about it, she explained that from time to time she simply thought of something funny. She never shared her wit with others, though. She once told him that she was terrified of trying to say something funny in front of people she didn't know. She was afraid that no one would laugh and everyone would just stare at her.

Erika, on the other hand, was no shrinking violet. She *used* her brains and enjoyed the spotlight. Her broad shoulders and Scandinavian features contributed to her air of confidence. And, of course, there was her figure—fuller than Sarah's, less angular, yet obviously firm. Not that there was anything wrong with Sarah's figure . . .

He turned his black Chevy Caprice into the driveway of the parsonage and sat for a few minutes with the engine running, thinking about Erika and Sarah, but mostly about Erika. Finally, he eased his foot off the brake. *For God's sake, David, you're a minister—and you've got a wife, remember?*

To his left, Sarah stepped out the kitchen door onto the concrete stoop. She folded her arms across her chest as he edged past. David took a deep breath and pulled the car into the garage.

chapter 4

Sarah shut the oven door and twisted the timer knob. In the distance, thunder rumbled. Through the open window above the sink she saw the trees in the backyard shiver, then go still, as if listening. The air was thick and damp, and perspiration beaded on the back of her neck. She moved away from the heat of the oven, picked up a dishcloth, and wiped it across the yellow Formica countertop.

She looked over her shoulder at David. He was sitting at the kitchen table, twirling a metal saltshaker between his fingers. Their eyes met. He turned away.

Sarah considered her words carefully. She had no interest in playing the jealous wife. On the other hand, on several occasions she had observed the way David looked at Erika Balik—the kind of looks that only a wife would notice. His coffee date with Erika had fed Sarah's concerns. She knew that she was probably being paranoid. Still, she needed reassurance. The problem was how to get that reassurance without a confrontation.

"What is Erika Balik like?" she said, her back still turned to him.

"What do you mean, 'What is she like?'?"

"Is she nice?"

"I don't know. I guess so. We don't talk much—except about the Sunday school project."

"It looks to me as if she has taken charge of the committee. She must be talented."

"I wouldn't say she's taken charge. She's definitely influential. She's an executive with a major corporation. When she talks, we listen."

A gust of wind came through the window and tossed Sarah's hair across her face. She pushed the hair back and pulled the window shut just as the first drops of rain splattered the glass. Turning to face him, she said, "Do you think she's pretty? She's certainly got a figure."

"Pretty? I don't know. I never really thought about it, to tell you the truth." He lowered his eyes.

"She seems young. What would you say, thirty-two?"

"I have no idea." He twisted the top off the saltshaker.

"Do you think she is interested in you?"

"Oh, come on, Sarah!" David threw up his hands. Salt splashed from the saltshaker across the tabletop.

Sarah quickly turned back toward the sink.

David brushed at the salt. "Look, this is ridiculous," he said. "We met for a cup of coffee. That's all. Let's talk about something else. What are you cooking?"

"Strawberry bread. Georgia Fraley is having ankle surgery Monday. I thought I would take something to her. You'll want to come with me to see her Monday afternoon, won't you?"

"Georgia Fraley? Who's that?"

"You know Bill Fraley, the custodian at Jack's school. He's always so nice to Jack. Georgia is his wife."

Thunder cracked outside the window. Rain sprayed across the glass.

"Why do I have to go see Bill Fraley's wife in the hospital?"

"You're a preacher, for one thing." Her neck grew warm. She wiped the stove in tight, circular strokes.

"The Fraleys don't go to our church."

"It would mean a lot to them."

"Please don't pull the guilt thing on me again, Sarah. I visit lots of people in the hospital. Monday's my day off. Even Jesus went to sleep every night knowing he hadn't healed all the sick people."

"I'm not trying to make you feel guilty. I can go by myself."

"Fine." He crossed his legs.

Neither of them noticed Jack enter the family room next to the kitchen. He stopped near the kitchen door.

Sarah wrung the dishcloth and placed it across the neck of the faucet. She walked over to the table and sat down. "David, is something wrong? It's not just your meeting today. It's the way you've been acting for a while now. If something is bothering you, we should talk about it."

"Wrong? There's nothing wrong that I know of. Why do you ask?" He had organized the salt into a little pile in front of him. He absent-mindedly swept it off the table.

Sarah knitted her eyebrows as she watched a granular shower sprinkle onto her tile floor. She glanced toward the hall closet where she kept her broom, but she didn't get up. She placed her hand on his. "You've not been around much, and when you are here, you don't seem to be particularly happy about it. You never talk to me anymore. I'm wondering where my charming old husband has been."

"It's difficult to be charming when I'm swamped with work. Do you know how many pictures of classroom chairs I've got sitting on my desk right now? Sixteen—and no one on the committee wants to make a decision on which style we want."

"I know you've had a lot to do. This is not about chairs, though. It's about our marriage. If you would let me, I would gladly help you select the chairs."

"You know that won't work. You aren't even familiar with the plans. I'm sorry that I can't just tell the church to stop for a while so I can take a break and chat with you. I can't believe you're getting on me about this."

"What?" She removed her hand from his. "I am not getting on you. I just offered to help."

"The best way you can help me is to be supportive. I would appreciate that a lot more than criticism."

"Okay," she said, softly. "I obviously have not done a very good job of expressing my point. I love you. I just want you to know that if you ever feel unhappy, we should talk about it. You would talk to me if something were wrong, wouldn't you?"

"Of course I would."

Sarah spotted Jack's head poking out from behind the doorway. "Jack, honey, I didn't see you there. Can I get you something to eat?"

"Hey, pal. Come on in," David said. "What do you say we watch the rest of the ball game?"

Jack walked into the room, his hands in his pockets. "It's rain delayed. I just turned it off," he said.

"How about a game of Monopoly to pass the time until it quits raining?" Sarah said.

"Sure." He pointed up. "Ceiling's leaking."

Sarah and David looked up just in time to see a drop splash to the floor.

"Go get the game out of your closet," Sarah said. She went to the cabinet, pulled out a saucepan, and positioned it under the leak.

As Jack left the room, David looked at Sarah and frowned. "Do you think he heard us?" he whispered.

"I don't know. I hope not."

Here, Sandy!" Jack squatted and clapped his hands. No response, not even a glance. Some dog.

The thunderstorm had finally let up and it was good to be outside, away from the tension in the house. He stood and stretched his arms into a breeze that was unusually cool for July in St. Louis. To the west, brilliant tubes of sunlight pierced the clouds and bored to the ground. It wouldn't stay cool for long.

What he had heard in the kitchen only confirmed what he had suspected for a while. There was something going on between his parents and it wasn't good. As much as he'd rolled it around in his mind, though, he couldn't figure out what was wrong.

"Sandy, get over here!" he yelled, smacking his hands against his jeans. Again there was no response. He muttered and started for the wooded creek that wound behind their house. The storm gutters of the ranch-style parsonage gurgled and spat behind him as his canvas sneakers squished across the soggy grass.

He and Sandy had been inseparable since the spring, when his dad found the flea-infested, half-starved puppy wandering in the brush at

Lake Gilmer. Her spunky personality had endeared her to the entire family, and any thought of adopting her out had quickly faded.

As Jack approached the creek, Sandy wobbled around on her hind legs beneath a massive oak tree that towered over the steep bank. She was yapping at a squirrel that was leaning over a low branch and chattering angrily back at her. Jack looked over the edge and took a quick step backward. The water was rushing furiously, no more than six feet from his shoes. He'd never seen it so high. The din muffled Sandy's excited barking.

He squinted up into the dripping leaves. "You're wasting your time, Sandy. That squirrel's not dumb enough to come down here." A gust of wind shook loose a shower that drenched his hair and face and shoulders and sent him scampering from beneath the tree. He was leaning forward, flipping his hands through his hair, when a high-pitched yelp spun him around. Sandy's eyes flashed with pleading panic as she dropped tail first down the embankment. The wet soil was falling away beneath her like a trap door.

"Sandy!"

In response to his voice, the puppy worked her front paws frantically in the crumbling earth, and for a moment seemed to slow her fall. But it was hopeless. In the next instant she was gone.

Jack sprang toward the bank and scanned the water. Sandy was nowhere in sight. He sprinted downstream, then stopped to thrash at the prickly brush and look through to the creek below. Just as he pushed his head between two shrubs, he heard a faint whine. Soaked and muddy, Sandy was clinging to a spindly tree that jutted at a forty-five-degree angle from the opposite creek wall. She strained to pull herself onto the tree, but the current was grabbing her hind legs, trying to sweep her away.

The closest place for Jack to get across was at least five hundred yards downstream. He looked around for options. There were none.

DAVID SLOGGED THROUGH THE MUD along the side of the house, dragging a ladder under one arm and holding a hammer and jar of roofing nails in his free hand. After an hour of watching rainwater drip from the kitchen ceiling, he was going to fix that leak if he had to climb on the roof and plug it with his thumb. Besides, he was looking forward to the time out of the house. He needed to ponder some things— things that were difficult to think about with Sarah close by.

What attracted him so much to Erika (and he had to admit to himself that he was attracted) was her self-confidence. She was a woman of achievement. He felt that he had reached a point in his own career where he could legitimately consider himself to be a man of achievement. Erika had practically told him as much at the diner.

He wondered whether, under different circumstances, he would have chosen a woman like Erika instead of Sarah—that is, if he had known what he would become. But he hadn't known. He had chosen Sarah, and he *did* love her. He knew that what he was experiencing was temptation, plain and simple. But he could handle it. Still, it was somehow thrilling to wonder . . .

As he rounded the corner of the house he saw Jack standing at the creek, peering through the shrubs. David was just opening his mouth to yell at his son to get away from there when Jack took several steps back, ran and leaped into the water.

HURTLING DOWNWARD, Jack instinctively pulled himself into a crouch. When he splashed into the creek, the cold rainwater shocked the air from his lungs. He came up gulping. As the current swept him past

Sandy, he reached out and locked his arm around the tree above her head, painfully scraping a patch of skin from his forearm. Wrapping his other arm around her, he pinned her against the tree.

"It's okay, girl," he said, his voice shaking. He yanked his leg against the current and swung it over the base of the tree trunk. Then he sat up, straddling the tree with his back pressed against the muddy creek wall. He pulled Sandy to his chest.

"Jack! Are you okay?"

Jack looked up and saw his dad, hands on his knees, peering across the creek from the opposite bank.

"Don't move a muscle!" his dad shouted. "I'll get across downstream and come get you!"

"Oh, brother, Sandy. We're gonna get it this time," Jack said. He pressed his stinging forearm against his side, leaving a red splotch on his soaked shirt.

His leg was beginning to feel numb, so he shifted his weight and transferred Sandy to his other arm. The little tree shuddered beneath him. Then, before he could react, the roots tore away from the soggy soil. The tree lurched and crashed into the water. It bobbed tentatively, then rolled, pitching Jack and Sandy into the stream.

When they hit the water, somehow Jack kept Sandy wrapped in the crook of his arm, like a football. To his right he spotted the little tree. Caught in an eddy, it was bouncing and twisting like a tennis shoe in a washing machine. He grabbed it with his free hand just as the water carried them past. He maneuvered Sandy's front legs over the tree trunk.

The tree shot out into the middle of the creek, dragging Jack and Sandy sputtering up and down through the water. Sandy's legs slid off the trunk. He tightened his grip and pulled her back up. The current ripped at his hands and arms. He was swallowing so much filthy water that he could feel the grit crunch between his teeth.

Knowing that he couldn't hold on to Sandy and the tree trunk for long, he looked at the bank, not twenty feet away. *God, please don't let us die.* He took a deep breath, clutched Sandy to his side, and released his grip on the tree. Kicking away, he windmilled his arm in a lopsided backstroke. They went nowhere.

The current clenched him and rolled its weight on him, wearing him down. He thrashed at the water. *Dad! Where are you?* His head slid under. The cold darkness jolted him. He fought his way back up, sucking in air and foam as he reached the light. Again the current pushed him under. He kicked and strained and broke through to the light once more. Finally the current's strength overwhelmed him. Every muscle in his body burned. He tried to fight, but he could barely move his arms. His hope gave out. He allowed himself to slip beneath the surface.

As he loosened his grip on Sandy he felt a thud against his side, like a strong branch, wrapping securely around his waist and pulling them both out of the water.

"I've got you, Jack. I won't let go." It was his dad's voice, and it was his dad's arm, pulling them, coughing, to safety.

Jack wanted to talk, to thank his father, to tell him he believed him when he said he would never let go. But he couldn't say anything. He just wrapped his arms around his dad's neck, held on, and cried.

THAT NIGHT DAVID AND SARAH TUCKED JACK IN, despite his protests that they were treating him like a baby. When they returned to their room and got into bed, neither of them spoke for a while. David lay on his back and crossed his arms over his chest. He had been wondering all evening whether it had been his fault that Jack ended up in the water. After all, God couldn't be pleased with the thoughts he had been entertaining lately. It was one thing to be tempted. It was another thing to dwell on it, to find titillating pleasure in it. He shook the notion out of his head. He simply didn't believe the Lord threw kids into flooded streams to teach parents a lesson.

Sarah rolled onto her side, facing David. "It's so frightening I can't make myself think of it," she said. "Thank God you were in the right spot to save him. What would we have done?"

"I don't know."

"I have this awful feeling, David. I'm so afraid." She placed her hand on his shoulder.

"So am I. I suppose that's natural after something like this. It will probably take a while for us to unwind."

"No, not just this. I mean us—our family. I have this sense that everything is slipping away, that nothing is secure anymore."

He took her hand in his and turned to look into her eyes. "It will be all right. God gave us a gift today. Jack is safe. That's the most important thing."

"I love you, David."

He moved his hand to her cheek. "Things will get better now, Sarah. You'll see."

Before long he heard her breathing settle into a slow rhythm. Rolling onto his back, he stared at the ceiling. Sarah was right. Life had been crazy lately. He had to take control—starting with Erika. From now on he would be self-disciplined, all business. A few more meetings and they'd be done with the planning for the building project. Then everything would return to normal. Jack was okay. That was what mattered. *Thank you, God, for saving my son. I'm going to change. I promise.*

Soon his breathing slowed and fell into step with Sarah's. A collage of thoughts moved in and out of his consciousness before coalescing into a single vivid dream . . .

David reached down from the sparkling gold rail of an ivory sailboat and desperately grabbed at his son's extended hand. A massive wave lifted Jack and hurled him against the side. In an instant the wave disintegrated. Jack fell, flailing. David leaned over the side and snagged the boy under the armpits. He hoisted him toward the dazzling ship. Just before David got him over the side, David's arms inexplicably went limp. Jack slid back toward the water. David clawed at him, digging into his son's skin until it bled. But his hands had no strength. As Jack slipped into the sea, the boy raised his head and searched his father's face, as if puzzled at how things could possibly have come to this. David lunged at Jack one more time. When their eyes met, David recoiled. The person looking up at him with terrified eyes was no longer Jack. It was David.

David lurched from his sleep. He raised his head, blinked his eyes against the blackness, and looked around the room. Sarah was still sleeping next to him. He dropped his head to the pillow. Jack was fine. He was in his room, safe in his bed.

Hours passed before David fell back to sleep. He shuffled and tossed under the sheets as he committed himself over and over to change. He recalled a Bible verse, something the apostle Paul had said, he thought. Or was it Peter? *Resist Satan and he will flee from you.* He would resist. He had to. Despite his resolve, though, he remained uneasy as sleep finally enveloped him. Like Sarah, he couldn't shake the feeling that things were slipping away.

chapter 6

Jack watched the ball over his shoulder as his shoes pounded across the patchy grass. "I'll get it this time," he yelled. His legs and arms pumped furiously. The ball reached the peak of its trajectory and began to drop, passing directly over his head. At the last moment he stretched out his glove. The toe of his shoe stubbed a clump of grass. He tumbled onto his side and rolled, raising a cloud of dust. The ball fell six feet beyond him, wobbled, and nestled into the grass. He stood up and scowled. Reaching down, he picked up the ball, wheeled, and heaved it.

In the middle of the vacant lot, David instinctively raised his glove to catch Jack's throw. He lowered it as the ball sailed hopelessly out of reach.

"What in the world was that?" David said.

Jack's shoulders drooped. "I'm never gonna get this. It's too hard. Can you just throw me some easy pop-ups?"

It had been three weeks since David fished Jack out of the creek. They were in their usual spot, across the street from the parsonage. And they were playing their usual game—David providing instruction

31

and throwing an assortment of flies and grounders to Jack. They'd been playing ball together since Jack was three years old. The boy's skills had developed quickly. He had inherited the hand-eye coordination that had helped his dad play shortstop in the minor leagues.

An inability to hit first-rate breaking pitches had ended David's baseball career. That's when he had settled for the ministry. His father had been a minister, and a good one. Practically raised in a church, David had never questioned his faith. But he had dreamed of being a major-league ballplayer, not a pastor.

David walked over and picked up the ball. "Sure, we can do some easy pop-ups. Sooner or later, though, you've got to learn to do this. You'll never be outstanding at catching a ball that's hit over your head until you learn to take your eye off it and then pick it up again. Don't get so frustrated. It's not the sort of catch a player learns to make in one day."

"Why is it so important anyway?" Jack said, as he jogged over to his father. "I catch the ball fine my way. Besides, my coach told me I should always keep my eye on the ball."

"That's good advice. There is only one exception that I can think of—the ball hit over your head. It's the one play where you have to take your eye off the ball and have faith that it will still be there when you look back up. It is simply impossible to run as fast while looking over your shoulder as you can while looking straight ahead."

Jack shaded his eyes and looked skeptically at his father.

"Trust me on this," David said. "The ball will be there. I've made lots of over-the-shoulder catches in my life. But don't wait too long to look up for it. If you do, the ball may fall right in front of your feet. Instead of catching it you'll stumble over it and fall on your face."

Jack smacked his palms against the legs of his jeans. Dust puffed into the air. "I can fall on my face doing it my way," he muttered.

"It takes some work, but once you learn to do this you'll never forget. Sometime, when the pressure's on and you really need to make the catch, you'll find that your training takes over. You can do this, Jack. I've got confidence in you. But if you want some easy ones, I'll throw you some."

David lobbed the ball underhand. It dropped at Jack's feet. "There, how's that?"

"Very funny." Jack picked up the ball and slapped it into the pocket of his glove. "So you think I can't learn this in one day, huh?" He tossed the ball to David.

"I just said it's not the kind of thing . . ."

"Oh yeah? Watch this." Jack turned and trotted away from David. "Throw it over my head. If I catch it, you owe me a Dairy Queen," he said, over his shoulder.

David pivoted onto his right foot and brought his arm back. He imitated the voice of Jack Buck, the St. Louis Cardinals' play-by-play announcer. "It's a long fly ball," he shouted. He squinted into the late Sunday afternoon sun and threw the ball in a long, looping arc, trying to place it just where he figured Jack's outstretched glove would reach.

Jack eyed the ball as it left David's hand. Then he turned his back on it and sprinted. Behind him the ball curled upward, seemed to pause, and then hurtled toward the ground.

David continued his play-by-play. "The hitter really smoked this one, folks. It's way over Parst's head. I don't think he can get to it."

At the last moment, Jack turned and looked over his shoulder. The ball was ten feet away and falling fast. He followed it over his shoulder and stretched out his glove. The ball settled softly into the webbing.

David threw his hands into the air. "Parst, the young rookie from O'Fallon, makes a sensational grab! Who would have believed he could get to that one! Listen to the crowd!" He cupped his hands in front of his mouth and made a classic roaring-masses sound. "*Aaahhh! Aaahhh!* They love this Cardinal rookie in St. Louis! *Aaahhh!*"

Jack turned and fired the ball back to his dad.

David grinned as he watched Jack trot toward him. "Great catch. I think you've figured it out."

"Just like Curt Flood," Jack shouted, referring to the Cardinals' former Gold Glove center fielder.

"Yeah, right. Don't get a big head. Remember, pride goes before a fall."

"Huh?"

"That's what King Solomon said. It means that if you get cocky, you're in for big trouble."

"Geez, I was just joking about Curt Flood, Dad."

"I know."

"You must have made a million catches like that," Jack said. "I'll bet you were the best shortstop in the whole minor leagues." He tossed the ball to David.

"I made a few catches, I guess. Unfortunately, I also only made a few hits." David chuckled and swept a thick shock of hair off his forehead. He carefully tucked his beat-up old glove under his arm. He looked at his watch. "It's time to go in or we'll be late for the evening service." His mind had already turned to the meeting Erika had scheduled for them at the architect's office after church.

Erika had arranged for one of the finest architects in St. Louis to design the new Sunday school complex, and at a cut rate. As she pointed out, when the guy did twenty stores a year for her company, how was he going to say no? The trade-off, she had said, was that they had to arrange things around the architect's schedule. Still, a Sunday-evening meeting was unusual. He had considered saying no, but how could he miss a meeting with the architect?

He hadn't exactly lied to Sarah about it. He had told her the Architectural Subcommittee was attending the meeting. Technically there wasn't an Architectural Subcommittee. Essentially, Erika filled that role. He felt bad about the half-truth, but didn't see what else he could do. Since the day at the creek, he'd focused on being more attentive to Sarah, and things were getting better between them. Sarah seemed happy again. When thoughts of Erika pushed into his mind—and they still did with alarming frequency—he pushed them right back out. There was no use causing a stir. If he could get through this one meeting, everything would be all right.

David and Jack walked to the edge of the curbless street. The windows of their tan brick house stared across the road at them from beneath a hood of towering elms. A hundred yards to the right of the house, across the asphalt chasm of the church parking lot, the white steeple of their sprawling church pointed expectantly upward.

They waited for a VW Beetle to sputter haltingly by and then crossed the street. David did some coaching on the way. "Remember to run on your toes when you go after a fly ball." They arrived at the front stoop of the house and stopped. "If you run heel-toe, your head will wobble around all over the place, and the ball will bounce around in your line of sight; but if you stay up on your toes, your head will stay still and the ball will stay steady."

"That's what I did that time, and it worked," Jack said. He tossed the ball into the air and caught it one last time before they walked up the three concrete steps onto the tiny front porch.

"I guess I owe you a Dairy Queen," David said. "But, actually, I never agreed to that bet."

"You did too. Anyway, I deserve a Dairy Queen for that catch!"

"I suppose you do. It may not be tonight, though. Now you'd better go clean up."

David held open the screen door. Jack ran into the house. Sarah was sitting on the couch in the family room, reading. David ducked his head and hurried past her without speaking. He didn't see her lower her magazine and watch him walk down the hall.

AFTER CHURCH, Jack and Sarah sat at the kitchen table eating peanut butter sandwiches.

"Can't you and I go to Dairy Queen tonight?" Jack said.

"Let's wait until your father can go with us later this week."

"We could go twice."

"You are a born negotiator." She reached over and squeezed the back of his neck.

"Is Dad coming home before he goes to his meeting?"

"He had better or he'll be walking." She pointed to the car keys dangling from the hook on the wall next to the back door. "Why don't you run into your room and get that shirt with the missing button? I'll sew it on tonight so you can wear it to Bobby's birthday party tomorrow. Please grab my sewing basket out of the hall closet too."

"Sure, Mom." Jack hopped up from his chair.

After he left the room, Sarah leaned forward and massaged her temples. Things had been going so well until today. David had been spending more time at home, and he was talking to her again. That was a big improvement in itself. The evening before, he had even reached over and held her hand while they were watching TV. This business about a Sunday night meeting had been an unpleasant surprise.

She sat back in her chair. She had never lied to David. There was nothing else to do but to assume that he would never lie to her.

The front door creaked open. David's footsteps approached across the living room. When he entered the kitchen, Sarah looked up at him. He looked away.

"I've got to run," David said. "I'm late for the meeting at the architect's. I don't know how long it will last, so don't wait up." He walked to the back door and took his keys off the hook.

Sarah stood. "David, do you have to go? It's late. Surely the committee can handle just one meeting without you?"

"Please don't do this, Sarah. I don't want to go anymore than you want me to. You know I can't miss this meeting."

She opened her mouth, but before she could say anything he was out the door.

Jack walked into the room carrying his shirt and the sewing basket. He stopped when he saw the look on his mother's face. "Mom, is there something wrong with Dad?"

"No, Jack, your father is fine." She forced a smile. "We're all fine. You had better go take your bath."

As he walked out of the kitchen, Jack looked over his shoulder at his mother. She was staring at the back door.

chapter 7

David strained in the fading light to make out the numbers on the row of flat brick office buildings that lined Tempe Street. Before he found the right number, he spotted Erika's Camaro convertible idling at the curb next to the painted white sign that identified *Selig & Associates, Architects.*

As he pulled in behind her car, Erika got out and strolled toward him. Her blonde hair swung about her shoulders with each stride. Hip-hugger bell-bottoms wrapped tightly around the firm curves of her thighs. David made a conscious effort not to stare at her low-cut peasant blouse. He was torn between regret that he had come at all and regret that he hadn't changed into something more "hip" for their meeting. He reached up and loosened his tie.

"Bill's not here yet. I tried the door already," she said as she neared the car.

David looked at his watch. He was fifteen minutes late himself. "Do you think he forgot?"

"I don't know. He's probably just running behind. Why don't you come sit in my car? It's nice tonight with the top down, and I've got a new eight-track, *Solid Gold Elvis.* I love Elvis. Always will."

"Maybe we should call," David said as he opened the door and got out of the car.

She squeezed her hands into the slits of her back pockets and shrugged. "I'm sure he's just running a little late. He's brilliant, but the absent-minded professor type."

They walked back to her car and slid into the front. She punched a button on the stereo. An instant later they were listening to "Suspicion" while the last rays of sunlight flickered and then faded off the hood of the car.

"A beautiful night, Elvis, the top down—this is tough to beat, isn't it?" she said.

"Too bad Bill Selig isn't here to enjoy it with us." David looked at his watch again.

"I wouldn't be surprised if he forgot to write it in his calendar," she said. "There's a parking lot in the back. Do you want to pull around and see if maybe he came in that way?"

David looked up and down the street. He knew that he should get out of the car. For some reason, though, his hands didn't move toward the door handle. "There would surely be some lights on if he did."

"It's worth a try," she said.

Before he could react, she put the car in gear and gunned it away from the curb. David's head snapped back. He looked at her and smiled. "Like to drive fast, Mario?"

"Sorry. I guess fighting rush-hour traffic every day has made an animal out of me." She zipped the car around the corner. "What did Sarah think of your meeting me like this?"

"I didn't exactly tell her."

She looked at him out of the corner of her eye. "Oh? I didn't exactly tell Ted either."

They pulled into the parking lot in back of the building. It was empty. After wheeling into a parking space, Erika switched off the ignition and turned toward him.

"I hope you don't mind my saying this, but I've always been curious about you and Sarah. What I mean is, you seem so different. She seems sort of quiet, uptight. And you're . . . well, not."

He laid his head back on the headrest. After a few moments, he looked at her and said, "I don't mind. You're not telling me anything I don't already know. I remember my friends saying that of all the women I'd dated, the one they never expected me to marry was Sarah." He turned and stared through the windshield at the red brick wall of the office building. He felt as if he had already somehow cheated on Sarah just by talking about her this way.

"So why did you marry her? Wait, I guess that sounded bad. I mean, obviously she's a great woman. But with you two being so different . . ."

"Why did I marry her? Because she's better than I am. She's made me a better person—softened me."

"Unless I miss my guess, softening you was no small feat."

He chuckled. "That's true. After all, I practically lived in locker rooms for most of the first half of my life. If you'd ever spent much time around high-strung, foulmouthed guys, you would know that it's not exactly the ideal place to prepare for the ministry."

"Oh, yes. I had heard you were a big star baseball player."

David wasn't certain whether she was impressed or just teasing. "Not a star, just a guy who could field a grounder but couldn't hit a curve. There are hundreds of us, believe me."

"You're being modest, I'm sure. How did you end up in the ministry?"

"My dad was a preacher—he was a great man, my dad—he died just after my first year in the minor leagues. When I realized I was never going to get a shot at the majors, it just seemed like the ministry was the natural thing to do. I can't say that I ever really gave it that much thought."

"When did Sarah come into the picture?"

"She's been there for most of it. We got married when I was in Double-A ball in the Chicago area. Her father owned a company that provided all the uniforms, socks, and stuff to the Cubs organization. They were well off. Her dad was a nice guy, a big baseball fan. He always liked me. He died about a year ago."

"Oh, so you're rolling in inherited dough?"

David cocked his head and looked at her. She didn't flinch. He decided to ignore the question. "Sarah could have had it easy. She quit college—she's very bright, you know—and basically supported us while I bounced around from town to town on old beat-up buses. I think her mother believed I was one step above a bum. She had always wanted Sarah to marry a doctor or lawyer. Anyway, I was only home half the time, and the living was tough. That's the way the minor leagues are. It's not very glamorous."

"Don't worry, 'glamorous' was not the word I had in mind."

"After my baseball career washed out, Sarah put me through seminary. She never complained, though, even when we were living on peanut butter and jelly. She just did it. I told you she's better than I am."

Erika looked at him and laughed. "Wow, and I have to tell you, I agree."

"Thanks a lot. I like you too" He rested his arm on the car door and ran his hand through his hair. "We were just kids. There's so much of life we missed by marrying so young."

"I didn't know preachers were allowed to say things like that."

He turned toward her. "You know, I get tired of people thinking that if you're a preacher you have to act like Saint Paul all the time."

"I see your point. It must be a downer to be in a job that requires you to be good."

"To be honest, sometimes I don't feel like being good. And sometimes Sarah's goodness wears me out. I find myself wishing she would do something wild or completely selfish, just to take the pressure off."

"Something wild, huh? That's interesting." She moved a finger to the neckline of her blouse, slipped it under the elastic, and slid it slowly from side to side. "You said you didn't 'exactly' tell Sarah what you were doing tonight. What *did* you tell her?"

"That I was meeting with the Architectural Subcommittee." Though fascinated by what she was doing with her finger, he forced himself not to look.

"I guess that would be me." Her hand glided down the outside of her blouse to the top of her thigh. David followed it from the corner of his eye.

"What 'exactly' did you tell Ted?" he said.

"That I was meeting the architect. I didn't mention that anyone else would be here."

"I suppose it's accurate to say that neither one of us was exactly truthful."

"David, does it seem to you that we're acting like two people who are doing something they shouldn't be doing—but without actually doing it?"

"There's a reason I'm acting that way. I'm feeling guilty."

She put her hand on his shoulder. "Let me put it another way. If you're going to feel guilty anyway, don't you think you might as well earn it?"

He sat for a moment, looking straight ahead. Then he reached up and lifted her hand off his shoulder. "Look, Erika. You're a beautiful, talented lady. But I'm a married man—a preacher at that—and you're a married woman. I think it's time we got out of here before we get ourselves into some trouble that neither one of us needs." He stepped from the car and swung the door shut. "I'll walk to my car."

"Okay, Saint Paul, anything you say. But I didn't get where I am by giving up easily. I'll be back, and my guess is that you will be, too." She started the car and put it in reverse. "If you ask me, you need to think about taking your own advice—try something wild for a change."

David watched her back the car out of the space. "You're wrong," he said, under his breath. "I won't be back. I've got too much to lose." But, though he wanted to turn away, he followed her with his eyes as the car spun out of the parking lot. For the briefest moment, he imagined what might have happened if he had allowed himself to be wild, just this once. And for that moment, he wished more than anything that he had stayed in her car.

chapter 8

While holding the phone to her ear with one hand, Sarah swept her other hand over the bedspread, smoothing the wrinkles. "Yes, Mother, I'm certain," she said. "I just read the situation wrong. Why is that so hard for you to accept? Frankly, I am a little bit ashamed of myself. At one point I actually called the golf course to check up on him when he told me he was playing with some friends."

"Well, was he?" said her mother, Elizabeth, from the other end of the line.

"Of course he was, and I felt extremely foolish."

"Don't be ridiculous, dear. What woman wouldn't have been suspicious? If you ask me, he has been acting like a big jerk. Besides, what makes you suddenly so certain that nothing *is* going on?"

"Sometimes I think you wish that there were!"

"Let's not get into that," Elizabeth said. "I know you think I don't like David. I have defended myself enough on that point."

Sarah picked up a pillow. As she straightened her back, she felt the same tingling in her left leg that she had noticed several times during the past month. She shook her leg, then tapped her foot on the floor. "All I know is that he's been a model husband the past two weeks— since the night that he met with, or was supposed to meet with, the architect. Just this week he sent me flowers for no reason at all. That's a pretty good sign, wouldn't you say?"

"Maybe. Could be guilt."

"Mother!"

"All right, it is a good sign. Has he been home much, or is he still working all of the time?"

"He's still working a lot. I think I'm just going to have to accept that, though, with the building project going." Sarah shifted the phone to her shoulder and struggled to keep the cord out of the way as she fluffed the pillow between her hands.

"Well, I suggest you lay down the law to him on that. Church or no church, he needs to spend time with his family."

"He's trying. He promised that this afternoon we would all go to the zoo."

"That sounds nice. Jack must be looking forward to it."

"Actually, Jack says the zoo is for little kids. He's going through an 'I'm nearly a grown-up' phase."

"Once he gets there, he will love it."

"Gets where? Grown up? Or the zoo? If you mean the former, I'm not so certain."

"Sarah, sometimes your sense of humor is too strange for words. You are so like your father."

"Whoops, I hear David coming in the door, Mother. I've got to run. Love you."

As she hung up, Sarah tapped her foot on the floor again; the tingling continued. She made a mental note to call Doctor Schiffman after Jack started back to school.

STANDING IN THE LIVING ROOM with Jack and David, Sarah tried to collect herself before speaking. She didn't want to make a scene in front of Jack, but she could hardly contain her surprise at what David had just told her. She looked at Jack. He was staring at the clock over the oven while he pushed his new baseball in and out of the pocket of his ball glove. With school starting in a week, he didn't have many days of freedom left. If they weren't going to the zoo, she knew that he would want to get outside as soon as possible to play ball with his friends.

She turned toward David. "It's all right," she said, her voice tightening with each syllable. "I was just under the impression that you had promised to take us to the zoo today."

"I'm sorry," David said. "But I don't have any choice. The contractor's meeting me in Kirksville to pick out the materials for the classrooms. He insisted on doing it today. If I don't go, who knows when I'll be able to get him again?" He waved his hand in Jack's direction. "Look at Jack. He'd rather go play ball anyway."

Jack bent over and tied his shoe as if he hadn't heard. It was obvious to Sarah that he didn't want to get pulled into the middle of this. David must have sensed the same thing, because he switched gears.

"Look, why don't you go over to Snyder's and look for a new dress?" he said. "They're open on Sundays now. I saw it in the paper. You haven't bought anything in forever. You deserve it."

Sarah's back stiffened. "I don't need a new dress. I need to spend some time with my husband!" She glanced at Jack and her tone lightened.

"You just go on David, I have plenty of things I need to get done around here. I'm a little disappointed, but I'll live."

"Well, can't you buy a dress even if you don't need it?" David said. "Just once, live dangerously."

She frowned. "Buying things we don't need isn't living dangerously; it's living irresponsibly. I'll buy a dress when I need it. I want to tell you something, though. I'll be glad when this Sunday school complex is built. I am getting pretty tired of this."

"Next Saturday we'll all go to the zoo." David looked at Jack, who was frowning up at him. "Or to a movie or something—a last fling before school starts. I promise. I've got to go now or I'll be late. I'll see you two tonight at church."

When the door closed behind David, Jack walked over to Sarah and put his hand on her shoulder. "Mom, I'll just stay home. I don't feel much like playing ball today anyway. We can get out the cards and play some gin."

She smiled and hugged him. "No way. I don't want you and Sandy tracking dirt around here all day. But thanks anyway, honey. You're a good boy. Now get out of here." She turned him around and gave him a push.

"C'mon, Sandy," Jack said. Sandy's ears perked up. She sprang off the chair where she had been sprawling disinterestedly. Jack opened the door just in time for her to shoot out past his legs.

When the door slammed behind Jack, Sarah sat on the couch in the empty room and folded her hands in her lap. She reached up and straightened her hair with one hand, then placed the hand back in her lap. The room was silent except for the ticking of the clock on the bookshelf. She felt incredibly small. She pictured herself curling into a tiny ball and disappearing between the cushions of the couch. She wished it could happen.

She thought of her father and wondered if he could see her. If only he could come and sit with her, just for a while. It occurred to her, though, that he would not have approved of self-pity. He never had. If he were there, she knew what he would have advised her to do. She lowered her head. *Oh, God, please save my family . . .*

chapter 9

Jack pulled open the sliding glass door, and he and Sandy walked into the house from the backyard. It was Sunday, a week after their aborted trip to the zoo. His dad had kept the promise he had made a week earlier. He had spent the whole day with the family on Saturday. To Jack's relief, they had gone miniature golfing, not to the zoo.

Today after church, though, David had gone to another meeting in a neighboring suburb. Jack and Sandy had spent the afternoon playing war down at the creek with some of Jack's friends. Now they were standing in the middle of the family room carpet, looking like characters out of a Dickens novel.

Dried mud caked in splotches on Jack's arms, while streaks of pasty dirt iced his face. His hair looked as if someone had dumped a vacuum bag on it and then given it a good shake. Sandy was even worse. She was just about black.

Sarah walked into the room, put her hands on her hips, and laughed. "Too bad we don't have time to run you through a car wash. Get in the bathroom and hop in the shower. We're going to be late for church."

"Can't I just wipe off over the sink with a washcloth?"

"You've got to be kidding! Get in there! I've got half a mind just to throw you both in the washing machine. Be sure the plug is out of the drain. I don't want a ring in the tub. And put Sandy outside. I'll hose her off."

"C'mon, Sandy, outside," Jack said. He slid the glass door open. "Sorry, girl. I'll see ya later." Sandy's ears drooped. She shuffled out the door with her tail between her legs, occasionally looking over her shoulder at Jack, as if hoping for a last-second reprieve.

In his bedroom, Jack grabbed some clean pants and a shirt out of his drawer and crossed the hall to the bathroom. He pulled off his clothes and tossed them in a filthy heap on the bathroom floor. Stepping into the tub, he turned the water on full. He hadn't realized how worn out he was until that moment. The thought of lying down in the tub and letting the water spray over him sounded good.

"Jack, hurry up! We've got to leave for church in ten minutes." Sarah had stuck her head into the bathroom. Her voice had assumed the nervous edge that had been routine for the past week.

"I'm going as fast as I can," Jack called from behind the shower curtain. The door clapped shut. Lowering his head, he let the warm spray rush over his hair and shoulders, carrying every variety of local silt to the bottom of the tub. He watched as chocolaty rivers formed at the backs of his ankles, split into separate tributaries, then converged just past his toes in a break-neck rush to the drain. A narrow rivulet formed on the bridge of his nose and tumbled off the edge in a waterfall. He noticed that by moving his head up and down he could make the waterfall bigger or smaller. He flared his nostrils and caused the water to split into two streams.

"Jack!"

That woke him up. He slid the soap rapidly over his face, arms, and legs, rinsed off, and jumped out of the tub. After a cursory toweling, he threw his clean clothes on over his dripping body and ran downstairs, stumbling to pull his shoes and socks on along the way. His mom was just opening the back door when he caught up with her. He fell into pace and they hurried across the parking lot.

"You boys must have had a great time today, judging by the amount of dirt that was on you and Sandy," Sarah said.

"You should have seen it. We tied a rope to that giant tree in Neil's backyard. We could swing across the whole creek and land on the other side."

Sarah frowned at him. "Haven't you had enough of that creek?"

"The water's only about a foot deep now. I couldn't drown if I tried."

"Don't say that, Jack, not even joking."

"Sorry."

Jack walked up the short set of stairs and opened the side door of the church for his mother. Sarah stepped into the front of the sanctuary, just next to the raised chancel. The sanctuary consisted of two long columns of pews, divided by a green-carpeted center aisle. In the middle of the chancel was a rectangular altar, covered with a white cloth. A plain white pulpit anchored the left side of the chancel. Behind the chancel was a loft of seats in which the choir sat on Sunday mornings. Above the choir loft, a huge stained-glass Jesus beckoned the congregation with extended arms.

Sarah took several steps toward the pews, then stopped abruptly. Jack stumbled into her from behind.

"Mom! What are you doing?"

She was staring up at the empty pulpit.

"Is something wrong, Mom?"

She shook her head. "No, I suppose not. I just had the strangest feeling, that's all."

Jack gave her a puzzled look as they slid into their usual second-row pew, right in front of the pulpit. Sarah turned and smiled at a new couple she hadn't seen at the church before. After a few minutes Jack's dad walked down the aisle and up the chancel steps, then took his seat behind the pulpit.

The platinum blonde head of the song leader, Ginger Halley, appeared above the pulpit as if from the ether. "Good evening! Let's praise the Lord in song!" she shouted in a heavy southern twang. Ginger was the bubbly star of the Sunday Evening Country Gospel Hour, one of David's most successful innovations. Not tall enough to see over the top of the pulpit, she stood on an orange crate to lead the singing. The base of the pulpit hid the crate from the view of the congregation. When it was time for David to deliver his sermon, he simply slid the crate with his foot into the hollow back of the pulpit to get it out of his way.

"We're gonna start tonight with an old hymn that was my momma's favorite back in Tennessee when I was growin' up. I've still got a soft spot in my heart for it. Please turn to page one hundred eighty-seven, 'Standin' on the Promises.' Isn't it wonderful to know that we have a promise worth standin' on? Let's sing so loud that the angels in heaven'll hear us!" As if winding up an invisible spring that powered her vocal cords, Ginger swung her arms up, down, and sideways during the pianist's introductory notes. "Standing on the promises of Christ my king," the crowd belted out.

Jack knew the words by heart, having grown up surrounded by all sorts of church music. He could hear his mother's sweet voice next to him, but nobody else could. She sang so softly that only those who happened to sit very close to her ever got to enjoy it.

When they finished the song, David stepped to the pulpit to pray. "O Lord, our God, we thank you for all of the blessings that you shower on us each day. We have nothing without your grace. Please strengthen our faith, Lord. We are all sinners, and we pray for your forgiveness. Breathe your Word into our souls this evening and straighten our ways. In the name of Jesus we pray. Amen."

The congregation echoed, "Amen."

Now it was Ginger's turn again. "If you're a visitor with us tonight, please take a minute and fill out one of the cards in the back of the pew in front of you. Just drop it in the offerin' plate when it comes around. We promise we won't call you and try to sell you anythin', but we don't promise we won't call you." The congregation chuckled politely. "While we're givin' everyone a second to do that, do we have any announcements?"

Pamela Ferris stood up. "We're planning the annual bake sale for the youth group. It will be two weeks from now, right after the Sunday morning and Sunday evening services. If you'd like to bake and donate some of your favorite cookies and treats, please see me after the service tonight."

"All right, Pam," Ginger said. "We'll all get to bakin' as soon as we get home tonight. Anyone else?"

Ted Balik rose slowly from a pew near the middle of the church on the opposite side of the aisle from Jack and Sarah. A paunchy man with thick black glasses, Balik was squeezed into a wool sport coat that was far too heavy for the St. Louis heat. Few of the church members had ever heard him say a word. Erika, who usually did the talking for him, was sitting to his right. She scowled and tugged at his sleeve, but he ignored her.

He stood silently for a moment, his head bowed. When he raised his head, he said, "I've been struggling with something for several days now. I've prayed and prayed about it. Finally, I realized the Lord was putting a burden on my heart to come here and let you folks know about it. I know many of you are aware how much hard work our preacher has put into the plans for our new Sunday school complex. It's going to be a great facility and a real blessing to this church." His voice trailed off. He lowered his eyes and ran his hand through his thinning hair.

This was unusual. Announcement time was for announcements, not speeches. People shifted around in their seats and rustled hymnal pages. Erika glared at her husband, her mouth open slightly as if on the verge of ordering him to sit down. Jack looked past the pulpit to his father, expecting him to be irritated at the strange interruption in the service. Instead, David was sitting stiffly upright, his eyes riveted on Ted.

"You folks have every reason to believe that your pastor is a fine man," Balik continued, "a real pillar of our community." His voice was regaining its strength.

David rose from his chair and walked quickly to the front of the chancel. "That's very kind of you, Ted, but there are many people who have put a lot of time into the building project and into this church. They all deserve our thanks. Thank you for your thoughtful words."

The page rustlers stopped. All eyes turned back to Balik. He threw his shoulders back. "I'm sure you would like for me to stop, David, but what you don't know is that you've been found out! You've been doing things in the dark, thinking that no one, not even God, would see. But you were wrong."

"Now wait a minute!" Fred Kramer, a member of the church's Board of Elders, jumped to his feet. "You can't come in here and insult Reverend Parst that way. You'd better leave now."

Jack's stomach churned. He sensed that something awful was happening, but he wasn't sure what. He glanced to his left and noticed that his mother was rocking, ever so slightly, her arms folded in front of her as though she were hugging herself. She wasn't even looking at Balik. In fact, her eyes were almost closed. Jack looked back up to the front of the church. His father still stood silently, alone in front of his flock.

Balik pointed a finger at Kramer. "No, *you* wait a minute. The Bible says, 'Those who sin are to be rebuked publicly, so that the others may take warning.' First Timothy five-twenty. You can look it up. I've read it a hundred times the past few days. That's why I'm here tonight—to rebuke the biggest sinner of all: our own preacher!"

The sanctuary was silent. David stared in Ted's direction, but anyone studying his eyes would have realized that his focus was actually just beyond Ted, on Erika. Her eyes brightened and the corners of her mouth lifted in a smirk. She winked. David fell back a step, as if he had been punched.

Ted continued, "Wednesday, when Erika thought I was at work, I was actually waiting down the street in my car, watching for her. I'd become suspicious that she was seeing someone, but didn't want to believe it was true. I followed her all the way over to the other side of Ferguson, on Route 16. When I saw her pull in to a motel, I sat in my car and cried. About half an hour later a car drove up. I recognized it immediately, but I refused to believe it could be true. Then out stepped Reverend Parst. He hustled up to the door like he didn't want to be seen. He didn't even have to knock. She opened it and let him in."

A woman in the back gasped. Fred Kramer slumped into his seat.

"Even then I couldn't believe it. I thought, maybe they're working on the building plans. But I knew that didn't make any sense. About an hour later David opens the door, sticks his head out, and looks both ways to make sure that no one is watching, just like the guilty man that he is. Then he steps out. Erika steps out after him, and they kiss, right there in front of my eyes. He got in his car and drove off."

Several women in the congregation sniffled. Others stared at their preacher in disbelief. But still no one said a word.

"I didn't know what to do. How could these two, of all people, do such a thing? I cursed them and I cursed God. But finally, when I was about to go crazy over it, I began to pray. Once I started, I just kept praying and praying. Yesterday God helped me come to grips with it. Now I know. God didn't cause this. It was just two people sinning, nothing more and nothing less. One of the sinners just happens to be our preacher. The other is my wife. I thought you had a right to know."

Jack sat staring for a few moments after Balik stopped. His mother moaned softly. Jack looked at her, then jumped to his feet and waved his arm at Balik. "You can't say that! Shut up! You shut up! My dad's not a sinner. He's a great man!" He slid down his pew to the center aisle. "My dad's a great man! He didn't do that! You're a liar!"

He stumbled across the aisle and grabbed Balik by the arm. He pulled him—trying to tug him out to the aisle, out of the church, as if that would put everything back together again.

Staring wide eyed at Jack, Balik moved his free hand to cover a bulge in the pocket of his coat. Instead of reaching into the pocket, he simply held his hand protectively over it. His eyes moved rapidly from Jack to David, then back to Jack. He lost his balance and took a stumbling step toward Jack, as if to follow him. Catching himself, he pulled his arm free and said, "I'm sorry, son. I didn't think . . . I didn't mean to hurt you. I suppose I couldn't even get this last thing right."

Harry Thompson, an old friend of Jack's parents, hurried across the aisle, put his arm around Jack's shoulder, and tried to lead him away. Jack jerked away from him and began tugging on Balik's arm again.

"Please, leave us alone! Go away. Leave us alone!" He was sobbing, wiping his face on his sleeve as he pulled at Balik.

Thompson glared at Balik and gently pulled Jack away again.

Jack looked to the front of the church at his father. "Tell him it's not true. Please, Dad."

David's shoulders slumped.

Jack turned and looked across the aisle at his mom. She was crying quietly and still rocking, still hugging herself as if there were no one else who could, or would. He broke free from Thompson and ran over to her. He sat down beside her, put his arms around her, and hugged her tightly for a long time. The congregation sat frozen.

Finally, gently, Jack helped Sarah up. He picked up her things, put his arm around her shoulder, and led her out of the pew. They walked together the few steps to the side door and left the church without a word.

WHEN THEY REACHED THE PARSONAGE, Jack opened the door for Sarah. She walked into the kitchen and sat at the table. Jack followed her into the room. A napkin was folded on the place mat in front of Sarah. She picked it up and dabbed her eyes.

Jack put his hand to his forehead. "What did we do to make him hate us, Mom? He said he loved us. What did we do?" He pressed his fingernails hard into his skin until a drop of blood trickled toward his eyebrow.

Sarah jumped up. Reaching for his hand, she pulled his fingers open and wrapped them in hers. "We didn't do anything," she said. "I want you to listen to me. Don't ever think that. This is not our fault."

"But he hates us."

"I don't know. Maybe he does. But I do know that we've done nothing to deserve this. I also know that we're going to be all right. That may seem impossible to you right now, but I promise you it is true. We will be all right, you and I. Do you hear . . ."

Through the open window came a loud pop. Tires screeched on the road out front. A woman screamed.

Jack pulled his hand free and ran to the window.

"Jack, don't . . ."

Before she could finish, he had turned and run out the door. He sprinted at an angle across the parking lot toward the front of the church. He saw a man running from the street toward the walkway that led to the church steps. The man's car was stopped at the side of the road, with the driver's door open. A woman sat in the passenger seat. She was staring toward the front door of the church with her hand over her mouth.

When Jack rounded the corner of the church, he ran along the grass toward the front steps. The church door opened. Two men rushed out. Jack recognized them as the Sunday evening greeters who sat in the back pew during the service. They looked down the stairs at the walk and stopped. One of the men tilted his head toward the sky and turned away. A row of low shrubs, bordering the concrete walk, blocked Jack's view.

The man from the street reached the walk before Jack. Looking toward the foot of the stairs, the man put both hands to his head. He turned to the men at the top of the steps. "We saw the whole thing from our car," he said.

As Jack approached the shrubs, he slowed to a trot. When he got close enough to see over them, he dropped to his knees. He doubled over and vomited. At the base of the concrete stairs, Ted Balik lay sprawled on his back, his head in a pool of blood. His shattered eyeglasses lay next to him. Where his right eye should have been, there was a dark, bloody hole where the bullet had entered. A few inches from his right hand was a black pistol.

chapter 10

David sat hunched over in the driver's seat, his forehead pressed hard against the steering wheel. Despite the blasting air conditioner, tiny beads of sweat crept tentatively down his brow. From time to time headlights pierced the dark interior of the car, gradually washed over him, and then receded, leaving him alone again in blackness. How long he'd been sitting on the side of this farm road he didn't know, didn't care. Everything was over now.

When the police finished questioning him at the church, he had gotten in his car and driven aimlessly. Somehow he had ended up in the country. No reason had compelled him to stop in this particular spot. One place was as good as another. There was little sense in going home. They would be gone. He knew Sarah well enough to know that.

What difference did it make? She could never forgive him now. He could never forgive himself; how could he expect forgiveness from someone else? He had murdered a man tonight, just as surely as if he had pointed the gun at those black glasses and pulled the trigger. And what had Ted Balik ever done to him? Nothing. Nothing except be quiet and meek and decent. Adultery and murder—he had covered the major sins now. What else was left for him but to die and face his judgment? He was so afraid when he thought of that.

And for what? For Erika Balik? He was nothing but sport for her. He'd known it all along. The look on her face during the church service had confirmed it. She enjoyed the whole scene, a good show. My, how different she had been when she was standing over the body, though. She hadn't seemed as cocky then.

He shook his head. He was beginning to pass the blame, and he wouldn't allow it. The blame was his. This hadn't been about Erika Balik. It had never been about her. It had been about his own pride, his belief that he had become something big—too big for Sarah and Jack and the things he'd give anything now to have back. He groaned. *It's finished. I'm lost.*

Something inside of him responded, *No, you're not lost.* It was not a voice but a sense. David raised his head from the steering wheel and looked around. *Lord, I'm so far away from you. How can you ever forgive me for this? It's too much.* He rested his head back on the steering wheel and whispered, "Lord, I have sinned against you, against Sarah, against Jack, and against an innocent man who is dead because of me . . ."

JACK STARED AT THE DASHBOARD and listened to the methodical flopping of the windshield wipers. His mother had barely said a word since they got in the car a couple of hours earlier. There had not been much to say after the police left. They both knew they couldn't stay. They had begun packing as soon as they got back to the house.

True to form, his dad had not even had the guts to come home. He was probably out laughing it up with Mrs. Balik. After all, she was the one who was important to him. Now that they'd gotten Mr. Balik out of the way, they could have a great time.

Jack punched his pillow with both hands and jammed it against the window. He'd never been able to sleep sitting up. He wished he'd gotten in the backseat with Sandy when they left the house. That way he could have stretched out. He had wanted to keep his mom company, though. It would be a long time before they got to his grandmother's house in Chicago. He looked in the back. Sandy was snoring lightly on her blanket.

He turned toward his mom. She was staring straight ahead, focused on the road, or whatever. When he thought of how she must feel, he wanted to kill his dad. Then he thought that maybe he *would* kill him someday. He imagined himself standing over his father, with a black pistol in his hand, sneering as the coward begged for mercy. The thought provided a break from his misery. He fell asleep feeling better than he had all evening.

chapter 11

David took one last look around the dreary little apartment. Funny how even this thimble of a place appeared bigger without furniture. He'd moved out of the parsonage two days after Ted Balik's suicide. No one had kicked him out. He had beaten them to it. He'd submitted his resignation along with the keys. Within twenty-four hours he had found this studio.

After six weeks of reporters' calls, neighbors' whispers, and relentless self-recrimination, it was time to move on, at least physically. He could easily have gotten in his car and left before noon. It had been loaded since early that morning. For some reason, though, he had been unable to get himself going until nightfall. He reflected gloomily that, after all, people like him were supposed to slink out of town after dark.

Although he had called Sarah at least twenty times, he had been unable to convince her to talk things through with him. Most times Sarah's mother, Elizabeth, answered and told him that Sarah could not come to the phone. One time Jack answered and immediately hung up. On the few occasions when Sarah answered, she was coldly civil and excused herself just after his opening apology. With no sign of progress, he was ready to move far away, to put miles of highway between this desolate part of his life and the next. Texas seemed a big enough place to get lost for a long time; that was exactly what he intended to do.

Flicking on the light in the bathroom, he looked in the closet and the rusted cabinet above the sink to make sure he hadn't missed anything important. Everything was empty, just as empty as he was. He walked over to the front door and sat down on the water-stained linoleum floor. The jagged edge of a brittle, curled-up tile pierced his pants and stabbed his hip before snapping off under his weight. He reached his finger through the tear and touched the spot. When he pulled his finger out, it was moist with blood. He was glad that it bled.

There was one more thing to do before he climbed into the car and left O'Fallon, Missouri, behind. Since Sarah wouldn't take his calls, he'd decided to try another way. He considered it his last hope. He picked up the pen and tablet of paper he'd left lying there on the floor. In the faint glow of a bare, yellow lightbulb, he began to write a letter he'd composed in his mind a thousand times. As he wrote, he did something he hadn't done for almost thirty years. He cried.

chapter 12

Sarah let out an exasperated sigh as she wrestled the clacking wheels of the shopping cart across the orange-and-white checked tiles of Domino's Super Market. One wheel insisted on pointing in a different direction than the other three, placing her in constant danger of veering into the row of milk cartons on her left. The balky cart made her think of a documentary about World War II that she'd seen a few nights earlier. A Japanese plane had hit an American battleship with a torpedo, damaging its rudder. The ship had limped helplessly around in a circle until the Japs finished it off. She glanced involuntarily toward the ceiling, wary of enemy cart bombers.

A few feet in front of her, Jack scanned the refrigerated shelves. He grabbed a large chocolate-colored can with a picture of a white cow on the front. The cow had the name *Moore's* written in cursive across its flank. The letters *M-o-o* were in boldface. He dropped it in the cart.

Sarah didn't speak. She simply shook her head from side to side.

"Mom! The ads say this stuff is supposed to give me *Moo*re muscle. Get it?"

"It's just chocolate milk, Jack."

"Chocolate milk fortified with tons of vitamins. Look at the label!"
She crossed her arms.

He picked the can out of the cart and replaced it on the shelf.

"If I'm going to be grounded, I should at least get to pick out something that will keep me healthy," he said. "I could waste away, you know."

"With all of the food you eat after football practice I don't think there is any possibility that you're going to starve. And don't start feeling sorry for yourself. You're grounded because you earned it. You can't smart off to teachers and expect that there will be no consequences."

"Why aren't you as understanding as my guidance counselor? Remember, he said, 'Some behavioral lapses are to be expected under the circumstances.'"

"I don't want to hear about circumstances. Bad things happen sometimes. That's life. It is no excuse for bad behavior. I just hope your teachers really accepted your apology and will give you another chance. You don't want a reputation."

They turned the corner and Jack pointed toward the checkout counter. "Long line."

"Maybe they'll open another register," Sarah said.

Sarah coaxed the balky cart up the aisle. Just before they reached the back of the line, she stumbled. She clutched the handle of the cart to keep herself from falling.

Jack grabbed her arm. "Are you okay, Mom?"

"I'm fine, just clumsy. I must have tripped on my own feet. Oh, look, I caught my pants on the cart." She leaned over and inspected a tiny tear in the leg of her tan wool pants. Straightening, she took a step but pulled up abruptly.

Jack watched her closely. "Are you sure you're okay?"

"Strange, my leg feels as if it's gone to sleep. I must have been leaning with my weight on it when we were talking back there." She took a short, timid step, then another. "I'm all right. My leg is tingly, that's all."

When they arrived at the back of the line, Sarah pulled her checkbook out of her purse. She squinted at the neatly printed ledger entries while she rubbed her leg with her free hand.

When their turn came at the checkout counter, Jack dug the groceries one by one from the cart and dropped them onto a black belt that carried them in short, jerky bursts toward the register. With stunning dexterity, the checkout girl snatched each item from the belt and slung it toward the bag boy with one hand while tapping out the price on the register with the other. Sarah searched her purse for a pen.

While fishing in the cart for the eggs, Jack heard his mother say, "Oh, no." He glanced up. Her face was flushed deep red. She looked down at her feet. Jack stopped, his head suspended over the grocery cart.

A little girl standing behind Jack pointed and said, "Mommy, that lady peed her pants!" The buzz of conversation in the line behind them stopped. Every head turned toward Sarah.

The little girl moved past Jack and squatted next to Sarah's legs to get a better look. The last trickles of a thin stream dribbled from the bottom of Sarah's pant leg into a small puddle on the floor between her feet. An acrid smell drifted past Jack and back through the line.

The woman with the little girl touched her hand to her nose.

A man muttered under his breath, "Poor woman."

Eyes wide, Sarah looked at Jack. She clutched her purse to her side and spun around as if to hurry from the store. With her first step, her leg buckled beneath her. She reached for the counter but could not hold on. As she spilled toward the floor, her purse flipped into the air. Her knees banged hard against the tile and her body twisted over, leaving her sitting on her side in the puddle. Her purse's contents rained down around her.

The checkout area was silent. A man from the line took a step forward, as if to help, but he bumped into Jack, who seemed to have frozen in place.

Sarah reached up to the counter and pulled herself to her feet. The hem of one leg of her pants was hitched up to midcalf. The wet, stained wool clung heavily to her hip and the insides of her legs.

Still holding on to the counter, without looking at anyone around her, Sarah gingerly tested her weight on the leg that had given way. When it held, she limped out of the aisle and out of the store, without a word.

Jack looked at the young woman at the cash register. She batted her eyes sympathetically.

"I'm sorry. She's sick," he said. He knelt on the floor. Picking up her purse, he quickly scooped up the wet, scattered contents and dumped them in.

The checkout girl said, "Don't forget this." She reached down and handed him Sarah's checkbook.

"I'm sorry," Jack said again, straightening up. Red faced, he turned and ran after his mother.

chapter 13

As she tucked her blouse into her skirt, Sarah stared at the shiny array of doctor's instruments spread neatly on the white counter to the left of where she stood. She felt her eye twitch. That was what she hated worst, maybe even worse than the humiliating scene in the grocery store the day before. At least she'd wet her pants only once. The twitching was becoming frequent and it was driving her crazy.

She had such a sense of foreboding that she was not sure she wanted Dr. Raines ever to come back into the examination room. On the other hand, not knowing what was wrong was killing her. She reached down and rubbed her tingling leg. There was a knock on the door.

"May I come in?" said a man's voice from the other side of the door. "Yes."

Dr. Raines, gray and plump, opened the door and peeked around the corner. "All put back together?"

"I guess you'll have to answer that question." She forced a smile and leaned back against the examination table.

"Yes, well, let's get to the point, then." He walked into the room and shut the door behind him. "I don't know for sure what is wrong with you, Sarah. I do have a very strong suspicion, but only time will tell if I am right. In the meantime we'll have to continue running some tests. Basically, we'll attempt to rule out the other possibilities, and that will help us make certain that my tentative diagnosis is correct."

"I don't really want to ask, but what do you think it is?"

He took off his glasses and wiped them on his white lab coat. "I'm ninety-nine percent certain it's multiple sclerosis—but there are other things it still could be."

Sarah squeezed the table with both hands.

"I have a lot of written information that I can give you about the disease," he said. "The more you learn, the better you'll be able to deal with it."

"I never imagined . . . I suppose that's what explains my having problems with my eye and leg at the same time."

"That's correct. Weakness in the legs, twitching eyes, urinary incontinence—all are possible symptoms. The odds are against anything else causing that combination."

"You said it could be something else. What?"

"Pinched nerve, for example. But I seriously doubt that. It would be strange for that to affect your eyes *and* legs for this long. It wouldn't explain the bladder, but that could be something else, maybe an infection. The culture I just took will tell me that. It could also be some other sort of neuromuscular disorder. I don't want to mislead you. At your age the odds are that it's MS."

"How did I get it? Neither of my parents had it."

"It's not contagious, and it's not clear that it's inherited. We don't know what causes it. You've probably had it for a while, but the symptoms were so mild that you didn't notice. Often something happens that triggers more severe symptoms. Have you been sick? Had a death in the family? Anything that could cause unusual stress?"

She chewed her lip. Then she chuckled.

He raised an eyebrow.

"During the past six weeks I've separated from my husband; I've witnessed a suicide; I've moved halfway across the country to live with my mother, who is simply giddy that I'm free of the aforementioned husband; and when I'm through here today I'm meeting my son at his new school to talk to his counselor because he's not making any friends and he's already had run-ins with two of his teachers. I don't think it's an exaggeration to say that my middle name is Stress."

"I see. I suppose that would do it."

"What am I going to do now?" she said, under her breath.

"Pardon me?"

"I've got a son and no husband around. It's not just me I have to worry about."

"If you don't mind my saying, Sarah, you seem like a strong woman. If I'm correct and this is MS, you can deal with it. It is a misconception that all MS patients end up in wheelchairs. Many, perhaps even the majority, lead normal lives in most respects. For many others the symptoms come and go and never get any worse. It's just impossible to predict."

Sarah's face flushed. "A wheelchair. Things become less abstract at the mention of it."

He nodded. "I didn't mean to frighten you."

"Would you do me a favor, doctor? Would you give me a minute before we continue our discussion?"

"Yes, certainly." He left the room, closing the door behind him.

Sarah sat on the edge of the examination table. Looking around the room, she thought how sterile it all appeared, figuratively and literally: a horrible place for a person to receive bad news. She crossed her arms and clasped her shoulders in her hands. She closed her eyes. *God, when will it stop? Why are you letting this happen to me? . . .*

SARAH TOOK A DEEP BREATH and knocked on the door of Jack's room.

"Come in," Jack said.

She opened the door. "Doing your homework?"

Jack was sitting at his desk with the reading lamp on. He turned and said, "Yeah. I've got a social studies test."

Sarah walked in and sat on the bed. "I need to talk to you about something."

He pushed his book aside.

"You know I went to the doctor today," she said.

"I know. Is there something wrong with you?"

"Yes, there is." She rubbed her hands together. "It explains what happened in the grocery store."

He looked away.

"I've had some other things happening lately, also, things you didn't know about: tingling in my legs and some problems with my eyes."

"Are you dying?"

She stood up, walked over, and put her arm around him. "No, honey. I'm not dying. It's fairly serious, but it won't kill me. They're pretty sure I've got multiple sclerosis."

"Isn't that the Jerry Lewis disease? I thought only kids got that."

"Actually, I don't know if it's the same thing."

"Are you going to be crippled?"

"I certainly hope not. The truth is I don't know. Some people end up . . . crippled. Some don't have much of a problem at all. Mine may get worse or it may not. It could even get better."

"When will you know?"

"When it happens. There's no way to predict it."

He flipped the pages of his book with his thumb. "How did you get it?"

"The doctor said I've probably had it for a while. He said that the symptoms I'm having now could have been triggered by stress."

"You mean Dad caused it."

"No, your father didn't cause it."

"He killed Mr. Balik. Why not kill you too?"

"Your father did something very bad. I'm not going to minimize that. He did not kill Mr. Balik, though."

Jack looked her in the eye. She looked down at the bed.

"I wish he was dead," he said.

"Don't say that. He's your father. God would want you to treat him with respect, even if you're angry with him."

"I hate God."

"What did you say?"

"Nothing."

"I heard it. You said you hate God. That's an awful thing to say, but I understand why you feel that way. As time passes, you'll change your mind."

"Sure. Can I do my homework now?" He glowered at his social studies book.

"We're going to be all right, Jack. We really are." She leaned over and kissed him on the head. He continued to stare at his book. She wondered if he had read her, if he had sensed her doubt seeping through the veil of reassuring words. She turned and walked out of the room.

chapter 14

Later that week, Sarah and Elizabeth stood in the kitchen, talking in low tones. Jack wheeled around the corner from the living room.

"Hey, Mom, guess where I'm going Saturday?" he said. He noticed a half-moon wrinkle curled over his mother's eyebrow, a sure sign that she was concentrating hard on something. He pulled up short.

Sarah was holding a torn envelope and a folded piece of white paper. "Hi, Jack," she said.

He thought her voice was too soothingly soft. "What's going on? Somebody die?" He smiled weakly.

Neither of the women smiled back at him.

"Jack, your father is coming," Sarah said. She held up the envelope and paper. "He wrote us a letter. I called him today after I read it. He wants to see you."

Jack stuck his hands in his pants pockets. "So? I don't want to see him."

"The letter is addressed to you too. Why don't you read it and then decide?" Sarah held it out to him.

"I don't want to read it. I hate him and I never want to see him again."

Elizabeth nodded.

Sarah frowned at her. "He says some things I think you should hear," Sarah said. She moved across the room toward him, limping noticeably. He studied her halting gait and scowled.

She hugged him. "I know this is difficult, honey, but he's still your father."

"He didn't think that was a big deal." Jack turned to Elizabeth for support, but this time she didn't respond.

"He's very sorry," Sarah continued.

"Yeah, I'm sorry too. Not as sorry as Mr. Balik, though. Most of all, I'm sorry for what he did to you. You can hardly walk."

Sarah took a step back and looked him in the eye. "Listen to me, Jack. We've been through this. Your father did not give me MS. It just happened."

"You said the doctor told you stress could cause it."

"The doctor said stress could *trigger* it, not cause it. They don't know what causes it."

"If they don't know what causes it, how do you know he didn't cause it? You didn't have it before he treated you like dirt. And what about what happened in the grocery store? That never happened before either."

"Losing control of my bladder is a symptom. There are ways to deal with it. If your father didn't cause the MS, he couldn't be responsible for the symptoms. Anyway, hating him won't do anyone any good."

"It sure makes me feel better."

"Don't say that. You have to try to forgive him."

"Have you?"

She folded her arms across her chest. "I'm not going to lie to you. No, I haven't forgiven him. It's going to take a while. Frankly, though,

I'm trying to do it for me, not for him. As time passes I'm sure that will change."

He shrugged. "Sure, if you say so. Can I go upstairs now?" He turned to walk out of the room.

Sarah placed the letter and envelope on the counter. "I'll leave the letter here in case you change your mind."

When Jack had gone, Elizabeth turned to Sarah. "I'm going to go talk to him," she said.

"I don't think you should, Mother. Let him mull things over for a while. I'll go up and talk to him later."

"Sarah, I am not going to leave that boy alone in his room at a time like this. You just give me a few minutes with him. Sometimes a little talk with Grams is just what's needed." She headed for the kitchen door.

"Mother, please!"

"I'll just check on him and come right back down," Elizabeth said. She was up the stairs before Sarah could respond.

When she reached the door to Jack's room, Elizabeth knocked twice, then opened it. He was sprawled on his side on the bed, twirling a caramel-colored baseball between his fingers.

"Are you all right?"

"I'm okay," he said, without looking up.

Elizabeth walked over to his bed. "You know, Jack, it's only natural that you're angry with your father. No one can blame you for that."

He dropped the ball onto the wood floor. It bounced twice and rolled under his desk. "He makes me sick. I don't want to see him. If you came up here to talk me into it, it's not going to work."

Elizabeth patted his arm. "Frankly, dear, I don't want to see him either. Just think of what he did to your mother. He ruined her health and then tossed her away like an old shoe."

"Mom said he didn't have anything to do with her MS."

"Sometimes mothers fudge the facts a little to protect their children, dear. All I know is that she didn't have any health problems before."

Jack looked at her out of the corner of his eye. Loose furrows ran from her cheekbones to her jaw, where they disappeared into the folds of her neck. He wondered how such a small woman could have so much skin.

"I'm going to see him, though," she continued. "I will be civil to him too—nothing more and nothing less. I'm going to do it for your mother. As for his pathetic letter, I don't blame you a bit. If I were you, I wouldn't read it either."

He propped himself up on his elbow. "It'll just be a bunch of lies, like before."

"A person can't do what he did and then expect to make everything right by just writing a letter," she said. "This is important to your mother, though, so you're going to have to talk to him when he's here. You can say hello and go through the motions. We'll get through this together, okay? That's the least we can do for your mother." She winked at him.

Jack smiled. "You're something, Grandma. Okay, we'll get through it together, you and me."

She put her hand on his head. "You're a good boy." She got up and walked out of the room.

Sarah was filling a glass with tap water when her mother walked back into the kitchen. "Well, how did it go?" she asked.

"He said he would see David when he comes," Elizabeth said. "I think he's going to be fine."

chapter 15

David pulled his rental car to the curb in front of Elizabeth's stately Georgian house. He reached in his pocket, pulled out an antacid tablet, and popped it in his mouth. Driving through his mother-in-law's fashionable neighborhood reminded him how much comfort Sarah had given up to marry him. She'd gone from this to peanut butter and jelly, and she'd never complained once. No matter how badly things might go today, he knew that he deserved even worse.

During the past few days, he had allowed himself the hope that his visit might not be futile. After all, Sarah had called when she received the letter. That was a good sign. She had also agreed to see him. That was more than he had dared dream.

When he got to the front door he reached for the doorbell, but it had pulled loose from the brick and was dangling from three color-coded wires. He rubbed his earlobe, wondering whether he would get a shock if he pinched the button between his fingers. He decided to knock.

After a few moments he heard footsteps coming toward the door. He sucked his stomach in and threw his shoulders back. Elizabeth opened the door.

"Hello, David." Her mouth was so taut that her lips barely parted when she spoke.

"Hello, Elizabeth. Is Sarah here?"

"Yes. Come in." She turned and strode across the oak-floored entryway toward the formal living room.

David stepped into the house and absentmindedly pushed the door behind him. The huge door swung heavily. He turned and grabbed for the knob, too late. The door slammed, rattling picture frames on the entryway table.

Elizabeth stopped in midstride. A purple vein bulged until it nearly glowed from the side of her pasty neck. David felt his armpits becoming damp. He couldn't take his eyes off the throbbing vein and wondered how engorged it could become before it finally burst. Elizabeth's shoulders shuddered, then rose and fell in a deep breath, but she did not turn around. She continued walking. David lowered his head and hurried to catch up to her.

Arriving at the living room, Elizabeth gestured toward a blue wing chair with ornately carved legs. "You can sit down. I'll get her." Without waiting for a response, she left.

David looked around the room. The grand piano, the carved stone fireplace, the porcelain vases—thinking back, he could not recall a single time when he had ever actually sat in this room. During their summer visits he and Jack had always hung out in the den, where they could talk in normal voices and didn't have to worry about breaking something that mattered.

He had often wondered how Sarah, having been raised in this environment, could have ended up so uninterested in material comforts. As far as he could tell, she had never cared one bit whether she wore an expensive designer outfit or a sundress from a discount store. Her father's influence, he supposed.

Just as he was about to sit down, Sarah stepped around the corner. He was shocked to see that she was using a cane. She was far thinner than he had ever seen her. She wore gray sweatpants, and her ponytail fell loosely over a yellow sweatshirt that seemed to swallow her.

He raised his hand in a sort of half wave. Realizing how pathetic it looked, he quickly dropped his arm to his side. "Sarah—it's good to see you."

"How was your flight?" Her tone was businesslike. His heart sank, but he had prepared himself not to become easily discouraged.

"Fine. No, bumpy, actually. What happened to your leg?"

"Nothing. I hurt my ankle."

"How?"

"It doesn't matter. Can I get you something to drink?"

"A glass of ice water would be good, if it's not too much trouble. I didn't have anything to drink on the plane."

When she left the room, he sat in a different chair than the one Elizabeth had offered. Sarah was back in a few minutes. Elizabeth followed her into the room, carrying two tumblers of water. David kicked himself for not having thought to offer to help Sarah get the water.

Elizabeth placed his glass on a silver-rimmed coaster on the mahogany end table beside him. Then she crossed the room and placed the other glass on a similar end table next to a floral settee.

"Thank you," David said. He took a long drink and set the glass on the coaster.

Elizabeth did not acknowledge him. She walked out without a word.

Sarah sat on the settee. When she leaned her cane against the seat, he made it a point to check her finger for her wedding ring. She wasn't wearing it.

"How have you been? How's Jack?" he asked. He twisted his own wedding band between his fingers.

"Jack's school is generally good. He's had some trouble making friends, but that seems to be improving. Football has helped. He's gotten into a little bit of trouble."

"Trouble?"

"Nothing real serious, but enough to worry me. He's been in detention twice. I think he's still learning to deal with things."

"What did he do?"

"The issue seems to be a smart mouth, according to his assistant principal."

"Jack?"

"I know. His guidance counselor says he's working through some things and that it will take some time. I sat him down a couple of weeks ago and let him know that the rules haven't changed. He seemed to get the point. He hasn't had any problems since."

David shook his head. He had always been amazed at Sarah's ability to lay down the law when she had to. "Is he here?" he said.

"Yes, I'll get him." She leaned forward and placed her hand on her cane.

"No, wait—I was hoping we could talk first."

She sat back.

"You didn't tell me how *you* were doing."

"It hasn't been pleasant, if that's what you mean."

"No, of course not."

She held up her hand. "You don't need to worry about me. I'll get by."

"But I do worry about you."

She looked at him impassively.

"You've lost weight," he said.

"I suppose that pleases you."

"No, what I mean . . . is something wrong? Are you okay?"

"I'm fine. I've just been too busy to eat much since we got up here."

"I'm sure you have trouble believing that I worry about you. I can tell you, though, that it's true," he said.

She continued to look steadily at him.

"I thought that if I could see you again . . ." He twisted his wedding band more rapidly. "I guess the point is that I've always been able to talk my way out of anything. That's my problem: all show, no go. Well, I can't talk my way out of this one. For the first time in my life, I see myself clearly, and I don't like it."

Sarah took a drink from her glass. A few drops of condensation slid onto her sweatpants. She placed her other hand beneath the glass and rested it on her leg. Still she said nothing.

David looked into her eyes. "I thought that if we could talk face to face, instead of just hearing what I'm saying, you could feel it. You could feel how sorry I am. Then you would believe me—and let me come back."

She knitted her eyebrows. "Your letter was good, David. I believe you're sorry and I'm trying hard to forgive you. Someday I think I'll be able to. But I can't let you come back."

His shoulders slumped. He had anticipated that she would at least be willing to discuss the possibility. Otherwise, why had she allowed him to come? He leaned forward. "Sarah, this can't be the end of it. We can't just throw away our family without trying."

"Wait a minute. *We're* not throwing away anything. *You* threw it away, remember?" She set her glass on the end table.

"Yes, and I hate myself for what I did to you. But is it really possible that there's no second chance—that one mistake can cost me my whole life?"

"You've got to understand, I loved you, David. I really loved you." Her eyes moistened. She frowned and swiped her sleeve across her cheek. "I told myself I wasn't going to cry. The fact is that apparently you didn't love me as much as I loved you. But no matter. Will I take you back after you gave what was mine to that woman? No, I won't do that."

"Sarah, that was craziness. I can't even explain to myself how I let it happen."

He stood up and moved across the room toward her. Bending over, he wrapped his arms around her.

Her eyes opened wide and she recoiled, pulling her hands to her chest, as if he were covered with mud. "Please don't touch me!"

His mouth fell open. He fell back several steps.

From the next room, Elizabeth called, "Are you all right, Sarah?"

Sarah turned toward the door. "I'm fine!" She looked at David and lowered her voice. "You didn't *let* it happen. You *made* it happen. Don't insult me by acting as if you were a victim of some tragic event. And please don't try to touch me again."

He slumped back into his chair. In his wildest imagination he had never anticipated that she would respond with such physical revulsion. Gathering himself, he said, "I know it's going to take a long time for you to see me the way you saw me before. It will happen, though, if you'll just give me a chance. I could move up here. I don't mean necessarily in the same town, but close by. We could talk every once in a while. I could spend time with Jack. I know I could prove myself to both of you."

"It won't work," she said, shaking her head. "Can't you see that? I'll forgive you eventually. I'm sure of that. But we can never go back. You broke the bond. We were one person. Now we're two. Maybe some marriages can be glued back together like broken china, but mine can't. It's over."

"You're being rash. You can't just throw our lives away like this without even giving yourself a chance to digest things! There's too much at stake. Think about Jack."

"Don't lecture me. You have no right."

"I'm sorry. Of course I don't."

They sat silently, facing each other across the room.

David struggled with where to go from here. It seemed that all was lost already, but there was so much more that he had intended to say, that needed to be said. He clasped his hands in front of him. His voice became plaintive. "There is one thing I want you to know for sure before I leave here, Sarah. I love you. Yes, I broke the bond, and I deserve whatever I get for that. But I'll never stop loving you."

"I'd like to believe you, David. Maybe I will someday. Time can accomplish many things. I've learned that since my father died."

He leaned back in his seat. "So where are we now? Are you going to ask for a divorce?"

"I don't know what I'm going to do. I never thought I would be in this situation."

"I hope you won't ask for a divorce. You said time can accomplish a lot. I'll wait. Who knows? Maybe you'll change your mind. Maybe in a year or two . . ."

"As I said, I need to think about it," she said. She put her hand on her cane and pushed herself up. "Jack is upstairs. Do you want to see him now?"

David knew he was in no condition to talk to Jack after this conversation. What was he going to do, though, come back later? "Yes," he said. He watched closely as she maneuvered away from the settee with her cane. He looked at her ankle and noticed that it did not appear to be wrapped. "How does he feel about my being here?"

"Honestly? Not good. What did you think? Right now he says he hates you. I'm not feeding his feelings, believe me. I don't want you two to be estranged forever. That's no good for him. Don't expect too much, though. He's very bitter."

"Did he read my letter?"

"No. I tried to convince him to, but he wouldn't."

"Okay, at least I'm prepared."

"I'll be right back." She made her way out of the room.

David heard Elizabeth and Sarah whispering in the hall. Then Elizabeth said, "I'll get him."

David balled his fists and rapped them against his temples. Cursing himself for being such a fool, he stood up and walked to the fireplace. He wondered if this could really be happening. It seemed so unreal, like a horrible dream. Sarah was gone, probably forever. And Jack . . . of course Jack hated him. How could he not? David tried to think of what he could possibly say that would change his son's feelings. He heard footsteps coming around the corner. When he looked around, Sarah and Elizabeth were standing with Jack in the doorway. Jack was frowning.

"Jack, your father would like to talk to you. We'll leave you two alone," Sarah said.

Jack turned as if to follow her. Elizabeth caught his eye and nodded her head toward David. Jack stopped and faced his father.

"Hi, Jack. How have you been, pal?" David made a movement toward him. Jack stuck his hands stiffly into the pockets of his jeans. Remembering Sarah's reaction a few minutes earlier, David stopped.

"I've been okay."

"I heard you're playing football."

"Yeah."

"What position have they got you at?"

"Quarterback. Can I go now?"

"Jack, I know you're mad, and I don't blame you. I did something bad, very bad. But I want you to know that I love you more than anything. I'm hoping that you'll give me a chance to be your dad again."

Jack shifted his weight from one foot to the other and studied his tennis shoes. After a few moments, he looked David in the eye and said, "Don't you know what you did to Mom? I hate your guts." He turned and walked away. A second later the front door slammed.

David went to the window, placed his hand on the pane, and watched Jack jog down the walk, across the street, and out of sight. Leaning forward, David pressed his forehead against the cold glass. An overwhelming fear washed over him—the fear that he wouldn't see his son again for a long, long time.

chapter 16

The back tires of the pickup sprayed a cloud of orange dust as they skidded to a stop in front of the diner. David turned off the ignition. The engine coughed and bucked before settling into a restless, clicking siesta. David stepped out onto the rocky clay that passed for soil after two months without a drop of rain. He looked at the cloudless sky and recalled a slick tourist brochure that he had picked up at a rest stop six months earlier, when he first drove into Texas. It had pointed out that East Texas was the part of the state that was supposed to get all of the rain. He shook his head. Judging from the comments of the natives, this was the hottest, driest spring on record.

Reaching back through the open window of the truck, he grabbed a threadbare towel from the front seat next to his tattered Bible. He wiped it across his glistening face. It was only noon and it had to be ninety degrees. It occurred to him that he should have listened to the farmer who sold him the old truck. The farmer had warned him that a vehicle with no air conditioning might be a better choice for a young-ster. David wondered if Texas was the only place with people honest enough to try to talk a man *out* of buying their truck. The price had been right, though. He tossed the towel back through the window.

Before opening the diner door, he wiped his work boots on a green doormat that said *Cowboys Welcome, Cows Not.* A tiny bell jingled above his head as he stepped over the threshold. A rusted window air conditioner just to the right of the door blasted icy air onto the side of his neck. He paused to enjoy it. Two farmers in a booth near the front turned in unison, looked him over, and tipped their John Deere caps. David nodded and slipped onto a stool at the counter.

A pear-shaped waitress with impossibly yellow hair leaned her elbows on the counter in front of him. "What'll ya have, darlin'?" she said, with a big smile. She swished a wet dish towel over a coffee stain near his right hand. "Sorry, missed that one."

He scanned the menu, posted in black magnetic letters on a white board behind her head. "How's the chili?"

"Pretty fair, most would say. It only won the cook-off at Canton."

"Is that a big deal?"

"Fifth largest chili cook-off in the state."

"Fifth largest? How in the world do you determine that?"

"Don't have to. People have been callin' it that since I was a baby. Must be somethin' to it, don't you think?"

"I'll take the chili, then, and a Pepsi."

"One red hot!" she yelled into the little kitchen through the rectangular cutout in the wall behind her. She turned back to him. "You'll like it. I wouldn't steer you wrong. You from around here?"

"Where is here? I didn't see a sign when I drove into town."

"The metropolis of Elsa. No cow jokes, please—that's Elsie."

"It never occurred to me. Now I understand the welcome mat."

"You must be a dull one. First thing that pops into most people's minds." She laughed good-naturedly. "I'll get your Pepsi." She turned and walked to the other end of the counter.

David pulled his wallet out. Twenty-two dollars. He hadn't had a job for more than a week, and he hadn't had a decent job for more than a month. There had been plenty of times in his life when money was tight. For the first time, though, he wondered what a person did when the money ran out completely. He was already sleeping in his truck most nights. What would he do for food, for gas?

"Say, you wouldn't happen to know anyone who needs a handyman, would you?" he said.

"Mister, in this part of Texas everybody lives next door to a handyman."

"Yeah. I'm starting to figure that out."

She placed a Pepsi and a big white bowl in front of him. She reached beneath the counter, pulled out several packages of crackers, and put those in front of him also. "I've got to go in the back for a minute. If you need anything, just yell. My name is Margie."

He nodded. "Thanks, Margie." Digging his spoon into the chili, he pondered his position. There was no question that it was time to declare the situation critical. Even if he headed for Dallas, where the jobs would surely be more plentiful, he wasn't likely to find anything before his money ran out—and it was a lot easier to sleep on the side of the road in East Texas than in the city. On the other hand, at least the city would have shelters where he could get a meal and a cot to sleep on.

The bell over the door jingled. He took another bite of his chili.

Good Lord, so this is what I've come to. It's between sleeping on the side of the road and looking for a soup kitchen. In his mind, he pictured the parsonage in O'Fallon. He saw himself sitting at the kitchen table with Sarah and Jack. He dropped the spoon in the bowl and put his head in his hands.

A few minutes later someone tapped him on the shoulder. "Excuse me. Do you happen to know anything about carburetors?" said a gravelly female voice.

David turned. In front of him was a tiny, white-haired woman in a green cotton dress. Standing behind her was a tall, bald-headed man wearing huge, black-framed eyeglasses.

"Carburetors? On a car?"

"Laws a'mighty, Willard, I think we've asked the wrong man," she said, looking over her shoulder.

"No—of course it's on a car," David said.

"Well, that's progress. Do you think you know how to fix one?"

"I think so. Why?"

"Our car's been fussin' at us all the way over here. Spittin' and hackin' is the best way I can describe it. Would you mind takin' a look at it? We'll pay you what it's worth to fix it."

"I'd be happy to. But don't you have a mechanic here in town?"

"Yes, we do. Would you like for me to ask him to fix it?"

"No! To tell you the truth, I could use the money right now."

"I'm Leta Hodgkins. This is my husband, Willard."

"I'm David Parst."

"Happy to meet you."

"Which one is your car?"

"You shouldn't have any trouble findin' it. It's the only one out there other than yours." She handed him her keys.

David looked at the booth where the two farmers had been sitting.

It was empty. "Ma'am, with all due respect, you don't even know me. You're going to give me your car keys?"

"That's your truck out front, isn't it?" she said.

"Yes."

"Is that your Bible in the front seat?"

"It is. How did you happen to see that?"

"If you live long enough, you learn how to learn about people. Your Bible's good and worn. I'll take my chances with you. Willard's toolbox is in the trunk."

David walked out the door. Ten minutes later, he came back into the diner. He approached the booth where Leta and Willard were sitting. "Mrs. Hodgkins."

"That's Leta, thank you."

"Okay, Leta, I started your car and ran it for a while. It seems to me to be running fine. Are you sure there's something wrong? How did you say it sounded?"

Leta looked across the table at her husband. "Willard, have you ever seen anything like it?"

Willard lifted his coffee cup and took a drink. "Nope. It's a world-class shocker, hon."

"You're one whale of a mechanic, mister," Leta said. She reached in her purse, pulled out a twenty-dollar bill, and pushed it into his hand.

"Why, I can't take that, Mrs. . . . . Leta. I didn't do anything. I'm not even a mechanic. Your car wasn't broken."

"It was broken when we came in."

"I don't think it was, ma'am. Maybe you got some bad gas or something."

Willard took another sip of coffee. "David, I'm gonna give you a tip," he said. "It'll come in handy if you're gonna spend any time around here. If Leta says somethin's broken, let it be broken. When she says it's fixed, let it be fixed. It's sort of a rule of nature." He smiled at her.

Leta swatted Willard's arm. "You don't have to listen to this senile old buzzard. Just let him go on. If he wasn't so cute I wouldn't keep him around."

David scratched his head.

"So if you're not a mechanic, what are you?" Willard said.

David stuck his hands in the back pockets of his jeans. "I'm nothing, I guess."

"Mercy, you must really be down on your luck, to say somethin' like that," Leta said. "You seem like a nice fella to me. Tell me, what were you before you became nothin'?" She looked directly into his eyes.

For years, David would look back and wonder why he answered her question at all, let alone truthfully. "I was a preacher," he said.

Leta looked at Willard and whooped. "Willard, the Lord works in mysterious ways."

Willard lifted his cup in a toast and then drained the last few drops. "Hot dog," he said.

part 2

chapter 17

Leta Hodgkins smiled appreciatively from her wheelchair as David forced an oozing yellow-and-green forkful of her Vegetable Surprise into his mouth. Around them, the three hundred or so members of the First Christian Church of Elsa, Texas, buzzed from table to table, enjoying a potluck dinner in David's honor. On the wall hung a hand-painted banner: *Happy 10th Anniversary, Pastor Dave.*

David stared at the banner and shook his head. Could it really have been ten years since Leta and Willard walked into his life in that ramshackled little diner? He knew that the Bible said we sometimes entertain angels without knowing it. If ever he had met angels, they were Leta and Willard. That was certain.

He reached over and patted eighty-five-year-old Leta on the knee. "Leta, all in all this old church has done pretty well, hasn't it? Who would have thought?"

"You saved us, preacher. That's a fact."

"I didn't save anything. Where would I be without you?"

"Shovelin' pig pens, just like the prodigal son, I suppose," she said.

He looked at her and smiled. "Or dead somewhere on the side of the road."

"Laws a'mighty, I don't think things were quite that bad. Besides, if I hadn't found you sittin' there cryin' in your chili that day, somebody else would have. The Lord's plans don't depend on an old woman like me. I just happened to be the one who walked through the door of the diner."

"What were the odds, though, of you and Willard walking into that particular diner on that particular April day, and during the particular week that your preacher quit? It was a miracle."

Leta harrumphed. "Some miracle. Willard and I had been goin' there for coffee every Friday for fifteen years."

"Okay, but what about my being there? I'd never even heard of Elsa."

"I'll grant you, that was a nice little coincidence. In my life, the Lord has worked more often by takin' advantage of coincidences than by callin' fire from the sky."

"And that charade about your carburetor!"

"Pastor Dave, as beaten down as you looked that day, I think God would have struck me deaf and dumb if I hadn't done somethin'."

"I still say it was a miracle."

She smiled at no one in particular. "All right, then."

He raised another forkful of Vegetable Surprise to his mouth. "Leta, I don't know how you do it," he said. "You're not only beautiful, but I don't believe the Lord has ever done such a job teaching one woman to cook." He took another bite and chewed with a vigor that suggested enthusiasm but actually reflected contortions designed to shift the awful concoction away from his taste buds while he pulverized it sufficiently enough to swallow.

"Preacher, you are a scoundrel. You're flattering me again." She smacked him on the arm.

Looking down at his plate, David resolved to take strength from his environment. Rapid fire, he shoveled several huge globs into his mouth, all the while struggling not to gag. Finished at last, he turned to Leta and said, "That was so good I almost forgot to leave room for the fried chicken." He looked hungrily at the crispy chicken breast that anchored the medley of remaining food on his plate—the Lord's reward for a small act of kindness.

"I don't think anyone else liked it nearly as much as you. It's hardly been touched," she said. She nodded toward a plain white casserole dish, sitting forlornly full in the middle of the makeshift buffet table along the wall, like a gangly teenager spurned at the high school dance.

David looked at the dish, then longingly at his fried chicken, then back at Leta. Reaching up to straighten her silver-blue wig with her hands, she smiled sweetly. He backed his chair out. "They don't know what they're missing. I'd better hurry before they figure it out." He walked over to the buffet, his blue short-sleeved shirt and wrinkled slacks draped loosely over his thin frame. After grabbing a clean paper plate, he scooped up several gooey helpings, enough to elevate Mrs. Hodgkins' neglected dish safely above wallflower status.

When he arrived back at the table, Leta leaned over, pinched the sleeve of his shirt, and whispered, "I didn't know you liked my Vegetable Surprise so much. I'm going to whip up a special batch for you and have one of my grandbabies bring it over to your house this week. But don't tell anyone."

David smiled wanly and struggled to keep his face from turning green.

"Gotcha, preacher!" she shouted, throwing a skinny, age-flecked arm into the air. A number of heads turned to see what had happened. Leta laughed so hard she began to cough and wheeze. When she caught her breath she said, "Don't you think I've figured out by now that everyone knows I can't cook a lick? I just bring the stuff so people won't say the old broad's tryin' to eat for free."

David looked around sheepishly. Everyone sitting near them was laughing. His green eyes sparkled. "Leta, you old coot. What have I done to deserve you?" He put down his fork and picked up his fried chicken.

"Not a thing, preacher, not a thing." She slapped her thigh. "But you've got me anyway, you lucky dog."

"Dog, maybe. Lucky, questionable." He took a huge bite from the chicken breast.

Her face turned serious. She leaned toward him and in a low voice said, "I understand you're meetin' with Jeff Mirer this afternoon."

David wiped his mouth with a paper napkin. "How did you know that?" he whispered.

"Because I'm the one who told his wife to make him meet with you, that's how. He's been spendin' way too much time playing pool with the boys over at the Highway House—so he says anyway. And them with that little girl at home." She shook her head. "I figured you could do him some good, let him know a little somethin' about life."

David knew exactly what she meant. Leta knew everything about David's past. So did most of the older members of the church. He had told the hiring committee the entire story during his first interview. He was the most surprised person in Elsa when they offered him the job. Initially he had taken that as a testament to just how hard it was to attract a minister to a tiny town like Elsa. As the years passed, his view had changed. He had come to appreciate that it was more of a reflection of something inside of the people of Elsa.

Elsa was an East Texas town that had flourished while the oil held out, but the glory days were long gone. A few locals who still held producing oil leases had gotten rich with the high oil prices during the late seventies and early eighties. For most folks, though, the strengthening economy of the first few years of the eighties had been nothing more than a headline on the national news. The people of Elsa were accustomed to scratching hard to get by. They didn't expect perfection of one another or anyone else. There was only one thing they seemed to despise, and that was a quitter. So when Leta suggested that David could teach Jeff Mirer something, David took no offense.

"I'll do my best to straighten him out," he said.

Leaning over, he nudged Leta's arm. "How about if I pick up a double cheese pizza and bring over a deck of cards tonight? We can play some gin."

"Why, that would be first rate, preacher. Penny a point, as usual, so bring your wallet."

David simply smiled.

chapter 18

David was making coffee in the kitchen of his tiny white frame house when he heard a knock at the front door. "Come on in and have a seat," he yelled. He poured a pot of water into the machine, hit the switch, and walked into the scantly furnished living room. Jeff Mirer was settling his lanky frame on the beat-up old couch, shifting this way and that in an effort to find a spot that did not jab him with an insistent spring.

"Hi, Pastor Dave. How've you been?" He nervously moved his fingernail in tight, rapid circles on the leg of his blue jeans.

David was well aware that Jeff would rather be just about anywhere than the pastor's living room on a sunny Sunday afternoon and that he wouldn't be there at all if his wife, Teri, hadn't made him come. David couldn't have cared less. He wasn't going to sit by and watch this kid ruin his life. "I've been great, just great. How about you?" he said.

"Getting by pretty well, thanks."

"How about those Rangers? They're off to a good start," David said. He knew Jeff liked baseball.

"If their bullpen can hold up, they're going to be tough all right,"

Jeff said. "I sure like their rotation, with Hough, Honeycutt, and Tanana." He looked around the room, and his eyes stopped on a framed black-and-white picture sitting on the desk in the corner. It was David in his Peoria baseball uniform. "Is that you?"

"I played some ball when I was younger."

"Peoria. Is that the minor league team?"

"Yeah. Cubs, Double-A."

"Whoa. I'm impressed. You were a lot bigger then."

David could see that Jeff was having a hard time reconciling the athletic young fellow in the picture with the man sitting in front of him. "I've had a few problems. I have a little harder time keeping the weight on these days."

"Chocolate shakes, that's the key—one per day. It will fatten you right up. That's how I put it on for high school football. What position did you play?"

"Shortstop. Couldn't get past Double-A."

Jeff's eyes moved across the desk to another framed picture, this one faded a bit, of a boy in a Little League uniform, coiled in his batting stance. "Who's the kid?" he said. As one of the younger members of the church, Jeff had never heard about David's past.

"My son."

"You're kidding me. I didn't know you had a boy. How old is he?"

"Oh, he's a grown man now. That was a long time ago."

"He looks like he was a good little ballplayer."

"Yes, he was. Still is. Good range, great arm, good contact hitter. He plays in college now."

"Where?"

David looked at the picture and contemplated whether he wanted Jeff to know that. "He plays at a good school. It doesn't matter which one."

"I didn't mean to be nosy."

"You weren't. I don't see him anymore. Actually I do see him—just about every other weekend this time of year, during baseball season. In fact, I'm going to see him play next Saturday. He doesn't see me, though. He hasn't for ten years."

"I don't get it. You see him, but he doesn't see you?"

David placed his hands on his knees and leaned forward. "I go to watch him play, but he doesn't even know it. If he did know, he'd tell me not to come. He doesn't want to have anything to do with me, and there's a reason. Would you like a cup of coffee or a soda or something? I've got a story to tell you and I want you to listen carefully, because it's important . . ."

chapter 19

David balanced a quart bottle of Pepsi on the flimsy pizza box while he rapped three times on Leta's storm door, sending a violent tremor rattling through the glass.

"Hold your horses! I'm comin' as fast as my buggy will take me." Leta's scratchy voice came from the back of the house.

After a few moments the door opened.

"Your dinner, madame." David bowed, holding out the pizza box. "And a bottle of Pepsi's finest."

"Oh, you got me some Pepsi too? You know I shouldn't drink that at night. It's the devil's brew when you're my age." She cackled and snatched the bottle out of his hand. Securing it in her lap as if it were a sack of gold coins, she turned and nimbly guided her wheelchair across the wood floor of the tiny living room. As she approached the kitchen in the back of the house, she looked over her shoulder and said, "Double cheese?"

"Leta, you cut me to the quick. Have I ever ordered anything else for you?"

"I've got some paper plates and cups on the counter. You get some ice in the cups and bring the plates over. I'll shuffle the cards."

David cringed as she rolled onto the slick kitchen tile at an alarming speed. Deftly braking at the metal breakfast table, she set down the bottle and picked up the deck of cards that was lying there.

"Hurry up with those cups, would you?" she said. "At my age you have to take your pleasures quickly. I might just keel over dead before we get this stuff poured."

Before long they were resuming the longest-running game of gin in Macoupin County. For months Leta had carefully scratched their running score into her little spiral notebook. At one time she had been up on David by more than two thousand points, but recently he had fought his way back to within one hundred fifty.

"Gin!" He spread his cards on the table.

"Land's sake, preacher, you've been practicin' on the sly."

"I don't know what's happened lately, but I've been getting all of the luck, that's for sure." He swept up the scattered cards and began to shuffle them.

"You've been prayin' over our little card game, haven't you? I just don't think that's right, with you bein' a preacher and all. You've got a more direct line upstairs than I do." She took a big swig of Pepsi and smacked her lips, rattling her dentures.

"I doubt if anyone's got a more direct line than you do," he said. He pointed at her paper cup. "You'd better take it easy on that stuff. I don't want to have to pull you out from under the table."

"You don't have to worry about me, young man. I can handle my Pepsi." She slapped the table and smiled. "This chick's been around."

David laughed as he dealt the cards. "You know, Leta, even after all this time it seems strange playing cards without Willard."

"Willard was a good one, that's for sure. But I'll be gettin' on to see him soon enough. I figure he doesn't have it too bad where he is."

"You mean heaven?"

"I sure as heck hope so, preacher! Do you know somethin' I don't know?"

"Well, of course not. Certainly he's in heaven. I just didn't . . ."

"Oh, don't go wafflin' around on me. I'm just givin' you a hard time. Say, how did your talk with the Mirer boy go today?"

"Pretty well, I think. He seemed to listen, anyway."

"Oh, he listened, all right."

"What makes you so sure?"

"He called me after he left your house, that's what." Leta laid a card on the table.

"He did? Why?"

"He had a question about you."

"About me? I thought I told him my whole life story." David picked a card off the deck.

"He wanted to know why you've never remarried."

"I see—and what did you tell him?"

"I told him you still *were* married."

"I'll bet that ended the discussion."

"Nope. He was surprised, though. He said he figured you must have gotten divorced after all of that mess you stepped in. Then he asked why you never date anybody."

"What did you tell him?"

"I said, 'Didn't you hear me, son? He's married!'"

"What did he say then?"

"He didn't seem to know what to say. Some things a person just has to be older to understand, I suspect."

"Don't be too hard on him. I'm not sure I understand it myself sometimes." David laid down his cards. "I'm out with seven."

"You snake." She leaned over and peered at the cards. Unable to play on his discards, she counted the points in her hand, touching her index finger to each card. "That's thirty-two. Speakin' of marriage, have you talked to Sarah lately?" She pushed her cards across the table to him.

"A few weeks ago. It's all very strange, but I'd say we've settled into a sort of long-distance friendship. She's made it clear that's all it's ever going to be. Better than nothing, though. And, as King David said, 'Who knows what the Lord will do?'"

"Amen."

He shuffled the cards and dealt.

"How's that boy of yours doin' on the baseball team?" Leta said. "I haven't heard you talk much about him lately."

"Hitting three-thirty. Looks like he's on his way to his second straight conference Gold Glove at shortstop. I told you the Cardinals drafted him in the sixth round, didn't I?"

"Only about ten times. But I don't blame you for bein' proud. Lord have mercy, he is as big a star as his daddy was."

"Oh, he's a much better player than I ever was. He's got a real shot. With a little luck he could make it to the big leagues."

"Are you gonna go see him play next weekend?"

"Yep."

"Are you gonna stop by the locker room and see him this time?" She casually studied the cards fanned out in her hands.

"Don't sit there acting nonchalant, Leta. We've been through this before."

"Just askin'. No need to get a bee in your bonnet."

"He won't talk to me. You know that."

"What I know is that you haven't tried for years." She drew a card from the deck and placed another on the discard pile.

"Yes, but I beat my head against that wall for years. He wants me to leave him alone, and that's what I'm going to do."

"When you were wanderin' around Texas for six months before you came here to Elsa, did God leave you alone?"

"What does that have to do with anything?" He picked up the card she had just put down and laid a jack on the discard pile.

"Nothin', I suppose." One eye peeked at him from above her cards.

"That was different. I was looking for God. Jack wants nothing to do with me."

"I'm sure that's true. I did notice, though, that you haven't answered my question."

"No. God didn't leave me alone. He was on me the entire time and wouldn't let up. There, are you satisfied?"

"Oh."

"What do you mean, 'Oh'?"

"Why, I didn't mean anything."

He stared at the backs of her cards, which were blocking her face. "I know what you're doing, Leta."

From behind the cards, her voice rang out. "I don't know what you're talkin' about. You're a lot smarter than me. I suppose you've figured a perfectly good reason why you should be less persistent with your son than the good Lord has been with you."

Picking up his discarded jack, she spread her hand out on the table. "Gin," she said. "That's just what I needed. I feel a change in the weather coming."

David wasn't so sure.

chapter 20

Sarah Parst sat alone, facing the door of the restaurant. In front of her a swarm of red-vested waiters buzzed from table to table. For this special occasion she had reserved the prime corner booth at one of Austin, Texas's finest eateries. After all, her son would be engaged only once, God willing. She wanted to celebrate it properly. That is, if Jack and his fiancée, Katie Seers, would just hurry up and get there.

To save their table, Sarah had taken a cab straight from Jack's University of Texas baseball game to the restaurant. Jack and Katie were to meet her there after Jack showered and changed. If they didn't arrive soon, Sarah would have to cut their celebration short to catch her flight back to Chicago.

It had been a long, bumpy ride for Jack from junior high school to the April before his college graduation. At times Sarah had doubted that he would make it to college at all. Junior high and high school had been a struggle for him—not academically or athletically, but behaviorally. He had even been kicked off his high school football team for part of a season.

Leery of Jack's attitude problems, recruiters from most of the big-time college baseball programs had shied away from him despite his gaudy batting average and slick fielding. For some reason, though, UT had looked past his disciplinary issues. To Sarah's relief, Jack had really gotten his life in order during his four years at UT. There had been a few minor scrapes with the coach—one recently, about which Sarah intended to talk to Katie—but nothing serious.

The weekend before, Jack had called Sarah to tell her that he had proposed. Sarah thought the match was perfect. Katie had played a huge role in Jack's attitude adjustment since he arrived at college. Upon hearing the news, Sarah had immediately made plans to travel from Chicago to Austin and celebrate with them. Fortunately the news had come during one of her good spells. She was getting along fine with a cane these days and hadn't had to think about using a wheelchair for months.

Sarah looked at her watch, then took a sip from her water glass, and told herself to relax. There would be other flights.

The door of the restaurant swung open. Jack and Katie hurried in breathlessly. Katie spotted Sarah and waved. The couple wound their way toward Sarah through a maze of white tablecloths. Jack wore a navy blazer, striped tie, and gray slacks. Katie was dressed in a simple khaki skirt and blue oxford blouse. As usual, she had on scant makeup. Nevertheless, Sarah noticed more than one man's head turn as Katie's firm, athletic figure and flashing auburn hair brushed past.

"So this is how the other half lives," Jack said, as he leaned over and kissed Sarah on the cheek. He scanned the sea of suits around him.

"I thought you'd gotten lost," Sarah said.

"We had to stop and get gas." Jack stood aside to let Katie slide into the semicircular booth next to Sarah.

"What's wrong, didn't you have a suitcase full of money to donate to OPEC?" Sarah said.

Jack laughed. "You're behind the times, Mom. OPEC is on its way out. We're learning about it in economics. Cartels fail because members cheat. Classic economic theory, and it's exactly what's happening. Prices are coming down, hadn't you noticed?"

"I'm impressed. Then you must have plenty of gas money."

"You're confusing macroeconomic theory with my microeconomic reality. I'm broke, as usual."

"Well, if you're learning that much in school, I guess the least I can do is give you some gas money. Remind me before we leave. Of course, one solution is to walk more."

"Oh, he's all for walking," Katie said. "Not for him, though, for me. He told me that if we ran out of gas, I would have to walk to the station to get some because he was too tired. I pointed out that going one-for-eight with three strikeouts shouldn't have worn him out too much." She smiled, revealing the slightest gap between the front two of her otherwise perfect teeth.

Jack ran his hand through his closely cropped hair. "Good grief, two of their pitchers were all-conference last year. It wasn't exactly easy up there. That last guy must have been throwing a hundred miles an hour. I was just trying to keep from getting killed."

"Oh, I thought I recalled that you were all-conference last year too. Shouldn't that make it a fair fight?" Katie said.

"I'm not going to be all-conference this year if I keep going one-for-eight, that's for sure. I'm just glad those two guys are leaving town."

They opened their menus. Soon Jack and Sarah fell into a lively discussion about the relative merits of spinach casserole, which Sarah recommended, and garlic mashed potatoes, which sounded far better to Jack. When their main courses arrived, Jack sliced into his filet mignon and began to shovel in alternating bites of beef and potatoes at an amazing rate.

Sarah watched him for a few minutes, eyebrow raised. Finally, she set her fork on her plate and said, "Are you ever going to swallow, or is this something you do to keep your teeth filed down?"

Katie laughed and covered her mouth with her napkin. When she got control of herself, she looked around to see if any of the other diners were staring at her. "Sorry, I couldn't help it. Can you tell we never go to nice places?"

"I wouldn't care if we were at Hamburger Hamlet. Jack's table manners are atrocious," Sarah said. "Jack, repeat after me: 'I was raised by humans, not by wolves.'"

Jack continued chewing until he could finally swallow. "I'm glad you two are having such a good time at my expense."

"Actually, it's at my expense, remember?" Sarah said.

"Good point. By the way, thank you. This is great. We usually go to Pirrilli's on Sunday evening. You can buy a house salad for two dollars and thirty-eight cents and they give you all the bread you can eat."

Katie rolled her eyes. "It's very romantic."

"This is incredibly unfair," Jack said. "You're ganging up on me. I'll have to go back to eating all my meals in the jock hall. At least they appreciate me there."

"It's not so much that they appreciate you as that they're in awe of you. You're the only athlete in that building for the past decade who's had higher than a three-point-five grade point," Katie said.

"You're stereotyping. Bill Kilowski has a three-point-eight in physics."

"He's not an athlete, he's a placekicker."

"So? Placekickers are jocks, sort of. Anyway, let's talk about the baseball team. Tico has a three-point-six."

"Who's Tico?" Sarah asked.

"Center fielder," Katie said. "You've got a point. The baseball players do generally have positive IQs. Actually, so do most of the football players. They just don't act like it."

"Are you going to abuse me this much after we're married?"

"I certainly hope so," Sarah said. "He needs this. Otherwise he gets a big head."

Jack wiped his napkin across his mouth. "I thought we were celebrating an engagement, not roasting Jack."

"That's a valid point, honey. Let's get down to business." Sarah nodded at the waiter, who scurried out of the room, then reappeared with a bottle of champagne and three flutes. He filled the glasses, smiled, and slipped away.

"Well, well, what's this?" Jack said. "Katie, you should know that I have never before seen my mother take a drink."

"This is a special occasion. I want to make a toast." Sarah raised her glass. "Katie, I want you to know that I couldn't have handpicked anyone I'd rather have my son marry. I am so happy right now that I'm about to burst. I'm finally going to have a daughter after all these years. May the two of you enjoy all of the happiness marriage can bring, and may God bless you every single day." She clinked her glass against Katie's and then Jack's.

"That was so sweet I think I'm going to cry," Katie said. "Thank you."

"Excuse me for interrupting this love fest, but does anyone remember me, the groom-to-be?" Jack said.

"Of course we do. Honey, the air conditioning is getting a little cool for me. Would you mind running out to your car to get my sweater? I left it in the backseat this morning."

"I'm glad I play such a critical role around here. I'll be right back. I hope my steak doesn't get cold."

"If it does, I'll have them take it back and warm it for you." Sarah smiled sweetly. "No need to hurry on my account. Katie and I have lots to talk about."

"I'll bet. That's what worries me."

After Jack left the table, Sarah said, "I've never seen Jack so happy, Katie. I know he'll be good to you."

"He's a real sweetheart. Do you know that sometimes he sneaks notes into my books? I'll open my book in class and there's a note that says 'Thinking of you' or 'You're beautiful.' My sorority sisters think he's a dream man."

"My Jack writes love notes in your books? I didn't think he had it in him. You're obviously good for him. You know, I've been rooting for this engagement to happen since that first Mom's Day weekend when I met you."

"Really? Back then, I thought you didn't like me. You're so quiet and self-assured. I was intimidated. Nothing makes me more frantic than a pause in the conversation. I worried that we'd never be able to talk. Now look at us."

Sarah picked up her fork. "First impressions . . . Tell me, how is Jack's spat with his coach going? Have they patched things up?"

"It's still pretty tense. For some reason, Jack doesn't trust him. He's convinced he's looking for an excuse to shove that freshman in front of him at shortstop. I don't understand where Jack's coming from. After all, the man named him captain of the team."

"He's suspicious of anyone who's got authority over him—has

been since he was young. I'm sure it's because of what happened with his father. You and I have never talked about his father. He told you, didn't he?"

"Yes. I'm sure that losing his father at such a young age had a big impact on him."

"It did. It was traumatic for both of us. They were very close, and Jack was at such an impressionable age."

"How did he die?" Katie asked.

"Who?"

"Jack's father."

Sarah's fork stopped short of her mouth.

Just then, Jack returned to the table and sat down. "Not that it seems to matter to either of you, but I'm back. Here's your sweater." He reached past Katie and handed it to Sarah.

"You're pouting. Very unbecoming for a blissfully happy man," Katie said.

Sarah put her fork back on her plate and placed her hands in her lap.

Jack looked at his watch. "If you're going to get to the airport, we're going to have to start eating more quickly. I do appreciate your taking the late flight so you could see my game, though, Mom."

"You're welcome. You were the best player on the field, as usual." Sarah's hands remained in her lap. She looked at Jack, then at Katie.

"Are you okay, Mom? You look a little peaked."

"I'm fine. Just tired, I guess."

When they finished and were about to get up to leave, Sarah touched Katie's arm. "When I'm here next month for graduation, I think we need to have a talk," she whispered.

"Sure, about what?"

"About Jack's father. It's a talk we should have in person, not over the telephone. Please don't say anything to Jack. I want to talk to him first."

Katie studied Sarah's face. "Now I'm curious. I'll look forward to it." She helped Sarah out of the booth and handed her cane to her.

"I'm not sure you should."

They caught up with Jack. "Please, I'm counting on you—not a word," Sarah mouthed to Katie as they walked out the door.

chapter 21

Jack balanced the phone between his ear and shoulder while he pulled a polo shirt and pair of jeans out of a drawer and stuffed them into his athletic bag. "I didn't want to go into the whole thing with her, Mom. It's embarrassing and just a big hassle."

"So instead you told her your father was dead? That's a great way to start a relationship."

"I was going to tell her. I was just waiting for the right time."

"Jack, I can hardly hear you with that music playing so loud."

"That's the boom box you got me for Christmas. Works great, huh?"

"Fabulous."

He reached up to the shelf and turned the knob. "What's wrong, Mom, don't you like Michael Jackson?"

"That's much better, thank you. You mean that awful noise was from that cute little Michael Jackson who sang 'A-B-C'?"

"Same guy. Only now he's that grown-up, streetwise Michael Jackson who sings 'Beat It.'"

"What a shame."

"He doesn't think so. He's made about a gazillion bucks."

"Let's get back to the subject. So when were you planning on telling Katie about your father—at the altar?"

"Okay, okay. I'll tell her. But I've got an awful week coming up. We've got a game today at noon. I've got a finance test Tuesday. Wednesday we go to Baton Rouge for a game. Then, over the weekend we've got a big doubleheader against Baylor. I'm not going to be able to breathe, let alone talk to Katie about this stuff, until I get all of that out of the way." He switched the phone to his other ear, pulled his shaving kit off the dresser, and shoved it into the bag.

"Fine, but you *must* tell her soon. If you don't, I will."

"I already said I would tell her. I promise."

"It seems to me this is a good time for you to give your relationship with your father some thought."

He mashed his bare feet into the beat-up penny loafers that were sitting on the floor next to his bed. "I don't have a relationship with my father."

"My point exactly. Don't you think you should?"

"I don't see you inviting him up to Chicago to visit."

"Please don't use that tone of voice with me."

"I'm sorry, Mom. I can't even talk about him without getting ticked off."

"Believe it or not, I have a very civil relationship with your father. It would be nice if you could try also."

"I just don't see the point. I'm fine; he's fine. Let's leave it at that. Besides, it was his choice, not mine."

"That was ten years ago, Jack. For the past nine years it's been your choice. Are you going to ignore him forever?"

"I'm not ignoring him. He doesn't exist as far as I'm concerned. That's worked for both of us so far. Why fix something that's not broken?"

"It hasn't worked for him, I can tell you that. He's just given up, that's all."

"I don't know how you can even talk to him."

"Because I've moved on with my life. I've forgiven him. Every day I didn't forgive him only hurt me, not him. Besides, I have no desire to hurt him anyway. He's been punished enough."

"I don't want to punish him. I don't want to invest enough time in him to punish him. That's the point. As far as I'm concerned, he *is* dead."

"Jack!"

"I'm sorry, Mom. That's the way I feel."

"You will regret this someday, Jack. When you get older and he's gone, you will wish you had made the effort."

"I'll run that risk."

"I can see I'm getting nowhere here. At a minimum, though, you have to tell Katie."

"Next week. Not this week." One of his teammates stuck his head in Jack's dorm room and pointed at his watch. Jack nodded and slung the bag over his shoulder. "I've got to go. Batting practice."

"All right. Remember, be patient and keep your hands back until last."

He laughed. "Thanks, Mom. You're the best hitting coach I've ever had. I love you."

"I love you too. Promise me, you won't wait too long to talk to her."

"I promise, but next weekend. She's gone this long without knowing. Surely it won't hurt if she has to wait one more week."

chapter 22

Sarah shifted her weight to her strong leg and leaned her cane against her hip. As she pulled on her wool-lined gloves, she scanned the crowd milling around the church vestibule after the Sunday morning service. Her mother stood next to her with her back turned. Elizabeth was talking to a woman whose husband was helping her into a full-length mink.

"The weather was better in Texas," Sarah muttered.

Elizabeth turned. "I'm sorry, Sarah, did you say something?"

"I said the weather was better in Texas. This is ridiculously cold for April."

"That's the price of civilization, dear. The problem with Texas is that it has all of those Texans."

"Remember, your grandson is one of 'those Texans.'"

"So is your husband."

Sarah sighed. "Let's talk about something else." She felt a tap on her shoulder.

"Sarah? I'm glad I caught you."

She knew the voice immediately. When she turned, William

Connerly was thrusting a hardcover book in her direction. His brilliant teeth, meticulously combed gray hair, and unseasonable tan made Sarah think that he should have been a news anchor rather than a sales executive.

"What's this?" she said.

"At Bible study Tuesday you mentioned that you wanted to read Christine Malloy's new novel. I guess everyone else does too. I happened to be at the bookstore and noticed that there was only one copy left on the shelf. I thought I'd better grab it for you."

"That was thoughtful." She took the book. "Do you like to read?"

"Oh, yes, but nothing that would interest you. I like the career improvement books. You know: *Twelve Steps to Business Dominance*, that kind of thing." He threw his shoulders back. "The competition is fierce. A good executive has to stay on top of things."

Sarah nodded. "I'm sure." She pulled her purse off of her shoulder. "Here, let me pay you. How much was it?"

"No, no, I wouldn't think of it. Please consider it a gift."

"Well, thank you, William." She dropped the book into her purse.

"Will I be seeing you at Bible study again this week?" he said.

"I expect to be there. Unless it snows, that is."

"Isn't this awful? I've often said that April is the cruelest month in Chicago. Hopes are high but the clouds are low." He chuckled.

"That's very clever. I'll see you Tuesday, then, if the clouds don't get too low." Sarah turned back to Elizabeth and rolled her eyes.

"I don't know why you're being so smug," Elizabeth said, as they walked out of the church. She shivered and pulled her fur collar tightly around her neck. "He's a successful man, a senior vice president, as I understand it. Perhaps you should give him a chance."

"Give him a chance at what?"

"He's obviously interested in you." Elizabeth nodded and smiled at a distinguished-looking elderly man in a gray cashmere overcoat.

"Oh, please, Mother."

"When are you going to take your head out of the sand? Can you really not see that that man is pursuing you?"

"No, I can't," Sarah said. A young couple brushed past them on the narrow sidewalk. She lowered her voice. "And I wouldn't be interested if he were."

"Why not?"

"For one thing, he'd be quite surprised when he discovered I was married, wouldn't he? Besides, every time I look at him I think of Ted Baxter."

"Who is Ted Baxter?"

"The *Mary Tyler Moore Show?*"

Elizabeth looked at her blankly.

"Never mind," Sarah said.

"Perhaps you should not be so picky. The reality, dear, is that the available pool of men for a fifty-year-old woman who can spend months at a time in a wheelchair is not tremendously large."

Sarah looked at her with her mouth open. "Thank you, Mother. I appreciate that."

"I am just speaking the obvious truth. I know how wonderful you are, but at your age and with your medical issues, not many men are likely to be enticed into finding out for themselves."

"And who says I'm looking for a man?"

"Shouldn't you be?"

"I'm still married."

"And why is that? Is that not the question that cries out for an answer? Why are you still married to that man? Are you ever going to divorce him?"

As they stepped off the sidewalk and into the parking lot, Sarah stopped and leaned on her cane. "That was several questions. Are they all crying out for an answer?"

"You can be smart-alecky if you like. I am trying to be serious and I am trying to help."

"Okay, I'll be serious. I'm not ready to divorce him."

"Not ready? Sarah, it has been ten years! When are you going to be ready?"

"Maybe never. It's hard to explain." With her free hand, she fished through her purse for her car keys.

"Please try."

Sarah found her keys and began walking again. "All right, I will. It's sort of like the story that Jack told Katie about his father being dead."

"The more I think about that, the more I conclude that I cannot blame the boy one iota," Elizabeth said.

"Please, Mother, hear me out. Jack said his father was dead. Well, what we went through in O'Fallon *was* a lot like having David die. The man Jack and I knew was suddenly gone. Only we never had a funeral. Does that make any sense?"

"Minimally."

"When Dad died, we both grieved in our own way, right? You cried every day for a month. Crying isn't my way. Neither your way nor my way was right or wrong. We handled it the best we could."

"What does that have to do with your getting a divorce?"

"My point is I didn't try to tell you how to grieve. Please don't try to tell me. My husband is gone. Let me deal with it the best way I can."

"No one grieves for ten years, Sarah. Besides, he's *not* gone. He lives in Texas and you talk to him on the phone at least once a month. You always say that you have forgiven him. If that is true—and I never thought I would hear myself say this—why don't you take him back?"

Sarah stopped. Her brow furrowed as she reached down and gently squeezed the thigh of her weaker leg. "You're right. No one grieves for ten years, and I'm not still grieving. It's just that now that David and I are talking again, I don't feel that the time is right to think about divorce *or* about getting back together. He isn't pushing it."

They arrived at Elizabeth's black Lincoln Town Car. Sarah put the key in the door.

"Of course he is not pushing divorce," Elizabeth said. "He wants you back." Elizabeth looked at Sarah's cane. "Perhaps you are afraid to take him back." She walked around to the passenger side, opened the door, and eased into the car.

Sarah slid into the driver's seat. "I'm not going to dignify that with a response," she said. She started the car. "Let's get some heat going." She patted her gloved hands together.

"I am not trying to be harsh, dear," Elizabeth said. "I just do not want you to end up old and alone."

"I'm not alone. I have lots of friends and I think my life is just fine. As for David, there is a difference between forgiving him and letting him back into my house. I'm just not ready for that, and frankly, I don't know if I'll ever be ready."

Elizabeth took off her gloves. She pulled down the car's visor and inspected her hair in the mirror. "I am not getting any younger, Sarah. Just look at us. My vision is so bad you have to drive me around the way it is. Someday I'm going to be gone and you are going to be living in that big house by yourself. Please think about that. Who is going to take care of you?"

Sarah pulled the car carefully out of the parking space. "I don't need anyone to take care of me."

"That is easy to say when you are fifty. You may feel differently when you are seventy-five."

"Perhaps I will. My life has taken enough twists and turns already that I've given up on predicting. You, know, Dad used to say that we're only on this earth for a short while. Sometimes I think that I just need to get through all of this—that someday we'll be in a better place, a place where things last."

"That is dreamy metaphysics, dear."

"Interesting you would feel that way, considering that we just left church."

"Please do not be judgmental. It does not become you."

"I'm not saying that I want to ignore life. I've got friends, and I've got you and Jack, and now Katie. Actually, I'm fairly content. And I know I can do some good, help people."

"If we can stop waxing philosophical for a moment, I just hope you do not live to regret snubbing William Connerly. Men like him are not a dime a dozen."

"I'm sure they're not, Mother. I'm sure they're not."

Elizabeth pulled a nail file out of her purse and went to work. Sarah understood the signal that the conversation was over. She put on her blinker and waited for the traffic light to change. Her left leg tingled from her thigh to her knee. She was thankful that her right leg was the stronger. At least she could still drive.

She understood her mother's point. It was nothing she hadn't thought about a million times. *What happens when I can't drive? What happens when the good spells disappear completely?* She wondered if she was kidding herself. Was it childishly dreamy—or, worse yet, cowardly—to focus on something better than this life?

The green arrow flashed on. Sarah turned onto the parkway that led to their house. *Okay, maybe I'm a gullible fool. But my whole life I've cast my lot with God. I'm not changing now.* She peered into her rearview mirror. All of the traffic was catching and passing her. She chewed her lip and gripped the steering wheel tighter.

chapter 23

Katie stood on her tiptoes to see over the heads of the fans in the stands in front of her. Out on the field, Jack, his face contorted with pain, limped toward the dugout. His arms were draped over the shoulders of two teammates. Katie knew it had to be serious. Jack was from the old school. He didn't believe in making a fuss over minor aches and pains. Katie was glad that Sarah had come the week before and was not here to see this.

Jack had been turning a double play at second base when a Baylor runner rolled into his knee, dumping him in the dust. The trainer had worked on him for more than five minutes amidst a huddle of silent, shuffling teammates. When the trainer called for a stretcher, Jack refused and insisted on leaving the field on his feet. Katie had a sick feeling that he'd played his last college game. Apparently the UT crowd and the Baylor baseball players had the same concern. They were all standing and giving him an extra-long ovation.

Katie caught Jack's eye as they maneuvered him gingerly into the dugout.

"I'm okay," he mouthed, but he winced when his dangling cleat banged against the concrete step.

She turned and hurried up the stadium stairs toward the exit that would funnel her down the long pedestrian ramp to the locker room entrance. Just as she reached the top of the stairs, she felt a tap on her shoulder.

"Excuse me, Katie? I know you're in a hurry, but could you give me just two minutes before you leave?" The speaker was a thin, rumpled man with an unruly shock of gray hair. There was something vaguely familiar about him, but Katie couldn't place him.

"I'm sorry, I can't. That was my fiancé who just got hurt. I've got to get to the locker room to find out which hospital they're taking him to." She put her purse under her arm and looked him up and down.

"I know. That's why I wanted to talk to you. I'm as worried about him as you are. Would you let me drive you to the hospital?"

"Oh, you must be with the Cardinals." She relaxed her grip on her purse.

He smiled. "No. Actually, I wish I were." He looked directly into her eyes and his smile evaporated. "I'm his father."

Katie raised an eyebrow. "His what?"

"His father."

"I don't know who you are, mister, but that's sick."

The man seemed startled. "It's true, Katie. My name is David Parst. I was hoping you could help me see him. Here, I'll show you my driver's license." He reached into his back pocket and pulled out a leather wallet, so worn that it was difficult to tell whether it was brown or black. After fumbling in it for a few seconds he fished out a plastic-coated license.

She waved her hand. "Don't bother. Jack's dad is dead."

The man cocked his head. "Dead?" His shoulders sagged.

Katie lowered her voice and said, "If you don't leave me alone, I'm going to get a security guard."

He held out the license. "Here, just look: 'David Parst,' see?" He straightened his shoulders. "I'm not dead—I guess that's obvious. I mean his dad's not dead. Katie, I'm his dad. Please give me just one moment and I'll explain—please."

Her eyes darted from the license to his face and back again. The dark eyes, the thick hair, an eerie resemblance . . . but it was all too bizarre. Then she remembered Sarah's strange remark the weekend before. Surely this wasn't what Sarah had intended to talk to her about. Why would Jack lie about his father being dead?

"You could have had that license made up," she said. "If Jack told me you're dead—not you, his *father* is dead—why should I believe you?"

"Unfortunately, the truth is that he just wishes I were dead. That's why he won't see me. He won't even talk to me. I was hoping you could help. Look, I can prove I'm his father. His mother's name is Sarah. She lives in Chicago. You can call her and ask her about me if you'd like. I'll give you her number. What else can I tell you? He grew up in O'Fallon, Missouri, until he was twelve. I was a preacher, still am. Then, well, something happened and he moved to Chicago with his mother. Have you met Sarah?"

"Yes. In fact, she was here not too long ago."

"Then you'll know when I describe her. She's a quiet woman, and kind—one of the kindest people I've ever known—but really funny when you get to know her."

Katie smiled, recalling Sarah's crack about Jack's table manners: *raised by humans, not by wolves.*

"Let's see, what can I tell you about Jack?" the man continued. "He hates broccoli, at least used to. He's a whiz at math. He's got a double cowlick in the back. It makes his hair stick up . . ."

"Stop, stop!" Katie didn't know for sure that this man was Jack's father, but she had a strong hunch—and he didn't seem dangerous. "Let's find out where they're taking him and we can continue this conversation in the car—not your car, mine."

"Thank you." He hurried to keep up as she strode to the exit.

chapter 24

Katie guided her yellow Honda Civic expertly through the mine-field of potholes that guarded the exit to the stadium parking lot and turned onto the access road to I-35. "Mr. Parst—or whoever you are—if you're really Jack's dad, why would he tell me you were dead? And where have you been all of these years? He told me you died when he was twelve and that's why his mom moved back to Chicago."

"I did something bad. Let's just leave it at that. He can tell you someday if he wants to. Where have I been? I've been preaching in a little town called Elsa for the past ten years. It's about forty miles south-east of Tyler. I drive down for many of his home games, and I even go to some of the away games."

"That must be more than two hundred miles. How have you been able to come to all of those games without Jack seeing you?"

"This is a pretty big ballpark. I make it a point to sit in out-of-the-way places. I don't know if he'd recognize me anyway. I've changed a lot in ten years. Besides, I'm the last person he'd be expecting to see."

"What are the odds, though, that he would just happen to come to UT to play baseball? Did he know you lived in Texas?" She guided the car onto an exit ramp.

"Honestly, I don't know if he knows I live here. But it was more than a coincidence that he came to UT. You see, I used to play a little baseball myself. An old minor league buddy is an assistant coach here. I put a bug in his ear to watch one of Jack's high school games. He liked what he saw and recruited him. I made him swear never to tell Jack, though."

Katie clenched and unclenched her hands on the steering wheel. "So you're his dad, and you're not dead. Let's assume for a minute that's true. What do you want from me?"

"I was hoping you could convince him to talk to me. He hates me, I know. But how long can a person keep hating?" David turned and stared out the window. "You just can't imagine what it's like to have a son who hates you so much that he won't see you, he won't talk to you—that he wishes you were dead." He shook his head. "Believe it or not, I was a good dad once—in fact, most of the time. I loved him more than anything. I still do love him more than anything."

Katie flushed. If he was an actor, he was a good one. "What do you want me to do? I'm not saying I'll do it, but if I were willing, what is it you're asking?"

"Katie, I've got a hunch this injury is bad. I've seen guys blow out knees before. If this is the end of his baseball, I want to be there for him. My gosh, I taught him to play. I thought that maybe if he knew . . . if you told him how I've come to his games, maybe that would make a difference. What do you think?"

"I think that if you're really his dad it would have to make a difference. I know Jack. He puts up a hard-boiled front sometimes, but he's got a good heart. I can't imagine he wouldn't agree to talk to you. If you want me to do this for you, though, I've got to know: what did you do that made him so angry that he hasn't talked to you for ten years?" She watched him out of the corner of her eye.

As if he had guessed what she was thinking, he replied, "I didn't abuse them or anything—nothing like that. I guess you're going to find out anyway, so I may as well be the one to tell you. I was unfaithful to Jack's mother."

"I thought you were a minister?"

"That's right."

Katie turned onto Memorial Drive. She didn't understand how anyone could cheat on Sarah. On the other hand, if you could judge repentance by body language, this guy was one step shy of self-flagellation. "So you cheated on Sarah. Don't get me wrong, I think that's awful, but is there something else? I mean, he's stayed angry for ten years. Didn't you talk to Sarah? Didn't you tell her you were sorry?"

"There is more. The husband of the woman I had the affair with— he killed himself. He did it on the front steps of the church. Jack was one of the first ones on the scene. He saw the body. It was a very gruesome thing."

"How did he do it?"

"How did the man kill himself?"

"Yes."

"He shot himself in the head. There had been a big scene in the church beforehand. He must have had the gun with him. He went outside . . . that's where he did it. So that's the story. I had an affair and I killed a man. That's what I am." His shoulders slumped.

Katie squinted through the windshield. She cleared her throat but said nothing.

"The whole thing was very public and very humiliating," he said.

"For me, for Sarah and Jack, for the church. How do you apologize for something of that magnitude? Sarah's an extraordinary person, though. We talk fairly regularly now. I'm convinced she's forgiven me, but she will never take me back."

"If she's forgiven you, why wouldn't she take you back?"

David rubbed his earlobe between his thumb and forefinger. "You have to understand the kind of woman she is. It would never have occurred to her in a million years to cheat on me, so it was impossible, I guess, for her to take me back. I don't blame her one bit. At least she forgave me. I can tell you I've never forgiven myself, and never will. I don't deserve her back. But, Jack—he's my son. I'll never quit hoping that he'll change his mind."

Katie eased the car up to a stoplight. She stared at the license plate of the car in front of her. After a few moments, she tapped her palms on the steering wheel. "Here's what we'll do. You come into the hospital with me and wait in the waiting room while I go see him. If he's still in a lot of pain, or if he's all drugged up, we may have to wait. On the other hand, maybe some medication will soften him up. Anyway, I'll play it by ear. If I think the timing's right, I'll tell him all about what's happened today. Then he'll agree to let me bring you in." She reached into her purse, fumbled for a mint, and stuck it in her mouth, as if priming her vocal cords. The light changed and she pulled forward.

"That's so kind of you, Katie. I can't tell you how much I appreciate it. But please don't underestimate his feelings toward me. I don't think it's likely to be as easy as you think."

"Just remember, you might be underestimating his feelings toward me, also. If I ask him to do it, and he can see it's really important to me, he'll do it. Just watch. It will all be so emotional. I just hope I don't start bawling."

"You're quite a gal. I don't think I'll be making the mistake of underestimating you."

"By the way, how did you know who I was today at the stadium?"

"You'd be surprised what a fellow can learn over time by keeping his eyes open. And it doesn't hurt to slip ten bucks to one of the ball boys occasionally. I've known about you for quite a while."

"What exactly do you know?" She fidgeted in her seat.

"For one thing, that congratulations are in order. I heard that you're engaged."

"Yes, we are."

"Have you set a date yet?"

"Not yet. We were waiting to see how things went with the Cardinals. Go on."

"You're a Tri Delt. According to the ball boy, you're a 'real brain.' And my son is, well, head over heels in love with you—that's the cleaned-up version of the way the ball boy phrased it. I believe he said something about 'whipped.' Typical high school kid—he didn't know I was a preacher. Oh, and he offered one personal opinion."

"What was that?"

"He said you're, uh, strong-willed enough to hold your own with Jack."

She smiled but kept her eyes on the road. "Are you sure you're not CIA?"

He laughed. "Hardly. I'm lucky if I can find my own shoes in the morning. But, as they say, where there's a will there's a way. It was important to me to know something about you. Here's something I don't know, though. How did you meet Jack?"

"At the YMCA."

"The YMCA?"

"My favorite place to hang out—just kidding. Actually, we were tutoring third graders from one of the inner-city schools. The Y has an after-school program."

"Something the athletic department sponsors?"

"No. Jack and a couple of his buddies from the team did it on their own." She glanced over at him. "He's a good guy, Mr. Parst. A really good guy." She turned into the hospital parking lot and slid the car into a parking space. Turning off the ignition, she looked at him and said, "Well, here goes nothing."

chapter 25

After several hours in Jack's hospital room, Katie pushed open the swinging double doors that led back into the waiting area. David stood up to greet her. She could see that he was studying her. After a moment, his face and shoulders sagged. He turned and stared out the window.

"How is he?" he said, without looking at her.

"It's pretty bad. A torn ACL, whatever that is, and serious cartilage damage too. He's depressed. I should have waited. I'm sorry." Katie walked up to him and put her hand on his arm.

"It's all right. I appreciate your trying. Is he in a lot of pain?"

"No. They gave him something. As soon as the swelling goes down, they'll operate. It could be a day or two."

"That sounds bad. He won't be playing in the summer rookie league, that's for sure."

"There's no way. He'll have almost a year of rehab. The doctor said he won't even be able to think about playing seriously until the middle of the summer after next."

"How's he taking it?"

"Pretty well, really. He's talking about whether he should give it up and go to law school. He's been accepted at some good schools. The University of Illinois is probably where he would go. I've been accepted to their graduate journalism program, so that works well for both of us."

"God works in mysterious ways. This will turn out for the best, somehow."

"Mr. Parst, Jack told me a little bit about what happened, but not the whole thing. One thing he did tell me, though, I thought you should know because it might help you understand where he's coming from."

"What is it?"

"He said that his feelings toward you were not just because of what you did to his mom, although I'm sure you know he's very protective of her."

He nodded.

She took a deep breath. "He said that when he was growing up, everything in your family was about God and the church. He said he believed it all. He thought that was the way things were and the way they were supposed to be. Then you showed him it was all a lie, that he was nothing but a fool. He's told me before that he doesn't believe in God. I suppose this explains it."

David's eyebrows narrowed. "It's not a lie. I was the liar, not God."

"Apparently that's not the way he sees it."

"So I've led my own son away from God. Are there any sins left for me? I've cheated and murdered, why not steal too? Do you know what the Bible says about a person who leads someone away from his faith? It would be better for him to have a boulder tied to his neck and be thrown into the ocean. How much worse for a father who does it to his own son?"

"I don't know what to say."

"Do you believe in God, Katie?"

"Well, yes," she said, shoving her hands into the pockets of her jeans. "Of course I do."

"Do you go to church?"

"I grew up a Methodist. I have to admit that I haven't gone to church much since I came to college. But I definitely believe in God."

"Does it bother you that Jack feels the way he does?"

She shifted her weight from one leg to the other. "I don't know. I hadn't thought about it that much."

"Please begin to think about it. You're going to have kids someday. Do you want them to grow up not believing in God?"

A nurse walked past them. They waited for her to cross the room and pass through the swinging doors. Katie lowered her voice. "Of course not. But that's a long time from now."

"Katie, it's too late for me to reach him. That's obvious. But you can. You have to. Please don't ever forget that. You will have to be the one."

"I don't think it's my job . . ."

He put his hands on her shoulders. "It has to be your job. You're going to be his wife. You're young, Katie. I know it may not seem important now, but someday it will. Then, please remember what I'm saying."

"Mr. Parst, I'm sure his feelings toward you will change. I'll keep trying. I feel so bad for you."

"Don't bother about me anymore! This is about my son's soul. That may sound like preacher talk, but it's more important than me, more important than anything."

Katie took a step away from him. She glanced at the doors that led to the nurses' station.

His voice softened. "I've frightened you. I didn't mean to do that. I'm sorry." He pulled a pen and a small notepad out of his pocket, scribbled something, ripped off the page, and handed it to her. "Here's my number. Maybe you could give me a call once in a while and let me know how you're both doing. That way I could feel as if I'm still involved in your lives, if only from a distance."

"You didn't frighten me, Mr. Parst. I'm just not used to talking about things like this. I'll be happy to call you. He'll come around. Just wait and see." She folded the note and put it in her pocket.

He took her hand and squeezed it gently. "That's nice of you, Katie. Thanks. But please don't forget what we talked about tonight."

"I won't."

"By the way, call me David."

"All right, David. Let me drive you back to your car." They walked side by side out the doors to the parking lot.

KATIE PUSHED OPEN THE DOOR to her apartment and walked straight to the telephone on the kitchen wall. She tapped out a number and waited.

Sarah's voice came from the other end of the line. "Hello?"

"Sarah? It's Katie."

"Katie? Is something wrong? Where's Jack?"

"He hurt his knee in the game today. He's in the hospital."

"The hospital?"

"A runner slid into him. It's pretty bad. He's going to have to have surgery."

"My goodness. Is he in pain?"

"He was. They've got him loaded up on painkillers now, though. They don't know if he'll be able to play again."

"He must be terribly disappointed. At least there's next year. He'll just have to start looking forward to getting started with the Cardinals."

Katie shook the phone cord to untangle it, moved over to the kitchen table, and sat down. "You don't understand. They don't know if he'll be able to play again, ever."

"Oh, no."

"He's talking about forgetting the whole thing and going to law school."

"When is the surgery?"

"Whenever the swelling goes down."

"Poor Jack. He must be devastated."

"So far he's taking it pretty well, really. I'm surprised. It's probably the drugs."

Sarah chuckled. "Yes, that would matter in the short run."

"There's something else. I met someone you know tonight."

"Oh? Who?"

"David."

"David?"

"David Parst." Katie waited. There was silence on the other end of the line. "Sarah? Are you still there?"

"Yes, I'm here. Where in the world did you see him?"

"Not at the cemetery, that's for sure."

"Yes. I suppose it's time we had a talk."

"That's what I was thinking . . ."

chapter 26

Davidavid peered out over the headlights of his Datsun, focusing on the yellow dividing line. A cold front, or what passed for a cold front in Texas, had blown in while he and Katie waited at the hospital. The temperature had fallen only fifteen degrees or so, but it was enough to cause thick fog to settle over every highway valley between Austin and Tyler.

He was thankful for the distraction the difficult road conditions brought. Brooding on the day's events was making him crazy. The rational side of his mind told him to give it up, that Jack would never let him back into his life. After all, Jack wasn't a kid anymore. Was it really likely that he would ever give David another chance? *What kind of person can go ten years refusing to forgive? Maybe he's not even worth knowing. Sarah must have turned him against me. She says she's tried to convince him to give me a chance. But I have no idea what she's really said to him.*

He shook his head. *That's pathetic, Parst. She's the good one, remember? You're the liar. She didn't turn him against you. He didn't need any help to think you're a creep.*

He worked his way up a long hill, out of the low-lying fog, and thought about his conversation with Katie. It all seemed so bleak. He gripped the steering wheel tighter. He couldn't allow himself to give up. He would just have to stay in touch with Katie. That was the only hope.

He reached for the thermos of coffee on the seat beside him. As he crested the hill he put the thermos between his knees, snapped off the plastic top that doubled as a cup, and set it on the seat beside him. While the cup jiggled with each jolt of the car, he picked up the thermos and began to pour the coffee, his eyes moving back and forth from the road.

Descending, his car again slid into the fog. Out of the corner of his eye, he caught a quick, shadowy movement. He didn't actually see the deer until it rolled up onto the hood and smashed into the windshield. The impact crushed the side of the animal's face and flattened it against the glass. Coffee splashed across the seat, burning David's chest and arm. He found himself looking into the one remaining, terrified eye of the hopeless animal. For an instant, the eye became Ted Balik's eye, the one the bullet had not obliterated. David blinked hard and jammed his foot on the brake. He yanked the wheel to the right, throwing the car into a skid. The deer slid off the hood and thudded to the pavement.

He released his foot from the pedal, but the brakes had locked. The car whirled through two complete turns before it smashed into the guardrail and flipped. Something smacked against his scalp. Things turned fuzzy and twisted. A grinding, scraping roar filled the interior of the car as it sledded down the embankment on its roof. The last thing he felt was a crushing pain in the back of his head. Then everything went black.

part 3

chapter 27

Jack Parst clicked print on his laptop, stood up, and walked out of his office to his administrative assistant's station. He peeled the document off the printer tray, scratched a couple of notes in red ink, and placed it in the in-box. Running a hand through his prematurely graying hair, he said, "I'm going down to Bernie's office." He lowered his voice and added, "If anyone asks, don't say where I am."

Cindy Davis looked at him quizzically but quickly returned to her typing. Discretion was something every administrative assistant in the legal business learned early. Jack turned and walked down the hall.

It had been more than eighteen years since Jack and Katie moved to Dallas. Fresh out of the University of Illinois College of Law, Jack had joined Challenger Airlines' rapidly growing legal department. During that time he had worked his way up to associate general counsel, the third-highest legal position in the company. Challenger's sixty-year-old general counsel, Bernie Heath, had been a great help in Jack's advancement. Whatever Bernie's motives (and Jack had often puzzled over them), he had taken an early interest in Jack's career, acting as a willing and effective mentor.

In his nearly two decades working with Bernie, Jack had never gotten a message like the voice mail he'd received several minutes earlier.
Bernie had simply said, "I need to see you in my office ASAP. It's
important. And keep it quiet." Jack had mentally reviewed all of the
things he could have messed up sufficiently to result in such an omi-
nous summons. Unable to come up with anything, he had concluded
that someone else was in deep trouble. Consequently he looked forward to the meeting with morbid anticipation, like a pioneer eager to
arrive at the town square for someone else's hanging.

When Jack walked into the spacious office, Bernie was on the telephone. The sleeves of Bernie's crisp white shirt were rolled up to just
beneath his elbows, and his striped tie was loose at the collar. He was
pacing as he talked. He motioned to Jack to close the door and take a
seat in one of the four leather armchairs that circled the conference
table in the corner.

Bernie's office was always full of gimmicky little toys. Jack picked
up a miniature wooden paddle with a rubber ball attached by an elastic string. With a flick of his wrist, he twirled the ball around the paddle, then flicked his wrist again and unwound it.

"Mitch, I'm telling you I don't know who could have done it,"
Bernie said into the phone. "Listen, I've got to run, someone just came
in. Let me call you back after I'm done here." A pause. "Okay, great.
I'll call you." He placed the phone in its cradle.

"Well, what's the big mystery?" Jack said.

Bernie walked over to the table and sat down next to Jack.
"Something's going on and I wanted to let you know about it. But you
have to keep it quiet or Mitch will chop off my head in a heartbeat."

"This must be good. You know I'm not going to tell anyone. What
is it?" Jack had never seen Bernie so agitated. Jack knew that Mitch

Zanella, Challenger's CEO, had been miffed at Bernie since the previous spring. Bernie had discovered some questionable barter transactions involving a vendor who was an old college buddy of Mitch's. After unsuccessfully raising the issue with Mitch privately, Bernie had surprised everyone, especially Mitch, by bringing it up at the next board meeting. When the board lined up unanimously behind Bernie, Mitch had no choice but to cancel the deals. Mitch was no choirboy. Anyone who knew him realized that he would not soon forget the incident.

"Something weird's been going on at Challenger Express," Bernie began. Challenger Express was a subsidiary corporation that Challenger had spun off and sold to the public a couple of years earlier. "It looks as if there may have been some embezzlement, but we're not sure yet. Anyway, some big money is unaccounted for."

The muscles in Jack's shoulders tightened. He was acting general counsel for Challenger Express. He placed the paddle back on the table and did a rapid-fire mental audit of his own exposure. Surely they wouldn't blame him for being asleep at the switch. He'd never even worked on any accounting issues for Express. The parent company handled all of that. Regardless of who was taking the money, Jack didn't see how anyone could try to say that he should have discovered it. His shoulders relaxed. "That sounds bad," he said. "Do you have any idea who's involved?"

"We've got some ideas, but nothing solid."

"What does this have to do with me? I don't handle accounting issues."

"It doesn't have anything to do with you directly. But something else is going on. When we announce this, it's going to trash Express's stock price, at least until we get to the bottom of it. It turns out there's been a lot of short selling in Express's stock during the past few days. It started August seventeenth, right after this all came to light. I know you're just a dumb litigator, but I assume you know what short selling means." Bernie smiled. "Someone is trying to profit when the stock price falls."

"Yes, even we dumb litigators know what short selling is."

"We're going to make an announcement tomorrow about the missing funds. As soon as the Securities and Exchange Commission puts two and two together, there's sure to be an investigation. Because of your position with Express, you're likely to be one of the first people they talk to. I know you don't have anything to do with this, but I wanted to tip you off so you didn't get blindsided."

"Wow, you weren't kidding. This is big. I appreciate the tip."

"Jack, you can imagine how this is being treated at the board level. We all basically took a blood oath not to tell anyone until the official announcement. That's particularly critical because of the unexplained short selling. I really struggled with telling you, but I finally decided I couldn't leave you in the dark. I think you've got a right to know."

Jack got up. "Thanks, Bernie. I guess I'll go prepare for the grilling."

Bernie stood up and slapped him on the shoulder. "It'll be okay. All you've got to do is tell them the truth. That's the easiest job in the world."

"I hope you're right." Jack walked out and closed the door behind him. As he headed back to his office, he wondered why Bernie really had told him.

chapter 28

Katie stood next to the bed, pulled her tank top over her head, and tucked it into her running shorts. Though she had turned forty-two earlier in the year, her figure was still firm and athletic. She worked hard to keep it that way. Having just returned home from her job as a part-time feature writer for the *Dallas Morning News'* suburban edition, she intended to run a couple of miles before dinner. First, though, she had to talk to Jack.

Katie considered herself lucky. She and Jack had been married seventeen years. He was a kind husband and caring father. After all these years, though, she was still frustrated by his unwillingness to trust people. That afternoon, he had told her over the telephone about the Challenger Express fiasco. Somehow he had talked himself into a cockeyed theory that Bernie was trying to make him the scapegoat. She intended to say plenty to him about that.

She heard the garage door go up. Bending over, she tied her running shoes. As Jack's footsteps came up the stairs, she sat on the bed, her back straight, and waited. When he walked into the room, she opened her mouth to speak, but closed it again when he pulled a bouquet of roses from behind his back.

"Roses for the rose of Edensgate Drive," he said and gave an exaggerated bow. He remained bent at the waist and looked up at her out of the corner of his eye.

She rose from the bed and took the bouquet. "You'd better stand up before you throw your back out, Sir Galahad. What are these for?"

"What do you mean? Aren't you Katie Parst?"

"That's me."

"Wasn't it your recent article regarding the scandalous condition of suburban day care centers that awakened a sleeping Metroplex to enraged action?"

"Oh, Jack, that's so sweet." She threw her arms around his neck and kissed him.

"I'm proud of you," he said. "I know how much time you put into that piece. I think I'm being unbiased when I say that it's got Pulitzer written all over it."

"Now that you mention it, I am expecting the University of Missouri to call any day to offer that journalism professorship." She lifted the roses to her nose.

"You may as well dream big. No out-of-town gigs, though. We need you here."

"I'd better put these where Bandit can't get into them." She walked into the adjoining master bathroom and set them in the sink. "I'll put them in a vase in a minute."

"I must say, the renowned journalist looks nice in shorts too." Jack whistled.

"Your eyes are suffering from age."

"I don't think so." When she came back into the room, he wrapped her up in his arms and kissed her. "Now, that's a nice way to take my mind off a brutal day."

She pulled back and looked into his eyes. "Are you worried about Challenger Express?"

"Not too much. I didn't do anything, so there's no way for me to get caught up in it. That is, if Bernie plays straight with me."

"Plays straight with you?" Her arms dropped to her side.

"Yeah. As long as he doesn't try to set me up somehow."

"Wait a minute. Bernie stuck his neck out—way out—to tip you off about it. Now you're afraid he's setting you up?"

Jack pulled off his tie and unbuttoned his shirt, leaving it draped open over his muscular chest. "Office politics can be tough." He shrugged.

"We really need to talk about this, Jack. This idea makes no sense."

"Wait a minute and hear me out. You might just change your mind."

"I doubt it, but go ahead."

"Don't you think it's a little suspicious that he, as you put it, stuck his neck way out just to keep me from getting surprised by this?"

"No, Jack, I don't. Bernie's always looked out for you. That's what he's doing now."

"This is different, Katie. We're talking about embezzlement and insider trading. This is not just making sure someone gets the next promotion."

"I can't believe I'm hearing this." Katie sat on the bed and leaned back against the headboard. "Bernie Heath has never done anything to make you question his integrity. This notion that he's setting you up is so cynical that it's stunning. Can't you simply believe he's doing you a favor? He likes you. He's always liked you."

"Think about it this way, Kate: What if he's in on the whole insider-trading thing? He's now put me in a terrible position. If anyone asks, I'll have to admit that I knew about it before the public announcement. Being in the know is not exactly a good thing in this situation."

"You didn't do any trading, so what does it matter? Besides, if he were in on it, how would he benefit from your knowing about it? It would just come out that he's the one who told you, so what would he gain?"

"Not if he denied that he's the one who told me. No one else was in that meeting today. It would be his word against mine."

Katie got up, walked over to Jack, and put her hand on his arm. "Listen to yourself. This man has been nothing but good to you for fifteen years. He is not setting you up. He's trying to help you. Can't you just accept that? You are a kind, honest man. So is Bernie. Give him some credit. This crazy idea is beneath you."

"I guess you're right. It just seems strange to me, that's all. Boy, this conversation sure hasn't turned out the way I envisioned it at the florist."

She laughed. "I want to make one thing perfectly clear. Nothing I have said should be interpreted in a way that would discourage you from bringing flowers in the future."

He took off his shirt and twirled it over his head. "Hey, if I put one of those roses in my mouth I'd look like a matador."

"Or a psychotic lawyer. Maturity is a wonderful thing. You should try it."

"Nah. Immaturity is much more fun." He turned and walked into the bathroom, leaving Katie smiling and shaking her head.

chapter 29

$\mathbf{M}$itch Zanella swiveled his black leather chair away from his computer terminal and turned to face Jack. Zanella picked up an elaborately carved silver letter opener and scraped it impatiently back and forth across the shiny sleeve of his Italian suit.

Sitting on the opposite side of Zanella's sleek marble desk, Jack watched the letter opener flash in the light as it moved. His mind conjured the uncomfortable image of a barber sharpening a razor on a leather strop. He thought back to his conversation with Katie the evening before and hoped he was doing the right thing.

"So you had to talk . . . it couldn't wait." Zanella said. As usual, he spoke in intense word bursts, like a verbal machine gun. As a company veteran, Jack knew that the hallmark of Zanella's style was intimidation.

"I hope it's important . . . I've got a lot going on," Zanella continued.

Jack unscrolled his mental outline. "Mitch, it's about this thing with Challenger Express. I've got an idea that I think will help."

Zanella's hand stopped moving. He leaned forward and pointed the letter opener at Jack. "*What* thing with Challenger Express?"

Jack shifted his weight in his chair. "I know about it, Mitch—the missing money. But I've got an idea."

"How do you know about it?"

"It doesn't matter. The point is that I've got a plan that I think will limit . . ."

Zanella rapped the letter opener on the desk. "I'll decide what matters. Who told you?"

Sucking in a deep breath, Jack reminded himself to remain calm. "I can't tell you."

Zanella stood up and walked around the desk. When he was close enough to tower over Jack, he said, "I'll put it another way; tell me or you're fired."

Jack craned his neck to get a look at Zanella's face. "Mitch, if you'll just let me explain my idea, you'll see that we can work our way out of this Express thing with minimal fallout."

"You've got one minute to tell me who told you." Zanella cocked his arm dramatically and looked at his watch.

Jack leaned as far away from him as possible, but found himself trapped by the arm of the chair. He escaped by standing and walking to the door. "You're going to have to fire me then, Mitch. I won't tell you."

Zanella's face reddened. Jack reached for the door handle. The two men stood looking at each other for several moments. Then, to Jack's surprise, Zanella shoved his hands in his pockets and smiled—not a friendly smile, but the disciplined smile of an experienced negotiator.

"I admire your guts. You don't have to rat on anyone. I know Bernie told you."

Jack looked him in the eye. He was certain Zanella was bluffing. "You can think that if you want, but I'm not telling. And you know as well as I do that there are any number of people who could have told me."

"But only one thinks of you as the son he never had."

Jack squeezed the door handle. He felt a surge of color move to his neck, then into his cheeks.

A new smile, this one genuine—a smile of victorious recognition—spread over Zanella's face.

Jack struggled to force the warmth from his cheeks, but the gut pump ran more slowly in reverse. It was too late. He knew he had fallen for an emotional sucker punch. Like a cornered toad, puffing itself up to appear larger to a coiled snake, he threw his shoulders back. "You're grasping for straws, Mitch. I hope you'll be sure you've got the right person before you do anything rash."

"Oh, I'll be sure . . . I'll be sure." Zanella patted Jack on the shoulder, opened the door, and guided him out into the hall.

chapter 30

God, *I love baseball,* Jack thought as he squinted through his wraparound sunglasses toward the sun-baked Little League infield. The game was a much-needed diversion from the stress he had felt since his meeting with Mitch Zanella that morning. He didn't know what Mitch would do next. The day had passed uneventfully, so maybe the answer was nothing.

Jack had wondered whether to tell Bernie what he had done, but what was the point now? Nothing would change. Besides, it was possible that Mitch wouldn't do anything. Then Bernie would be mad at Jack for nothing. Jack glanced at Katie, who was sitting to his left. There was no way he could tell her. He decided to try to forget the whole thing and focus on the game.

Like most Little League parents, he and Katie made a genuine effort to show interest in the whole chattering, spitting, dirt-kicking bunch of twelve-year-olds milling about the field. In reality, though, and again like most Little League parents, they reserved most of their attention for the chattering, spitting, dirt-kicking kid who belonged to them. That one was Patch.

Because things had always come easily to Jack, he was incredibly proud of his son, for whom things did not come easily at all. Born with a defective heart valve, Patch had been given less-than-even odds of surviving his first month. He had proved far tougher than the doctors imagined. After three years of needle sticks, IVs, and surgeries, he had emerged about as healthy as any other kid in their sprawling Dallas suburb of Preston, Texas. The only remnant of his medical ordeal was his nickname, which sprang from his pediatrician's chuckling observation about how often he'd been patched up.

Somehow the natural baseball talent that had blessed the prior two generations of Parsts had skipped over Patch. After much hard work, he had become a passable second baseman, but no more than that. He got to play three innings of every game only because league rules required it. Nevertheless, he loved baseball, perhaps even more than Jack did. Patch's idea of a great time was the same as Jack's had been when he was a boy: a good game of catch when his dad came home from work.

As hard as he had to work at baseball, Patch had to work even harder at school. While his little sister, Lizzy, made straight As without effort, Patch studied twice as hard as the other kids. For that, he got mostly Bs, with a C here and there. His social sphere was nowhere near the popular crowd. Short and wiry, with a nose a bit too round and eyes a tad too small, he was not a boy who caused the girls to pass notes and blush.

"Play's at second, Patch," yelled Marge Milner, who was sitting two rows behind Jack and Katie.

Jack gritted his teeth. *He knows that, you old witch.* The season before, Marge had made a cutting remark to another parent about Patch after he lost a game by letting a ground ball go between his legs.

Unbeknownst to her, Jack and Patch had been standing beneath the bleachers where she was sitting. When she realized that they had overheard, she tried to apologize. Jack would have none of it. Since that time she had gone out of her way to be nice to Patch. She rooted especially hard for him, even though her own son often had to sit out so Patch could play. None of it fooled Jack, though. He knew it was an act.

Patch had been so hurt that Jack expected him to quit the team. Instead, the next day, Patch told Jack he wanted to practice fielding grounders every afternoon until he could do it right. As far as Jack was concerned, that said it all about what kind of kid Patch was.

As the game unfolded in front of Jack, he was determined to ignore Marge. Patch's team was ahead by one run in the bottom of the last inning. If they could hang on, they had an excellent chance of making the playoffs. Unfortunately, the other team had runners on first and second with one out.

"Hey, batter-batter, no-hitter, no-hitter," the boys chattered.

The batter swung and clipped a pop-up into short right field. The parents around Jack and Katie emitted a collective groan. Jack clenched his fists. He glanced at Katie. She appeared to be praying. If he had looked over his shoulder he would have seen that Mrs. Milner appeared to be praying too.

PATCH SAW THE BALL COME OFF THE BAT and started back. He had worked hard with his dad on this play—catching a ball hit over his head. He turned his back and ran as fast as he could. His dad had taught him that by running without looking at the ball, he could cover a lot more ground than if he watched the ball over his shoulder. Unfortunately he hadn't exactly mastered the part about looking back up at the right time and finding it again.

His rubber cleats chewed and spit tiny wads of outfield grass as he ran. He fought the temptation to look too soon. *Not yet . . . not yet . . . the ball will be there when you look.* Finally he turned his head over his shoulder. For a second he couldn't find the ball. Then he saw it, fifteen feet above his head and falling fast. He strained with every muscle he had, but he could see that it was going to land just out of his reach.

The runners flew toward home with the runs that would win the game. At the last moment Patch lunged and threw out his glove. The ball hit in the web and stuck. He fell face first, skinning his chin along the grass, but he didn't let go. Remembering the runners, he jumped up, spun around, and looked toward the infield. The runner from first had already rounded second. Patch didn't even have to throw. He jogged to first base and stepped on it: an unassisted double play.

His teammates went crazy. So did all of the parents in the bleachers. Jack grabbed Katie and kissed her, then jumped around on the bleacher, slapping the other parents on their backs. Mrs. Milner hopped down from the bleachers, ran straight out onto the field, and hugged Patch just as if he were her own son. Patch was so happy he wasn't even embarrassed. He just hugged her back.

Patch looked toward the bleachers and saw his dad winding his way through the throng of yelling kids. When Jack got close, Patch yelled, "You were right, Dad. When I looked up, the ball was there."

Jack leaned over and hugged him. "It always is," he said.

chapter 31

Katie stood in her slippers at the kitchen counter and waited for the coffee to finish brewing. She smiled at Goofy, who was smiling back at her from the Disney World souvenir mug that Patch and Lizzy had bought her the previous summer. Pulling her hair into a haphazard twist, she fastened it with a clip from the pocket of her white terrycloth shorts.

The coffeemaker beeped three times. She filled the mug and padded around the breakfast bar that overlooked the adjoining family room. Her favorite overstuffed denim chair waited for her in the corner, in the muted glow of the reading lamp. Holding her cup high, she snuggled in with her legs curled beneath her. After a few tentative sips, she reached over and picked up her book of daily devotions.

It was five-fifteen in the morning, her favorite time of the day. The sun wasn't up yet and neither were Lizzy, Patch, and Jack. This was her time. She liked to spend it studying her Bible and talking to God. This morning she particularly wanted to talk about Patch's catch the day before. Patch didn't ask for much. She was thrilled that for once he had gotten to be the star. She closed her eyes. *Thank you, God, for giving that moment to my son.*

Opening her eyes, she split the pages at the bookmark and found the thought for the day: *God is working behind the scenes in your life.* It focused on a story about a king whose army surrounded a city where the prophet Elisha and his servant were hiding. When Elisha's servant looked over the city wall and saw the army, he panicked.

"Don't be afraid," Elisha said. "Those who are with us are more than those who are against us." Elisha prayed for God to open the boy's eyes and let him see what Elisha could see. The servant looked out again and saw chariots of fire completely surrounding the army. The enemy that had seemed invincible a moment earlier was actually in a hopeless situation.

Katie thought back to Patch's birth and all of his medical problems. The situation had seemed hopeless, but Patch had come out of it fine. God had worked behind the scenes to save her son, and Katie had come out of it much more serious about her faith.

During the past few years she had been trying with increasing persistence to convince Jack to return to his faith. The things that Jack's father had said in the hospital so many years earlier had come back to her as she got older. Life was fleeting. Neither she nor Jack was bulletproof. She was determined to do all that she could to ensure that her family would be all right, not just in this life but in the next one.

Katie closed the book. *Lord, I know you're out there working behind the scenes, but I sure wish you'd work a little faster on Jack. Deep inside, he still loves you. I know he does. Bring him back to you, please.*

"You look comfortable!" Jack's voice startled her, and she jerked, spilling coffee down the front of her Fighting Illini T-shirt.

Looking heavenward, she said, "I asked you to bring him back to you, not to me."

"What?"

"Never mind. What are you doing up so early?" She brushed at the front of her shirt.

He scratched the back of his head and nodded at the coffee stain. "Sorry about that. I guess you're probably thinking that the whole reason you get up so early is to have some time by yourself, right? I've been awake for more than an hour and couldn't get back to sleep. I thought I'd come downstairs and surprise you. Worked, huh?"

Katie raised an eyebrow.

"I know. Somebody must have told me once that I was funny, but I'm really not," Jack said. He'd heard the line so many times that he had gotten in the habit of preempting it.

"Well, I can see my quiet time is over," she said, with an exaggerated sigh. "May I buy you a bowl of Cheerios?"

"I'd be honored."

As they sat down over their cereal bowls, Katie reviewed the shuttle schedule for the day. "Okay, so you're dropping Patch at school, and I'm taking Lizzy. You're coming home from work early to drive Lizzy to ballet while I take Patch for his physical. Remember, she's got to be there by five-thirty, so you need to be home by five-fifteen."

"We need to start printing an itinerary or something. It's getting to be more complicated than running an airline," he said. He picked a milk-drenched strawberry slice from his bowl and popped it in his mouth.

Katie stared into her bowl, swirling figure eights in the milk with her spoon. "Jack, there's something I want to talk to you about."

"Let 'er rip. I'm all ears."

"Excellent point, Spock."

"A little early in the day for the pointy-ears jokes, isn't it?"

"It was irresistible."

He made a show of drumming his fingers on the table. "You wanted to talk about something?"

"Yes, where was I? It's about church, and about Patch."

"What about church and Patch?" He crossed his arms. "Patch goes to church."

"I know he does. But he's getting old enough that he's obviously wondering why, if it's so important, you don't go. He idolizes you. I can tell that he's starting to think that maybe it's not a thing that 'guys' do. I just want you both to go. It would set a good example for him."

"Look, you know how I feel about that."

"Jack, the fact that your dad did something awful thirty years ago doesn't mean that everything religious is some sort of hoax. And it doesn't mean everyone you deal with is out to cheat you. Can't you see how this affects you? This whole deal with Bernie is the same thing. You don't seem to be able to trust anyone. Your dad made a huge mistake, but that doesn't make everyone else in the world a liar."

"Bringing up my dad is bad strategy."

Looking at his face, she knew he was right. She shifted gears. "You know I'm only talking about this because I love you. I want you to be as happy as you can be. I want to be sure that if something terrible were to happen, our whole family would be together someday."

"What do you mean, 'together someday'?"

She looked down and began to stir her milk again. "In heaven." She looked up just in time to see Jack roll his eyes.

"Don't laugh!" she said. "I believe in heaven, and I believe in hell.

And you can try to act like you don't, but I know that deep down inside you do. The most important thing in the world to me is to know that my husband and kids are going to be with me forever, no matter what happens on this earth. If you think that's dumb . . . well, you're dumb."

He smiled. "Nice comeback."

She responded with a *make-fun-of-me-now-and-I'll-kill-you* look.

He lost the smile. "You think I'm unhappy?" he said.

Katie noted that the whole heaven-and-hell thing made him uncomfortable. He was shifting back to the last earthly point in the conversation.

"Well, I think I'm a pretty happy guy, actually," he continued. "How could an unhappy guy be as witty as I am?"

"Believe me," she said, "if I thought religion could improve your wit, I'd have physically dragged you to church a long time ago. No, I don't think you're unhappy. I just think that you're blocking out something that's a big part of you. Seriously, Jack, promise me you'll think about it. I wouldn't bring this up if I didn't love you."

Jack reached over and put his hand on hers. "I know. If you think it's important for Patch, I promise that I'll think about it. Frankly, I don't see him acting that way, but I'll think about it." He looked at his watch. "I've got to take my shower." He got up and took his cereal bowl to the sink.

After he left the room, Katie reran their conversation in her mind. She felt that it had gone as well as could be expected. She was certain that he really would think about it. She could have kicked herself, though, for bringing up his father. That had been a mistake. Besides, she wasn't even sure that David still cared whether Jack forgave him. What a strange situation that was.

Katie had called David a couple of months after they met in the hospital. Inexplicably, he had seemed depressed and uninterested—like a different man. She wondered if he had given up. Who could blame him? She continued to call during the first few years of her marriage, but she was never able to convince him there was hope. Finally she quit calling altogether. Unlike David, though, she hadn't given up.

In the early days she assumed that it was just a matter of time before she convinced Jack to forgive his father. She had grossly underestimated his feelings. Jack was obsessed. His hatred for his father had become part of the bedrock of his life, like a deeply ingrained habit. She'd heard him talk about "swing memory" in baseball. When a player had swung the same way hundreds of times, his muscles remembered the swing just that way and repeated it even when his brain tried to tell them to do it differently. It took long hours of concerted effort for the muscles to forget the old habit and pick up the new. Jack's hatred of his father seemed to her to be the same sort of thing. She had never been able to identify the incentive that would make him want to work to change it.

She closed her eyes. *Lord, please heal Jack. Create an opportunity for him to return to you.* As she rose from her seat, she felt the muscles in her shoulders and neck relax. She hadn't realized how tense she had become during her discussion with Jack. She took the sudden relaxation as a sign and began her day feeling more upbeat than she had for a long time.

chapter 32

J ack doodled in the margin as he struggled through the second page of a convoluted legal memorandum prepared by one of Challenger Airlines' outside law firms. He swiveled his chair sideways, leaned back, and propped his wing tips on the open bottom drawer of his desk. "How do these kids get through law school?" he mumbled.

He was in a bad mood, and it had nothing to do with the professional shortcomings of the hapless young associate who had written the memo. Since his talk with Mitch the day before, Jack had not been able to shake the uncomfortable feeling that another shoe was about to drop—right on his head. The excitement of Patch's big catch had been great, but only a temporary diversion.

True, the more time that passed, the more reason he had to hope that perhaps Zanella really had been bluffing. On the other hand, Jack knew Mitch too well, and trusted him too little, to expect anything but the worst. Unable to concentrate, he put the report down, reached over to the computer, and clicked to the stock report. The market was down fifty-five points, but Challenger stock was up a dollar. Good news for the employee stock ownership plan, bad news for the short seller, whoever he was.

"Cindy! Did you make that lunch reservation at Bingham's?" Jack called out the door.

"Yes, I did. Twelve-thirty, for three," Cindy's voice came back. "They're saving your favorite booth."

He was taking two of the legal department's new litigators to a get-acquainted lunch. Training young lawyers was a responsibility Jack enjoyed. He was proud of his reputation as a demanding but patient mentor who didn't chop someone's head off over every little mistake. Largely because of that reputation, Challenger's legal department had successfully recruited many top law-school graduates who would otherwise have opted for the higher pay of the big Dallas law firms. Before he could go to lunch, though, he had to get started on a report to Bernie about a new class-action suit. The mind-numbing memo on his desk was supposed to update him on the applicable case law.

Jack was just picking up the memo to give it another try when he heard Joel Burnham talking boisterously to someone in the hall. "You should have seen how red his face turned," Joel said, and laughed. "I told him if we don't have it, we don't have it. We can't just create it out of thin air. Boy, did that set him off!" Joel was a bright third-year lawyer, a real star whom Jack had hired and trained right out of law school. Jack treated him like a little brother.

"Hey, Joel!" Jack called.

Joel stuck his head around the corner into Jack's office.

"What happened?" Jack asked.

"We had a mediation with Wilson Tarpley today in the Melton case. You know how Tarpley gets all high and mighty. He's such a crusader. Anyway, he swears to the mediator that while Melton was still working here he saw an e-mail between Harris, down in Marketing and Steptoe over in Accounting that supposedly said that they needed to get Melton fired before he blew the whistle on bribes by Marketing to the Brazilian transportation office. 'Alleged' bribes, I should say. Tarpley claimed we had erased the e-mail and destroyed the files so we wouldn't have to produce it in the case. I told him, 'Hey, I can't produce what I don't have. If you've got some evidence that somebody destroyed something, then you need to bring it to the judge.'"

"Well, was there an e-mail ?"

"Uh, not to the best of my knowledge," Joel said.

"Don't give me that 'to the best of my knowledge' bull. Was there an e-mail?"

Joel seemed taken aback. "Hey, I don't know. What's gotten into you? I talked to Harris and Steptoe, and they said no such e-mail existed. So I assume that it didn't."

"How did you ask them?"

"Huh?"

Jack leaned forward and tapped his pen on the desk. "How did you ask them? What did you say to them when you asked them about the e-mail?"

Joel straightened his back. "I did it just the way you taught me, remember?"

"No, I don't remember. Why don't you fill me in?"

"Before I asked them if it existed, I explained to them all of the possible ramifications if it did. The company would lose twenty million dollars or so. They'd get fired. They'd probably get prosecuted. They thought about it for about three seconds and told me it didn't exist. After a couple of days, I asked one of the computer guys to double-check to see if he could pull anything up. He said there was nothing."

Jack dropped the pen. "Well, that's a real scoop. Did you really think there'd be something after two days?"

"Look, Jack. That's exactly the way you taught me to conduct that kind of witness interview. You even took me along and let me watch your technique in that ZyTech case, remember? You told me that doing it that way puts all of the responsibility on the witness, not on the lawyer. If you want me to do it another way now, then fine. But it isn't fair for you to get all over me about it."

Jack shifted in his chair. The things Katie had said that morning flashed through his mind. He wondered what Patch or Lizzy would think of him if they had heard this conversation.

"Look, Joel, we're going to have to have a talk. Give me some time to think things over, and I'll come by your office. You're right, though, I don't have any right to get on you. I'm sorry."

Joel cocked his head to one side. "Are you all right?"

"I'm fine. I'll come by in a while."

Joel turned to leave.

"Close it, please," Jack said.

Joel eased the door shut as he went out.

Leaning back in his chair, Jack massaged his forehead with his fingertips. *There was a time when you'd never have considered doing something like Joel just did. And now not only are you doing it, you're teaching a young lawyer to do it. Congratulations, Parst.*

A knock on the door interrupted his thoughts.

"Yeah, come in," Jack said, sharply.

The door opened. Bernie strode in, carrying a cardboard box. A picture frame jutted from the top.

Jack sat up straight. "Bernie! What's up?"

Bernie walked over to the desk and set the box on it. "This is what's up." He pointed at the box. "This is what's left of my career. Mitch fired me this morning. He told me you told him. I wanted to come by and thank you on my way out."

Jack stood up. "Bernie . . ."

"Save it, Jack. I really don't want to hear it." He picked up the box. "You know, I always looked out for you. I never would have believed you were capable of something like this. I guess I'm just an old fool." He turned around and walked toward the door.

"How could he fire you? I'll talk to him . . . listen, Bernie, it's not what you think."

The door slammed.

Jack swiveled his chair toward the window. He kicked the bottom drawer of his desk shut. It bounced back open and he kicked it again.

His intercom buzzed. He slapped the button. "What!"

"Rob and Shannon are here for your lunch appointment."

"Tell them something came up. I'll have to reschedule."

Jack sat for a half hour staring out the window at the flat, gray landscape of North Dallas. How had he allowed himself to get to this point? He thought of the things that Katie had said that morning. Maybe she was right. Maybe it was time for him to rethink some things. Surely this wasn't what he wanted to be.

There was one problem he knew he could begin to fix immediately. He got out of his chair and straightened his tie. It was time to have a long talk with Joel Burnham.

chapter 33

The Parsts swarmed into the house from the garage. Patch carried three McDonald's bags, one in each hand and one in his mouth. His Bible was wedged under his left armpit. "Hough-di-ugh-gugh . . . ." he mumbled. The McDonald's bag crackled in his mouth with each syllable.

"We can't hear you," said Katie. She pulled open the refrigerator door.

Patch put the bags and the Bible down on the table. "I said, 'How did I get stuck carrying all of the food?'"

"You have talent. We wouldn't want to waste it," Jack said. "It's a gift—sort of like those Saint Bernards that carry warm drinks to stranded skiers. If you'd just work on a bark you could have a real future."

"You're strange, Dad, very strange."

This was the third week in a row that Jack had attended church with his family. He seemed to have settled right into it. Katie was keeping her fingers crossed.

"What's on the agenda this afternoon?" Jack asked of no one in particular.

"Seth's coming over to play at three, and Lizzy's going to Amanda's. You're trimming the hedges," Katie said.

"You'll at least grant me a few minutes to read the sports section, won't you, your highness?" He lifted the bun and pulled the pickles off his cheeseburger. Then he licked the mustard and ketchup off his fingertips.

"I suppose, but only if you'll give me a foot massage while you're reading. These heels kill me." She kicked off her shoes and rubbed her feet together.

"You're dreaming," Jack said. "But I mean that in a loving way."

"My feet hate you. Lizzy, what are you and Amanda doing today?"

"We're going to help Amanda's mom wash their dog." Lizzy sneaked a fry out of Patch's bag while he was looking at Katie.

"What kind of dog do they have?" David asked.

"A greyhound. He was a racing dog and they adopted him when he got too old to race anymore. Is that a spider on the wall?" When Patch turned to look, she grabbed two more of his fries.

"Be sure to wear your swimsuit under your clothes," Katie said.

"I will. We should adopt a greyhound."

"Why?" Katie asked.

"They got four out of five stars on *Dog of Your Dreams* on TV. They're loyal, smart, and good with children. Besides, if they don't get adopted I think they get killed." She reached for another fry from Patch's bag.

Patch slapped his hand on top of hers. "Can they be trained to eat little sisters?"

Lizzy laughed. "I got about ten of 'em before you caught me. If you're no more observant than that, I doubt if you'd be much good at training dogs."

"Oh, a comedian, huh?"

"'Observant'—that's a big word for an eight-year-old," Jack said between bites. "Nicely done, Lizzy."

"How can you compliment her? She's a common thief," Patch said. "We can only hope she doesn't turn to the Dark Side. Imagine a brain like that dedicated to a life of crime."

Katie chewed her burger and smiled. This was the way she wanted her family to be. Everything was returning to order. It was time to take the next step.

KATIE PACED ACROSS THE BEDROOM, shifted the phone from her left ear to her right, and peeked between the plantation shutters to make certain that Jack was still working in the backyard. "I think it's time, Sarah. I'm going to call David today. When was the last time you talked to him?"

"Just last week. He calls me maybe twice a month these days," Sarah said.

"Hey, are you two getting back together?"

"Oh, heavens, no. I'd say we've become more like long-distance friends. It's strange after all these years. Anyway, when I talked to him I followed your instructions and mentioned the possibility."

"What did he say?"

"He was cautious about it. I think his view is that he'll believe it when he sees it. He's not going to get his hopes up. Listen, Katie, I'm worried that maybe you're moving too fast. Don't you think you should give Jack more time?"

"I'm not going to set anything up yet. I just want to make the first contact, to let David know what's going on."

"All right, if you say so. Just don't think it's going to be easy. I've been fighting this battle for thirty years."

Katie peeked out the window again. "Things will be different this time. Jack's almost ready. I can feel it. You know, last night he called Marge Milner, the Little League mom who said the mean thing about Patch last year. He's had a running feud with her. He told her he wanted to bury the hatchet. He's changing, Sarah."

"I hope you're right. There's another thing, though. David is different now too. Physically, I mean."

"How is he different?"

"I promised that I would never tell you or Jack. David doesn't want Jack to give him a chance out of sympathy. He's got some medical issues, let's leave it at that."

Katie sat down on the bed. "He's not dying, is he?"

"We're all dying. Let's just say he's not as strong as he used to be."

"Well, neither am I. I'm still going to call him."

"Good luck."

A few minutes later, Katie had David on the phone.

"No, I can't promise that he'll do it," she said, "but that doesn't mean we shouldn't try."

On the other end of the line, David eased into the beat-up wooden chair behind the desk that occupied much of his tiny living room. His German shepherd, Shelly, who was stretched out on the floor by the desk, lifted her head and shook it, jangling her metal tags. He reached down with his free hand and stroked her. "Katie, I can't tell you how much I appreciate this call. Sarah told me what you had in mind. She thinks the world of you, you know."

"She's been like a mother to me since my parents died. I love her very much."

"Yes, so do I."

Katie put her hand in the pocket of her jeans and wondered how to respond.

"I don't know about your plan, though," he continued, before she could speak. "Of course I'd like to talk to him. But so many years have passed. So much has changed."

"It will be different this time, David. The timing's not quite right yet, but it will be soon. He's started back to church, and I can see that he feels good about it. I'm certain that once he's had some time he'll be ready."

"Assuming he was willing to meet me, I wonder what he would think. I'm not the man I used to be. Thank God for that. But physically, I mean—"

"That doesn't matter."

"A person thinks of so many things in a situation like this," he said. He rubbed his earlobe. "It's hard to imagine how it would go."

"Let's just wait and see. I'll be praying about it, and I know you will too," she said.

"Of course I will. It's just shocking, coming out of the blue this way. I gave up a long time ago. But I never forgot. There's not a day that's gone by that I haven't thought of him, prayed for him. I'm sure he's a fine man."

"He is a fine man, David." She paused. "You would be proud of him."

There was silence at the other end of the line.

"David?"

His voice came back softer than before. "I'm sure I would be proud of him, Katie. There's so much that I've missed."

"He's also missed a lot, and so have Patch and Lizzy. They need to know their grandfather. I just want it all to be over. I want our family to be whole. I'll stay in touch, David. When the time is right, I'll let you know."

"Thank you, Katie. I'm very happy my son found you."

"I'm happy he found me too."

chapter 34

Patch slammed the locker door and slung his purple nylon backpack over one shoulder. He started down the crowded hallway toward the gym, where he was meeting Seth to walk home from school. Seth and Patch had been best friends since kindergarten. They were about as different as two boys can be. Seth was as big and hulking as Patch was small and lean. Schoolwork was as easy for Seth as it was difficult for Patch. Despite their differences, though, the two were inseparable.

School had been in session for a week. The temperature outside was nearly a hundred degrees. All Patch could think about was cannonballing into the pool. He pulled his tan Savannah Sand Gnats ball cap out of his back pocket and put it on. When he walked through the gym doors, he saw Seth sitting on the bottom bleacher, watching some boys play basketball. The staccato squeaking of gym shoes pierced a background hum of youthful voices.

"Hey, Stick," Seth said when he saw Patch.

"Hey, Fat Boy," Patch called back, playing out one of the mysteries of adolescence—the way that boys bond by insulting each other. "How'd the Spanish quiz go?"

189

"Who knows? I sure as heck don't understand why every grown-up in Texas thinks it's so important for kids to learn Spanish all of a sudden. By the time we're old enough to use it for anything, we'll be able to carry around a computer that'll interpret everything anyway."

"I used that same line on my mom the other day."

"What'd she say?"

"'Well, if you take that approach, why learn anything? You can just have a computer do everything for you.' So I said, 'Hey, that's my point, Mom. I'm glad you agree.'"

"What'd she do?"

"She smacked me with the newspaper."

"You have the coolest mom in the school," Seth said. "And she's definitely the biggest babe. She can smack me with the newspaper any time."

"Knock it off. We're talkin' about my mom here." Patch punched Seth on the shoulder.

"Can't you take a joke? Hey, how come the rest of the school is so cold and the gym is so hot? I'd like to know who's the genius who sets the temperature on the air conditioner around here?"

"The gym's not air conditioned, remember? We're going to be boiling by the time we get home. I can't wait to get in the pool. First, I've gotta water Mrs. Salantro's plants and get her mail for her. Did you remember your swimsuit?" Patch was already heading out the back door of the gym.

"I've got it." Seth puffed as he jogged to catch up. "Why do you have to water Mrs. Salantro's plants?"

"Because it's Thursday. Every Thursday I water her plants and get her mail. She's gettin' old and doesn't have any kids around to help her." Patch spied a rock on the sidewalk and began to kick it ahead of him.

"How much does she pay you?"

"Nothing." He kicked the rock again.

"Nothing? Are you nuts?"

"She's an old lady. What kinda idiot would make her pay?" Patch frowned when he pulled one of his kicks and sent the rock skittering off the sidewalk into the street.

"This kinda idiot. Oh well, I guess I see your point. But I thought Thursday was the day you cut *your* grass." Now Seth found a rock and kicked it.

"That's Wednesday."

"You've gotta be the most organized kid in Texas. Between all of your chores, baseball practice, and piano lessons, I don't see how you have time to breathe."

"That's the point. I'm not a brain like you, so I have to stay organized or I'll never be good at anything," Patch said, matter-of-factly.

The boys were approaching the pond in Patch's subdivision. Prim, cone-shaped cypresses and gangly cedar elms surrounded it, with a splash of red-flowered crape myrtle here and there. Foamy spray gushed from a fountain in the center.

"There's Jason," Seth said, as they caught sight of Jason Borders' backward Texas Rangers cap. Jason was every suburban mother's nightmare. At thirteen, he was not a criminal—yet. Every time the school tried to do anything to discipline him, his parents threatened to sue, an effective tactic that freed him up to terrorize with impunity.

Jason was blocking the path around the pond, tormenting Stacy Fontenot. Stacy was twelve and was the sort of kid for whom life was destined to be pretty miserable until college. She was taller than most of the boys her age and about twenty pounds overweight. Her frizzy hair encased her head like an army helmet. Extraordinarily large front teeth highlighted her metal braces.

Short and stocky, Jason had to look up to shout at Stacy. "Where'd ya get those shorts, from Shamu?"

"Leave me alone, Jason. No wonder no one can stand you," Stacy shouted back

Patch was impressed at the aggressive defense she was offering, although the color in her neck and the halting rhythm of her voice suggested she was about to cry.

"Your sister told me she can't stand you either," she continued, apparently taking courage from her successful first volley.

Unfortunately for Stacy, Jason had been in too many name-calling contests to be knocked off stride by an amateur. "When do you think you'll finally get a boyfriend? When you're thirty? Or when you get back from the fat farm? Wait a minute, you'll probably have to stay at the fat farm until you're thirty, anyway, just to get back to normal."

That was all Patch could take. "Leave her alone, Jason. She's gonna start crying and you're gonna get in trouble. You're real tough, picking on a girl."

Jason had been so intent on his taunting that he hadn't heard the boys walk up. "How about if I pick on you then?" He stepped toward Patch. Patch looked him in the eye and didn't budge. Jason hesitated.

Something thumped onto the path and both boys turned toward Stacy. She had dropped her backpack. An old-fashioned girl's dress-up doll popped out. This stroke of good fortune seemed to revitalize Jason.

"Ooh, did we hurt your dolly? Let me get her a Band-Aid." He pounced on the doll, and before anyone could move, he hurled it into the pond. "Hope the water helps her boo-boo!" he cackled and took off running down the path.

Stacy looked Patch right in the face for what seemed like a full minute. Then she sat down on the grass and cried.

"Jason's a creep, Stacy. Just ignore him," Patch said, while wondering why in the world she had brought a doll to school in her backpack.

"He's right. Everybody hates me, and I'm fat and ugly."

"Stacy, you're not fat," he said. He knew he was lying, but the situation seemed to call for it.

"That doll belonged to my grandmother. She brought it from France and gave it to me just before she left yesterday," she said, and sobbed louder. "I took it to school to show my social studies teacher. My parents will kill me!"

It was obvious to Patch that the doll was just part of Stacy's problem, but it was the only part that he had any chance to fix. He pulled off his tennis shoes and socks.

"What are you doing?" Seth asked.

Stacy peeked in Patch's direction and sniffled.

"I'll get your doll, Stacy," Patch said, striding to the water's edge. He pulled his T-shirt over his head, tossed it on the grass, and sloshed into the water. When he was up to his waist, he dove at an angle toward the point where the doll had sunk.

Seth walked to the edge of the water and paced, his eyes fixed on the spot where Patch had gone under.

A minute later, Patch broke the surface. He flipped his head to throw the water out of his eyes.

"I can't see a foot in front of me, but it's not very deep, and the bottom's smooth," he said. "I think I can run my hands along the bottom, and I might be able to find it." Before Seth or Stacy could respond, he dove back below the water.

Patch opened his eyes and squinted into the greenish haze. He went straight for the bottom and swept his hands through the slime. His fingers touched something, but it was much too big to be the doll.

When he got within a few inches, he could make out a small log, about the size of his arm. His lungs began to feel full from his body's urge to breathe. He pushed off the bottom and shot to the top.

"Nothing yet but an old log," he yelled.

"Grab me a bass while you're down there, I'm hungry," Seth joked, but his voice had a nervous edge to it.

"Heck, no, I'll get a mermaid." As Patch dove again, he worried that his wisecrack about a beautiful woman, even a make-believe one with flippers, might have made Stacy feel even worse.

He quickly found the log again and put his hands on the bottom just beyond it. A second later he got lucky. His fingers touched the legs of the doll. He wrapped his hand around it, got his feet underneath him, and pushed off the bottom with the balls of his feet. His foot slipped on the muck. Instead of going up, he lurched forward. He felt a sharp pain just below his ankle, as if someone had pulled thread hard against his skin. He twisted his body and reached for his foot. When he turned, it felt as if a whole wad of thread were wrapped completely around his ankle.

What Patch felt with his fingers made no sense. His lower leg was enveloped in a wispy beehive. He twisted his body again. The thread tightened around his foot. He tore at the mysterious web with his hands. With each movement, it seemed to contract around his leg. He envisioned something alive and horrible, with tentacles, grabbing him and holding him down. Then a chilling realization flashed through his mind—it was fishing line! He thrashed and pulled at the line, slicing skin from his fingers and releasing precious air from his lungs.

At the side of the pond, Seth and Stacy edged closer to the water as the seconds crept away. Seth stared at the peaceful surface and shifted his weight from one foot to the other. Stacy twisted her finger in her hair.

Beneath the water, Patch yanked at the fishing line. What was holding it down? His fingers found the strands that led to his foot. He grabbed the line with both hands and jerked twice. It was too strong. The pressure on his lungs was awful. A choking feeling filled his chest as he fought his body's reflex to breathe. He knew that he was seconds from dying.

He spun upright, knees bent. He drove his toes into the muck and his feet shot off the bottom. The line tore into his ankle. His head snapped back. He inhaled violently. Water gushed into his throat and lungs. Short, violent spasms racked him, tossing him from side to side. After a few moments, his legs and arms went limp.

While his body floated lifelessly, his mind continued to work. He pictured himself blasting through the surface of their backyard pool into the radiant sunlight. He shook his head from side to side, and the water sprayed into the air off of his face and hair. He grinned at his mom and dad, and Lizzy squealed with delight. "Do it again, Patch! Do it again!" The pool water sparkled clear and bright, and Patch felt so peaceful, so calm, not sad or frightened at all, as he slid gently, easily back beneath the surface.

chapter 35

J ack winced. The pump to his right rattled, then coughed and spat, as if choking. The long stretch of tattered canvas fire hose that wound from the pump to the belly of the pond heaved and collapsed, like an expiring lung. Gradually the compact waterfall tumbling into the street slowed to a trickle. But it was all lost on him.

He stared straight ahead into the scattered litter and muck that lay newly exposed in the center of the muddy ditch. The gray sky sprayed a hard mist that stung his face. He was thinking about nothing, focusing on nothing. In fact, he was consciously trying to think about nothing. He was tired, worn out by the oppressive weight of four days of relentless grieving and thinking since Katie had called him at work with the news about Patch.

She had been eerily meticulous, relating every detail that she knew. He couldn't even remember exactly what she'd said. It was the precision of her approach that he recalled. The whole thing had been so strange, so otherworldly. Her lack of emotion had made it seem even more surreal. He'd felt as if he were acting a part, almost as if he'd seen this scene before but in somebody else's life.

None of it mattered, though. Patch was dead. Yes, he was dead. Today, Jack had found himself repeating it, driving the point into his disbelieving consciousness. Maybe he was trying hard to convince himself finally that it was true, so he wouldn't keep expecting Patch to come around the corner of the house laughing and asking, "Hey, Dad, do you wanna play catch?"

Tears rose to Jack's eyes. He fought them back with the resolve that whatever else, he would not make a spectacle of himself.

"We'll be ready in about fifteen minutes, Mr. Parst. You can put on these hip boots." Tom Peters was holding the boots out to Jack. A fireman who went to Katie's church, Tom had volunteered to help drain the pond. Divers had cut the fishing line and removed Patch's body the day of the accident. The city had decided to drain the pond and clean it out before refilling it. The parents in the area were in a panic and would have insisted.

"Thanks, Tom," Jack said. No one was making him wade into the muck, of course. They didn't need him for anything. For some reason, though, he had to do it. He had to see and understand what had happened. So he was there by the pond, with a group of firemen and police officers he didn't even know, waiting to see just how his son had died.

The neighbors had been thoughtful. They'd done, or offered to do, everything the Parsts could have needed during the past few days. Perhaps the most touching thing was that they'd all stayed away from the pond today, when the pumping was almost done. They had to be curious, but they'd stayed away just the same. Jack appreciated that. It showed that they were decent, that they had some respect for his family.

The hip boots were awkward to put on. Jack had never been much of a fisherman. Sure, he'd gone fishing with Patch and Lizzy for bluegill, no more than thirty feet from where he was standing. He smiled. They'd really caught some bluegill. But he'd never been a serious fisherman. He didn't know anything about hip boots.

He got the left boot all the way on and stood on that foot while he tried to pull on the right boot. It was long and limp. His right foot slid easily into the top but then became wedged sideways, causing him to lose his balance. He hopped on his left foot. When he put his right foot down, the bottom of the boot folded over, caught his heel, and twisted him down to his knees. Several of the firemen looked in his direction. They quickly turned away, as if ashamed to have breached etiquette by watching a grieving man take an embarrassing spill.

Jack cursed himself. Patch deserved better than a bumbling fool of a father. He sat on the wet grass and pulled on the other leg of the boot. Then he stood up, grass matted to the seat of his pants, and waited.

"Ready, Mr. Parst?" Tom asked softly.

"Yeah. I'm ready."

"I don't know how mushy it's going to be. We might sink in quite a bit. So step carefully. Why don't you stay behind me?"

"Okay, fine. Whatever you say."

Tom stepped gingerly off the edge of the grass into the slimy bed of the pond. "It's not too bad, Mr. Parst. Mostly moss. Pretty firm, really."

"Yeah. I'm surprised it's not muddier." The men eased carefully toward the drop-off, about twenty feet from the edge. Ten feet beyond that, still partially submerged in the remaining puddle of water, was a gnarled tree trunk. That was where it had happened.

As they slogged along, Jack's mind wandered. Lizzy still didn't seem to understand completely what Patch's death meant. More than anyone, she seemed to think that this was all something that was real bad but would end. Patch would come back, and things would return to normal. Jack was worried about her. He didn't really know what to expect.

As for Katie, Jack couldn't understand her at all. She had cried, really cried, the first day when he had gotten home. Since then, though, she had behaved as if she were involved in some sort of business transaction. What color of casket, food, memorial fund? Who'll ride in which cars? When would Jack's mom arrive for the funeral? All of those things actually seemed important to Katie. She acted more like a concierge than a grieving mother.

Katie had gone into their room and closed the door a lot, especially since the funeral. He knew she was praying. Once, she had asked him to pray with her. Jack hadn't even tried to hide his contempt. What was he supposed to say in that prayer? *Thank you, Almighty God. Thanks a lot. This was our son! Who cares when the mourners arrive, or where people send their twenty-five-dollar checks? He's gone. And you couldn't have cared less. And you, Katie, what are you doing? Can't you see that nobody cared what color the casket was?*

"Be careful on the downslope, Mr. Parst. It's likely to be slick."

Jack took a tentative step down the drop-off toward the tree. They could already see the huge web of fishing line twisted around the trunk and around the long, slender branch that pointed out toward the shore. Jack shook himself. He needed to concentrate on what he was doing. It was too hard to keep thinking anyway. He didn't want to fall down again. He didn't want to think anymore.

chapter 36

Katie knelt on the polished oak floor of the family room and peeled a strip of packing tape from the long, bulging box that held their artificial Christmas tree. It was mid-December. She knew she was taking a risk, but she was unwilling to wait any longer for Jack to make up his mind. Lizzy was going to have a Christmas, and a Christmas tree, and he would just have to deal with it the best way he could.

"Here, Lizzy, you grab that end and help me lift it out of the box. Put it down gently. We don't want to break any of the lights."

Katie had almost concluded that Jack did not intend for them to celebrate Christmas at all. Just after Thanksgiving, when she had first asked when they were going to put up the tree, he told her that he wasn't ready yet. He said that things were too hectic because the Challenger Express investigation was coming to a head. A few days later, Challenger Express announced publicly the names of the embezzler and the short seller. With Jack visibly relieved to have the investigation completed, Katie had again raised the issue of the tree. He asked for a few more days, so he could get back to his normal routine. A few days passed, then a few more. Now there were only ten days remaining until Christmas. For Lizzy's sake, Katie was not willing to put it off any longer.

Lizzy had become withdrawn in the months after Patch's death. Shunning friends, she stuck close to Katie, as though afraid that Katie could go away as suddenly as Patch had. Since Thanksgiving, though, there had been some improvement. She seemed excited about Christmas. Katie was not going to let her down.

Shortly after they broke open the tree box, the tree was in its stand, the white lights glowing. Katie pulled open another, smaller box. "Take some ornaments and start hanging them as quickly as you can," she said. "I want to have the tree finished by the time your father gets home."

Lizzy stretched a skinny arm into the box and pulled out a reindeer ornament. "Why doesn't Daddy want us to have a Christmas tree?"

"Christmas makes him sad this year. It makes him miss Patch."

"I miss Patch too."

"I know you do, honey. So do I."

"I'm tired of being sad. Sometimes I just want to be happy and have fun."

Katie leaned over and hugged her. "You should have fun. Christmas is a time to be happy."

"Do you think Daddy will ever get happy again?"

"Yes, he will. People get over things in different ways. Your father's way is to be really sad for a long time, but it won't last forever. I'm sure that gradually he'll get happy again."

Lizzy rolled an ornament around between her fingers. After a few moments she said, "I don't want a tree. Let's take it down." She placed the ornament back in the box.

Katie sat on the floor and motioned with her hand. "Come over here."

Lizzy sat on Katie's lap.

Katie rubbed her palm in gentle circles on Lizzy's back. "I thought you wanted to be happy. What's wrong?"

"I don't want to make Daddy any sadder." Lizzy twisted Katie's hair around her finger.

"We're not going to make him sadder, we're going to make him happier. I think this Christmas tree is just what Daddy needs to cheer him up. It will be a big surprise for him."

"Maybe if I hang his favorite ornament right in the front," Lizzy said.

"I think that's a great idea. You do that."

Lizzy jumped up, went over to the box, and pulled out a ceramic Santa holding a baseball bat. She hung it in the center of the tree.

"I'm sure he'll love it," Katie said. "Let's hurry and get the rest of these up."

When they finished trimming the tree, Lizzy went upstairs to do her homework. Katie picked up a book and sat in the denim chair next to the tree. From there she could see past the breakfast bar and through the adjoining kitchen to the door that led to the garage. Jack would see the tree as soon as he walked in the door.

When she heard the hum of the garage door opener, she put her book on the little table next to her chair. She glanced at the tree in the corner and took a deep breath. Jack walked into the kitchen. Katie stood up.

"Hi," she said.

Jack dropped his keys on the table. "Hi. What's for dinner?"

"Linguini. Your plate's in the refrigerator."

He spotted the tree and stopped. "What's that?"

As nervous as she was, Katie almost laughed. She tried to formulate an answer that would address the issues that she knew were behind the question. After a moment, she gave up and settled on the obvious. "It's the Christmas tree. Lizzy and I decided to surprise you." She motioned toward the tree with her hand. "Do you like it?"

"Yes, of course." He looked away. "I'm a little bit surprised you didn't wait for me."

"I thought that maybe you would prefer it this way, just to come home and have it already up."

He unbuttoned his collar and tugged the knot in his tie. "You were wrong."

Katie stuck her hands in the back pockets of her black wool pants. "You didn't seem interested in helping us put it up. Lizzy was really looking forward to it. I didn't mean to leave you out."

"I told you I wanted to do it."

"No, you told me you needed more time. It's been so long, I assumed you were just dreading it, which is understandable under the circumstances."

"Don't patronize me, Katie. I don't need you to analyze whether my behavior is understandable." He started down the hall toward the front stairs.

She took a step after him. "Jack, I was just trying to do what's best for you. I'm sorry if it was the wrong thing."

He spun around. "You don't need to worry about what's best for me! I'm an adult. I can take care of myself." He walked back toward her.

She put her hands on her hips. "What in the world set you off? You have no reason to shout at me like that." She saw Lizzy step around the corner of the stairs behind Jack.

Katie opened her mouth to speak. Before she could get anything out, Jack bolted toward her. He grabbed Katie's arms and shook her hard, nearly lifting her off the floor.

"Am I the only one here who remembers what's going on? How can you act like everything is fine? Didn't you care about Patch at all?"

"Daddy, stop!"

Jack released Katie and turned around. Lizzy stared, wide eyed, at them for a moment, then ran up the stairs, sobbing.

Katie's face turned crimson. She stepped in front of Jack and stood on her tiptoes, her face within inches of his chin. "Don't you ever question my love for Patch! And don't you ever grab me like that again! I've never done anything to deserve that kind of treatment. I won't put up with it." She brushed past him and strode up the steps.

AN HOUR LATER, Katie walked into the family room and found Jack sitting on the couch, staring at the Christmas tree.

He looked up and said, "Can we talk?"

"I don't know, can we? I thought I *was* talking to you before you practically hit me."

"I'm sorry. There's no excuse for that. I just lost it."

"Yes, you did lose it—and it frightens me. If Lizzy hadn't come down the stairs, what would you have done to me?"

"There is no way I would ever hurt you. You know that."

Katie walked over and stood in front of him. "I used to know that. Lately I'm not so sure. Let's not pretend this is the first time. Remember two weeks ago when you grabbed my wrist in the bathroom?" She rubbed her arm. "That scared me too."

"That was nothing. I was just trying to get your attention."

"To get my attention, all you have to do is say my name. No grabbing is necessary. And you just happened to be shouting at the time, you remember that part, don't you?"

"Okay, I was out of line then too. I'm telling you I'm sorry. What else can I do?"

"You can get some help, that's what—some counseling. Jack, this isn't you. You've never been like this before."

"Counseling? Good grief, let's not blow this out of proportion. I just lost my temper."

"You didn't just lose your temper. You screamed at me and nearly picked me up and threw me. How do you think Lizzy feels about it?" She pointed toward the hallway. "She saw the whole thing and she's upstairs scared to death."

"I'll talk to her. I'll apologize. She'll be all right. You don't understand what I've been going through."

"What part do you think I don't understand? Have you gone through something I haven't? Besides, there is no excuse for attacking me."

"I didn't attack you."

"What would you call it? And you actually questioned whether I loved Patch. How could you say such an awful thing to me? Do you know how that makes me feel?"

"I didn't mean it."

"Yes, you did mean it. For months now you've been saying things like that. Do you really think you're the only one who hurts? Well, I hurt too."

"I know. But it's different for me, just like it would be different for you if it were Lizzy."

"I'm sorry, Jack, but I'm missing your point. I don't think it would be a bit different if it were Lizzy. Could I somehow miss her more than I miss Patch? Could I have even more days when I feel as if my heart is being ripped out of my chest?"

"Whatever the reason, you seem to have had an easier time dealing with it than Lizzy or I have."

"You mean because I don't wear it on my sleeve? What do you think, that I'm some sort of saint—that I sit around and praise God about this? Don't you think I've screamed at God and demanded an explanation?"

"Wait, Katie . . ."

"No, you wait. You're always telling me how bad it is for you. I want you to know how it's been for me. I want you to listen."

Jack leaned forward, his elbows on his knees. She turned and looked into the fireplace. Jack's eyes followed her. When she turned back toward him, she said, "For a while, the pain was so bad that I visualized it. I pictured a creature living inside of me, gnawing at my muscles and bones—something that wanted to pick me over until nothing was left." She clasped her hands in front of her and rubbed them together. "I asked God to kill me."

Jack rubbed the back of his neck.

"You didn't know that, did you?" she said. "Well, it's true. As soon as I prayed it, though, I took it back—not because I cared about living. I wasn't willing to leave you and Lizzy."

He reached out and touched her arm. She pulled away.

"Let me finish. I want you to know all of it. I prayed and prayed for God to help me understand. I asked for a sign, something dramatic that would clarify things. It didn't come. After a few weeks, I found myself unable to concentrate, unable to pray with the same intensity. I wondered if I was already forgetting Patch, and I cursed myself for it. I cursed God too. After all, why did he save Patch when he was a baby just to let this happen? I felt that I couldn't take it a single day more. It was then that something began to happen—something that I later realized was God answering my prayers.

"One morning a phrase crept into my head, something Jesus said. *I go to prepare a place for you.* I couldn't get it out of my mind. I began to dwell on it. I rolled the phrase over and over in my mind. Before long, when I closed my eyes I could picture Patch, clear as day. He was alive, happy, waving at me—not beckoning, just waving. That's when I began praying a different prayer, a prayer for strength to get through each day—until I can see Patch again. And I know that I will see him again. That's what's gotten me through, Jack. That's what gives me hope."

Jack sat back. "I wish I could have your faith, Katie. I really do. But I don't believe it. You're healing yourself. God's not doing it. I'm glad whatever you're doing is helping, because I love you. I don't want you to hurt. Don't try to convince me it's God, though. If God cared a bit about you and me, Patch would be alive."

Katie knelt in front of him and took his hands in hers. "Please don't say that, Jack. God will help you. You've got to ask him."

He pulled his hands away and stood up. "Thanks, but I'll work through this on my own. I'm going up to talk to Lizzy." He walked past her.

"Before you go, I want you to know something," Katie said.

He turned.

"I love you," she said. "I'll do anything I can to help you, even if you won't get help. But I won't let you abuse Lizzy or me. If you ever come after me again like you did tonight, I'll leave, and I'll take Lizzy with me."

chapter 37

Katie sat on the edge of the bed in the master bedroom and eyed the ball glove and trophy on the dresser in front of her. To her right, she could see Jack shaving at the sink just inside the bathroom doorway. She took a deep breath and let it out. This wasn't likely to be easy.

It was a Saturday morning in late May. Things had gotten worse, much worse, since Christmas. Jack had brooded darkly through the holiday. During the past five months he had become withdrawn, sullen. When they did talk, they argued. It was all taking a toll on Lizzy. Her schoolwork had slipped badly. The one bright spot was that Jack had generally controlled his temper. There had been no repeat of the frightening scene that occurred before Christmas.

Katie had prayed constantly for help, but no help had arrived. Jack's emotional state had continued to deteriorate. Recently she had decided that sorting through Patch's things might give Jack closure, help him get on with his life. She knew it was a long shot, but the situation was so bad that she felt she had little to lose. Worried about how he might react, she had waited until Lizzy was at a friend's house to raise the issue.

She would begin with Patch's glove and the trophy his team had gotten for winning the playoffs the year before. The day after Patch's funeral, Jack had placed them on their dresser. That was where they'd sat for nine months. Occasionally she had seen him standing near the dresser for minutes at a time, patting his fist mechanically into the oil-stained pocket of the glove.

There was no sense putting it off any longer. Rising, she picked up the trophy and walked to the bathroom doorway. She held it out to Jack. "I think it's time we went to Patch's room and decided what we're going to do with his things."

Jack turned his head. The right side of his face was clean shaven, the left side whipped in a blue meringue of shaving cream. Setting his razor on the sink, he took the trophy and rolled it over in his hands.

"We've got to decide what we're going to keep and what we're going to give away," she continued. "We can't—we shouldn't—keep it all."

"We're not going to give his stuff away," Jack said evenly. He put the trophy on the sink and picked up the razor.

Katie hesitated. "I didn't say we should give it all away."

"What did you say, then? I must have misunderstood." He swiped the razor through the shaving cream on his cheek, clearing a flesh-colored swath.

"We can keep the special things, the things that will help us remember him. The trophy's a good example. So is his glove. We'll never give those away. But his clothes, most of his games and sports equipment, we can give those away to someone who needs them. Patch would have wanted us to do that."

"How do you know what he'd have wanted?" Jack said. He rinsed the razor under the tap.

Katie bristled. She was determined, though, not to let the discussion deteriorate into another argument. "Okay, I don't know for sure. It just seems to me that he would have wanted some needy child to have fun with his things."

"You know what I think? I think he would have been shocked that we forgot him so quickly." His voice was rising. "So I guess we disagree, don't we?" He turned to face her, the razor still in his hand. The light glinted off the blade.

She took a quick step backward into the bedroom, her eyes riveted on the razor.

He looked at his hand. His face flushed. He tossed the razor into the sink. "Well, we've truly reached bottom, haven't we? What do you think I am, some kind of monster?"

"That's ridiculous, Jack. I was startled, that's all."

He picked up the trophy.

She lifted her hand in a stop sign. "Look, this was obviously a bad time to bring this subject up. We'll let some more time pass. We can talk about it later."

He waved the trophy at her. "You don't get it, do you? We're not just going to let some time pass. We are keeping his things!"

She took another step backward. "All right. We'll keep them."

"Yes, we will. I don't want you to go near his room. Don't touch my son's stuff!"

Katie clenched her fists. "*Your* son? Who do you think you are? You've sunk so low that you think you've got to drag everybody else down with you. Well, you can't drag me! You may be lost, but don't try to lose Lizzy and me too. I've had it. You and your self-pity make me sick!" She wheeled and stomped toward the door.

"Oh, I'm sorry. I forgot to pay obeisance to your moral superiority, didn't I? This is all God's will, so I'm just supposed to shut up and accept it like some dumb animal. No thought required. Go ahead, run away! While you're at it, ask that God of yours if he really needed our son in such a big, screaming hurry!"

Katie turned to respond. From the corner of her eye she saw his arm go back behind his head. She ducked through the doorway to the hall and slammed the door behind her. The trophy crashed against the other side of the door. She ran into Lizzy's room and locked the door. Standing with her back to the wall, her chest heaving, she listened. When she was satisfied he had not followed her, she slid to the floor and sat with her head cradled in her hands.

chapter 38

The next evening, when dinner was over and Lizzy had gone upstairs, Katie told Jack she wanted to have a talk. He sighed and slouched into a chair at the kitchen table.

"I've decided to take Lizzy to your mom's for a while," she said. "I called her. She said it's okay. I talked to my boss. He's going to arrange a leave of absence for me." She looked into Jack's eyes and was startled at how expressionless they were.

"Look, Katie, I told you I was sorry about yesterday. I just lost it."

"That's right, you lost it, Jack. And what if you lose it again? What if that trophy had hit me? What if you lose it with Lizzy?"

"I would never hurt Lizzy."

"Oh, but you don't mind hurting me?"

"I didn't mean it that way. I wouldn't hurt you either."

"You *did* try to hurt me."

"You know that's not true."

"You threw a trophy at me! Look, Jack, I love you, but I'm not ever going to sit around and play the victim for you. I told you that if something like this happened again, I would leave."

"What about Lizzy? You can't just pick up and take her out of school."

"There's only a week left. All of the serious work is over. I think getting away for a while will be better for her than anything she'd get out of the last week of school."

"How long is a while?"

"Your mom says there are some nice kids on her street, nice families. Lizzy should be able to find some friends quickly. I thought we'd take Bandit with us. That will make it easier on Lizzy. We've still got some of those doggy tranquilizers from the plane ride last summer. If Bandit starts acting up in the car, I'll load him up."

"You didn't answer my question. This sounds like long-term planning to me. How long are you talking about staying?" He shifted his weight in the chair and looked out the window.

"That depends. How long do you want us to stay?" She didn't anticipate an honest answer.

"I don't want you to go in the first place," Jack said, his voice flat and emotionless. He looked down and studied the place mat.

It was just the answer she'd expected, given just the way that she expected. "We'll just have to play it by ear," she said. Something inside of her made her try one more time. "Jack, we can get through this. Please, you've got to want to try. We can talk to Reverend Fagan. Or we can go to a counselor."

Jack slammed his fist on the table. "No! No Reverend Fagan!" He blushed, seemingly surprised at his own overreaction, but he continued. "We can get through it all right. You and I. We don't need any Reverend Fagan or any counselors to help us."

"How can we work it out when we can't even talk without fighting?"

"On second thought, you're right. It probably is best if you go for a while. When do you plan to leave?"

Katie's mouth dropped at his sudden change of direction. It was obvious that he just wanted to end the conversation. "Tomorrow afternoon if we can get everything packed." Her voice had an edge to it now.

"Okay, tomorrow."

"We'll talk to Lizzy tonight. Please try to act as if everything is okay with us. I thought that maybe you could stay home from work tomorrow morning and take her to the park or something before we leave. It would be nice for you to spend some time with her. I could finish packing while you're over there."

"Listen, you don't have to act like I think it's some kind of chore to spend time with my own daughter. You're not the only one who loves her, you know."

After all of the things he'd said about her relationship with Patch, the irony of his comment wasn't lost on her. "I'll start packing." She pushed back her chair, got up, and walked out of the room.

chapter 39

Sarah creaked slowly back and forth in her wicker rocking chair and followed the lazy progress of a doughnut-shaped cloud in the eastern sky. Just beyond the back porch where she sat, Lizzy was tearing around the yard, firing a squirt gun at Bandit. The chaotic scene barely registered in Sarah's consciousness. She was searching her mind for a plan.

Katie and Lizzy had arrived the afternoon before. After hearing the entire story, Sarah was glad that Katie had had the sense to get away. The situation had obviously been intolerable. Jack needed help and he needed it quickly.

Katie walked up behind Sarah, carrying two glasses of iced tea. "I'm happy we brought Bandit," she said. She stepped around the empty wheelchair that was parked to Sarah's left. "He really keeps her company." She handed Sarah a glass, crossed in front of her, and sat in the matching rocker to Sarah's right.

"That tea looks good," Sarah said. "It's so warm out here—not a breath of a breeze." She pointed toward Lizzy and Bandit. "They're best friends, aren't they?"

Katie propped her bare feet on the wrought-iron porch railing. "Yes, they are. Dogs are amazing. They seem to sense things. Bandit has been so protective of Lizzy since Patch died."

They watched as Bandit switched directions and jumped on Lizzy, knocking her down onto the grass. He jumped on top of her and went into a licking frenzy. She covered her face with her hands and laughed while he searched for an opening through which his tongue could reach her mouth.

"We'll soak those jeans tonight to get the grass stain out," Sarah said.

"Lizzy, get up! You're going to ruin those clothes," Katie said.

Sarah smiled. "Sorry, that's just like me to think about the laundry. Let her have some fun. We'll get her cleaned up just fine."

Lizzy escaped, picked a tennis ball off the ground, and flung it across the yard. Bandit scampered after it.

Sarah pressed her glass against her cheek, enjoying the cool dampness. "I've been thinking about what we can do to help Jack," she said.

"Me too."

"I don't think it's likely that I can convince him to see a counselor if you couldn't. Nevertheless, I was thinking that I should go down and stay with him for a while. Maybe over time I could get him to come around."

"I don't see how that could work, Sarah. How would you get around? He'd be at work most of the time and you'd be stuck in the house."

"It is unfortunate timing, with my having this bad spell." Sarah nodded at the wheelchair. "This may pass in a week or so, though. It comes and goes. If I could get back up on my cane I think I could do all right."

"It would be too hard on you, even if you were on your feet. For one thing, the bedrooms are upstairs. Where would you sleep?"

"If I couldn't get up the stairs I could sleep on the couch. Let's wait a week and see how I'm getting around then."

"It would be a bizarre twist, I'll say that: Lizzy and me up here and you down there. Sarah, I hope you understand that we would never have left if we didn't think we had to."

"No, no. You did exactly the right thing. I'm glad you came. The question, though, is what do we do now?"

Katie took a drink, then leaned forward and placed her glass on the rail. "I've been knocking around an idea. You'll probably think it's crazy, though."

"Why would I think it's crazy? Let's hear it."

"It involves David."

"David?"

"David Parst."

"I take it back. Maybe I will think it's crazy . . ."

chapter 40

Jack struggled from the leather cocoon that passed for the passenger seat of Joel's Italian sports car. Once liberated, he shut the door and waved. Joel tapped the horn. The car emitted a low growl before bounding away from the curb.

Standing alone on the front walk, illuminated only by the faded glow of a distant street lamp, Jack turned and looked at his house. He could not conceive that this brooding brick shell was the same place that for thirteen years had overflowed with the energy of a growing family. Lifting his gaze to the darkened dormer windows, he wished for a light, just a flicker. There was no one left to strike one. He pulled his keys from his pocket and walked toward the door.

It was Friday. After work, Joel had suggested they go for a beer. Jack wasn't much of a drinker, so he had surprised himself as well as Joel by saying yes. The house had been so lonely since Katie and Lizzy left. He hated the idea of going home. He had been working late just to avoid it.

Katie had called from his mother's Wednesday evening. As he jiggled the key in the lock, he replayed the conversation in his mind. "Hi, Jack. We're finally here," she had said. "What a long trip. I don't care if

I never drive again. It's kind of cool here. Feels good. How are you doing?"

"I'm fine," he had answered. "Busy on the shareholder case. We've got a bunch of depositions coming up next week. I'm swimming in documents." For some reason, talking about work had seemed more comfortable than anything else.

"Your mother's arranged for Lizzy to meet some of the neighbor-hood kids tomorrow. Lizzy's a little nervous about it. Just a second." There was a shuffling sound.

"Hi, Daddy. Grandma said we can help her walk the neighbor's dog tomorrow. They're on vacation. It's a Basenji. That's an African dog that acts like a cat! They can climb trees, and they don't bark! I don't think Bandit's gonna like it."

"What kind of dog doesn't bark?" Jack said, drawing on years of experience at acting more surprised than he really was. "It sounds like a cat-dog to me!"

"Yeah, a cat-dog!"

"I miss you, sweetie. You take care of Mommy, okay?"

"I miss you, too, Daddy. When are you gonna come see us?"

"Real soon."

"Okay. Bye. I love you."

"I love you, too, kiddo."

Then Katie was back on the line. "We'd better go now. We'll call again this weekend."

"Wait a minute. Is Mom there?"

"She went out to get some milk for Lizzy's breakfast cereal."

"Tell her I said hi. I guess I'll talk to her this weekend. I'll talk to you this weekend too," he said.

"We'll call this weekend," she repeated, as if she couldn't think of anything else to say.

That had been it—some conversation.

He continued to fumble with the key and finally got the front door open. Once in the house, he headed directly for the favorite refuge of men who have been drinking beer—the refrigerator. Not much there that could be eaten without preparation: an apple that looked and smelled dubious, some cream cheese, an open Pepsi can, skim milk. Milk . . . That was it: cereal. He pulled the carton out and got a bowl and a spoon. Opening the pantry door, he surveyed the lineup of cereal boxes. Corn Pops, Honey Nut Cheerios . . . his thoughts darkened; that had been Patch's favorite. He stopped himself. *Not now. I'm not going to think about that now.* Raisin Bran, Special K . . . *yeah, Special K.* He grabbed the box and shook it. Plenty there. He walked over to the kitchen table and plopped down in a chair.

The cereal crackled under the splash of milk as he shuffled through a week's worth of mail and newspapers that blanketed the table. He tossed aside two requests for political contributions and a credit card offer. Then he scanned a mutual fund quarterly report, a card-sized envelope for Lizzy—probably a birthday-party invitation—three clothing catalogs, lots more junk, and Katie's church newspaper. Pushing it all into a heap, he crunched through the cereal in five huge bites. He looked around for something to use as a napkin. There was nothing. He wiped his mouth on the sleeve of his shirt.

His stomach no longer yelping for attention, he noticed the emptiness of the house. Soon the relentless dripping of the kitchen faucet rang through the silence like a church bell. Just as he had done each night since Katie and Lizzy left, he began to picture morosely the way things had been. There was Lizzy, running through the back door shouting excitedly about the Indian arrowhead she'd discovered in the flower bed—an arrowhead that was nothing but a common stone, shaped by the influences of environment, time, and his little girl's imagination. There was Katie, teasing him mercilessly when he wallowed in self-pity after discovering the first wrinkle on his forehead the day after his thirty-fifth birthday. And there was Patch, emerging from the decidedly unthreatening shrubs of the backyard like a triumphant safari hunter, with an errant baseball in one hand and a bewildered bullfrog in the other. There was Patch, tossing the ball to Jack, tossing and catching, laughing and tossing some more. Patch, his pal, his son . . .

Despite his efforts to avoid it, his thoughts came around, as always, to the way Patch must have died. He had imagined it so many times, in such excruciating detail, that he had developed a mental image of it that was eerily clear—as if he had been there in the water, a companion diver, observing and recording the events for a public television documentary. He saw the greenish fog of the water, the panic on Patch's face as he writhed and grabbed and thrashed at the fishing line, the precious bubbles of air escaping between lips that could not close tight enough to seal them off. He felt the awful pressure in Patch's chest as his body's instinct to breathe began to overwhelm his mind's desperate struggle to prevent it from breathing. Worst of all, he pictured the terrifying moment when Patch must have realized that it really could happen, that Mom and Dad were not going to appear somehow from nowhere and make everything right. At that point the mental picture always ended in the same way, with Patch crying out in an agonizing question, *Dad?*

Jack leaned over and rested his forehead on the table. The emptiness of the house, the emptiness of his life, pressed in on him. He searched his mind for any glimmer of hope, but at every turn he confronted only darkness, the absence of anything to grasp and clutch as worthwhile. He began to think of what he might do—not tonight, but sometime—to end it. It was not the first time the thought had entered his mind, but it was the first time he had allowed it to dwell there for more than an instant. The longer he allowed it to remain, the more he wanted to relinquish control to it—to give up and allow the forbidden thought to suck him faster and faster toward its inevitable conclusion. So it was without any conscious decision that he stood up, walked over to the hallway closet, and pulled the gun box from the shelf.

chapter 41

David sat alone on the bed in his motel room. He reached over, felt for the bottle of aspirin on the nightstand, and shook out three tablets. The dull ache in his arm and neck had become progressively worse during the day. He knew what it meant, but he refused to let himself think about it. He pictured the muscles of his upper body as an unforgiving course of kinks and knots. On top of that, his head throbbed from the exertion of his trip. He'd been alternately downing Tylenol and aspirin every few hours since noon. He would wait a few more minutes and then call Jack one more time. If he still didn't answer, he would try him again in the morning.

David had already tried to call every hour since he'd arrived in town early that evening. There'd been no answer, and he fought the irrational temptation to believe that Jack was actually at home but had somehow figured out from caller ID that David was calling. Because he was dialing from a motel, David knew that was not possible, but he mused that three decades of rejection could influence the way a man thinks. One thing he knew was that this time he would not give up until he talked to his son.

That Jack's situation was serious was clear—Sarah and Katie had left no doubt about that when they called. How David could help was less clear. Katie had said that Jack would never work things out until he got things straight with David. Maybe, maybe not. But he knew that he had let his son down once, and he would not do it again, no matter what.

For the hundredth time, David ran the possibilities through his mind. The most likely was the flat rejection. He'd grown accustomed to that one. But this time he was prepared. He'd tell Jack that he wouldn't take no for an answer. If Jack would not agree to meet him, he'd camp out on his doorstep. He'd have to come out sometime.

Less likely was the possibility that Jack would agree to meet with him at some indefinite time in the future—the stall. David would not agree to that. He would insist on seeing him within twenty-four hours. His son needed help now. The future might be too late.

The least likely possibility was that Jack would agree to see him the next day. In some ways that was the scariest. It was difficult for David to envision how it would go after all these years. But he had prayed and prayed and was willing to trust that God would take care of it. After all, what interest did God have in a busted father-son relationship? Despite David's sins, the Lord must want him reconciled with Jack—especially now, when time was so short. That was his hope, anyway. David reached for the water glass next to him and threw back the pills. Then he picked up the phone and dialed.

chapter 42

Jack leaned forward on the couch, opened the cardboard box of cartridges, and shook it, listening with a hypnotic attentiveness to the tinkling of the bullets. It seemed incongruous to him that something with so severe a purpose could make such a childlike sound. As he shook the box a second time, the tinkling blended with another, louder jingling that seemed to be coming at him from a dream. He realized it was the telephone ringing. He started to rise, but stopped himself with the dark recognition that it would be absurd to interrupt this business for something as pedestrian as the telephone. He let it ring.

He placed the open box back on the coffee table and picked from it a single shell, the one that seemed to flicker the most garishly in the light. Musing that if *this* was the time, *that* was the bullet—the flashy one that seemed to dare him—he grabbed the empty revolver with his free hand and set it on his thigh. Perhaps this *was* the time. Why not? He could look out as far as his mind would take him and see nothing that hinted at improvement in his situation.

He picked up the gun, clicked open the cylinder, and deliberately slid the bullet into the first empty chamber. The shell's golden sparkle faded to a flat copper as it disappeared into the opening. He slapped the cylinder shut and sat tapping the loaded revolver on his knee while trying to force his mind to focus on the pluses and minuses of the situation. Katie would be fine, better probably, without him. Lizzy—that was more difficult. He couldn't formulate a picture of how she would react. Sure she would miss him in the short run, but in the long run she'd probably be better off too. There would be someone to replace him eventually—someone stronger, better. All in all, they would win in the deal. He felt certain of that.

It occurred to him to spin the cylinder, to play Russian roulette. That way it wouldn't be so certain. Fate could decide. He spun the cylinder once but quickly had second thoughts and discarded the idea. He was either going to do it or not, but he wouldn't trivialize it by treating it as some sort of game.

He stared at the gun for a long time, unable to concentrate enough to reach a jumping-off point. It seemed to him that something like this should be preceded by intense soul-searching, but any number of inconsequential thoughts kept passing through his mind, interrupting his efforts at introspection. Each time he was able to focus for a few moments, something would interrupt—the dripping of the faucet, the ticking of the clock. Silence was not all it was cracked up to be. He wondered: if he really did this thing, and experienced real silence, total silence, what would it be like? How black would infinite black be? Blacker than it had been for Patch under the water?

For some reason his mind caught on a memory: Patch coming home from summer camp, excitedly describing the details of how he had learned to shoot a rifle. Jack smiled. Patch had been so happy, so energetic, so willing to work, and so innocently accepting of the trials that nature had imposed upon him. No child could ever have made a parent more proud than Patch had made him. His smile disappeared. No parent had ever lost more than he had lost.

The doorbell rang. Jack practically jumped out of his seat. He looked toward the door and then back at the gun in his hand. He flipped open the cylinder to remove the cartridge. It rang again. *All right, all right.* He wondered who it could be at this hour, and why so persistent? It rang a third time. It struck him that it must be Joel. No one else would have the nerve to ring the bell so insistently at this hour. Jack closed the cylinder and placed the gun on the coffee table.

He walked to the door and flipped the switch to turn on the porch light. Squinting through the tinted glass, he couldn't make out who it was, but it obviously wasn't Joel. He turned the lock and opened the door. In front of him was a thin, elderly man with an unruly mop of gray hair. He wore opaque glasses, rumpled khaki pants, and a plaid shirt that appeared to be at least one size too big. Sitting at attention at his side was a dog—a Seeing Eye dog. In the background a taxi pulled away from the curb.

"Hello, Jack?" The man tilted his head slightly upward, as if catching a scent.

"Yes?"

"I'm sorry to come by so late, but I called and called and I had a strange feeling that something was . . . Well, it doesn't matter. I couldn't wait any longer."

Jack looked the man over. A glimmer of recognition flashed through his mind—but it couldn't be.

"Do you recognize me?" the man asked.

Jack's forehead creased. "I don't think that I do. Can I help you with something?"

"I'm your father."

"Dad?" He could have kicked himself for blurting the undeserved name.

"Yes, it's me."

"What in the world are you doing here?"

"I have to talk to you, Jack. This time I won't take no for an answer, so don't bother trying." He flicked his wrist. The dog stood and walked through the open door. They were in the house before Jack could think to protest.

By the time Jack realized that he had every right to react badly to the intrusion, he hesitated for another reason. The man was blind. Many times in his life he'd fantasized about seeing his dad unexpectedly. He had run through hundreds of verbal blisterings he could administer. But in each of the fantasies his dad was young and vigorous and arrogant. In front of him was a blind, frail old man. It didn't compute. It paralyzed him.

"I suppose I need to do some explaining," David said. "First, and I guess the most obvious: as you can see, I'm blind. A fluke thing, the doctors said. I was in a car wreck fifteen years ago. I was coming home from . . . Well, that doesn't matter. Smashed up my head. Damaged the optic nerve. At first, it left me most of my sight. Over time it worsened. The lights went out completely a few years ago. This is Shelly. She's my eyes now, and my best friend. You can pet her if you want. When she's not working she loves to be petted."

In the current bizarre situation Jack appreciated the relief that bending over and greeting Shelly provided. "Hey, girl. How are you doing?" he said. He scratched her behind the ears. "You're a good girl, aren't you, Shelly?"

As he petted the dog, Jack recovered his bearings. All of the darkness he'd experienced for the past few months began to focus on this contemptible old man and what he had done to their family. Jack decided the blindness was irrelevant. He raised his eyes to his dad. His voice turned cold. "You haven't answered my question. What gives you the right to come barging in here in the middle of the night?"

"I have no right. I'm worried about you. This time I won't leave until you talk to me. That is, unless you're going to throw a blind old man out onto the sidewalk for all of your neighbors to see."

Jack looked through the door glass toward the illuminated windows of the houses across the street. "Come on in and sit down," he said. "But it's late and I've got to get to bed soon." Shelly and David followed Jack to the family room, Shelly's tags jingling with each step.

When they entered the room, Jack turned and waited for his dad to sit, but realized the old man had no idea where to find a chair. Shelly paused, as if evaluating the situation. "There's a chair over here," Jack said. He took his dad's arm and led him to it. The old man settled in and whispered an instruction to Shelly. She lay down beside the chair, her chin resting on the rug between her paws.

Jack sat on the couch. He looked down and saw the gun on the coffee table. His shoulders tensed. His eyes moved toward his father. He saw the dark glasses and remembered. He relaxed.

"I suppose I should offer you something," Jack said. "A Pepsi? Coffee? Water?"

"Coffee? I'd love some, thank you. I'm embarrassed to say I've taken a liking to that Starbucks coffee that all the kids drink. Pick some up every time I go to Tyler. I shouldn't have it this late, though. At my age, it will keep me stumbling to the bathroom all night." David smiled. Jack didn't.

"Well, you're in luck. I've got Starbucks. It's decaf, though." Jack walked into the kitchen and went to work putting on a pot.

"Decaf is perfect."

While scooping the coffee, Jack looked over the breakfast bar into the adjacent family room. David was moving his head about in a slow arc, as if taking in the feel of the room. As much as Jack hated to signal even the slightest interest in his father's life, he could not fight his curiosity. "You said you go to the Starbucks in Tyler? What takes you to Tyler?"

"I've been living in a little town near there since . . . well, for a long time. I thought Katie would have told you."

"She told me you were in Texas, but not where. What town?"

"Elsa."

"Never heard of it. What do you do there?" Jack leaned over the sink and poured water into the decanter.

"I preach."

Jack turned off the faucet.

After a few moments of silence, David said, "Surprised?"

Jack walked over to the counter, poured the water into the coffeemaker, and hit the switch. "Nothing surprises me anymore," he said. He drummed his fingers on the counter while the coffeemaker puffed to life.

A few minutes later Jack walked back into the room and placed a warm mug in his father's hand. Then he sat on the couch.

David took a sip, tipped his head back, and smiled. "Thank you for the coffee. It's very good. A good cup of coffee is one of life's real pleasures, don't you think?" He sipped again.

"Look, it's late. Let's get to the point," Jack snapped.

Shelly's ears pricked.

Crossing his leg, Jack continued, "Exactly what do you want that brings you here in the middle of the night after thirty years?"

"I didn't want it to be thirty years," David said.

"Well, I didn't want a dad who fooled around on my mom and got a man killed. Excuse me if I don't feel terribly sorry for you."

David reached down with his free hand and placed it on Shelly's side. "You're right, of course. I didn't come here to make excuses for what I did."

"Then, once again, why *did* you come?"

"Your mother and Katie told me you were struggling with some things. I wanted to help."

"You talked to Katie? Where do you get off interfering with my family?"

"You may not know this, but your mother and I talk regularly. We have for years. She told me what was happening with you and Katie. Yes, I talked to Katie too."

"Did they tell you to come see me?"

"They told me you needed help. I told them I wanted to help. That's all."

"Stay away from my family. Do you understand? They are off limits to you." Jack's eyes dropped to the gun on the table.

"I don't have any desire to interfere with your family. Honestly, I don't." David took several more sips from his coffee mug and placed it on the table beside him. "This coffee is really very good. Thank you again for making it."

"You've got real nerve strolling in here and acting like you're out for a cup of coffee at the neighborhood diner. This is my house and my life. You're not part of it. That was your choice, not mine. Don't come blowing in here out of nowhere, expecting me to act like things are fine. That's not going to happen." Again Jack's eyes fell on the gun. Without thinking, he reached over, picked it up, and began to wave it around. He felt strangely exhilarated by his ability to get away with something so outrageous right in front of the old man's dead eyes.

"Look, I'm sorry about coming so late, and I don't expect you to act any way at all. I was hoping we could have a talk. Like I said, I was worried about you."

"You don't have to worry. I'm just fine. We'd both be better off if you just rode right back out of town and forgot all about me." After he said it, Jack had another bizarre impulse. He pointed the gun at his dad's chest and lipped, "Pow." Shelly lifted her head from her paws and looked at him. Despite an uneasy sense that he had truly gone too far, the feeling of exhilaration returned, even stronger this time. Jack tightened his grip on the gun. "I don't need your help."

"If you're really doing fine, then I agree with you," David said, oblivious to what was happening in front of him. "I don't like it, but I'll do what you want and leave you alone. From what I understand, though, you're not doing all right."

"You know, it's actually none of your business how I'm doing, is it?" Unwilling to end his silent game, Jack leveled the revolver at his father's heart. He lightly squeezed the trigger, just enough to cause the hammer to rise and shiver before settling back in its place. He experienced another satisfying rush from the idea that the old man would be scared out of his wits if only he could see what was happening.

"From your standpoint I'm sure it's none of my business. From my standpoint you'll always be my business. You say you're doing fine. Well, if you're doing fine under the current circumstances, then you're Superman. Let's face it, Jack, you're grieving over Patch, you're separated from your wife and daughter, and you're sitting alone in an empty house in the middle of the night, thinking about how much you hate your father. That doesn't sound fine to me."

The audacity was more than Jack could take. In his mind's eye he had viewed his dad as a whipping boy for so long that he was infuriated by this man's refusal to act his part. He pointed the gun at his father's forehead.

Shelly, who had been eyeing him from the floor, rose up on her hind legs and growled.

"Shelly! What's wrong with you?" David said. She stopped growling instantly but kept her eyes fixed on Jack.

Jack closed one eye and peered through the gun's sight. He pulled the trigger. The hammer snapped, echoing through the still room like a gunshot.

David rose halfway from his chair. "Son . . ." Shelly leaped to her feet and growled.

Jack froze, dumbfounded that the sound of the trigger had been so loud and recognizable, horrified at what he had done. He fumbled for an excuse to explain things, but couldn't think quickly enough to come up with anything plausible. He decided to pretend nothing had happened.

"What got into her?" he asked.

David eased back into his chair. "I don't know. Something must have spooked her." He reached into his pocket. When he pulled out his hand, it was balled into a fist. He put it near Shelly's mouth. Never moving her eyes completely away from Jack, she nuzzled David's hand until it opened and released a tiny biscuit. David placed his hand on her head. She backed up and sat at his side, still eyeing Jack warily.

The two men sat silently for a few moments. David leaned forward and rested his elbows on his knees. In a soft voice, he said, "Talk to me, Jack. I know you're not okay. That's why I came tonight. Somehow I felt that something was urgently wrong."

Jack didn't respond. He stared at the gun with wide eyes, as if it were an alien appendage that had just sprouted from his hand. Had he really pulled the trigger? Yes, he had—and that meant he was not okay, not okay at all. He placed the gun on the coffee table.

"Do you love Katie, Jack?" his dad continued.

Jack fidgeted. "Where do you get off asking me a question like that?" He was flustered. His voice had lost its hostile edge. To his surprise, he continued, "I'm not sure. I hope so."

"Hope is a good thing. I'm glad you said that. I hope you love her too. She loves you very much, you know."

"How do you know that?"

"Jack, how can you ask me that question? It's obvious to me, and I hardly know her at all. You've lived with her for fifteen years. You know it better than anybody. I'm right, aren't I?"

Jack knew he was right. He changed the subject. "Katie and I just aren't on the same page anymore."

"Then maybe you need to keep turning pages until you find her."

"Oh, God, how clever."

"I'm glad you brought up God. Katie said you've got a problem with God. Is that right?"

"How did I bring up God? Anyway, of all people, I don't expect to get a sermon from you about God. You taught me all about that. If there is a God, he's kicked me in the teeth enough. Excuse me for being sick of the whole idea."

"What I taught you about God is true. Don't ever assume that there's something wrong with God just because people like me do things that are wrong. God didn't do anything to you or your mother. I did."

"Yeah, well what about Patch? You didn't hold him under the water until he was dead. Where was God then?"

David leaned back in his chair. "Listen, Jack, I understand your bitterness. You wouldn't be human if you didn't feel some anger. But do you really believe that God wanted Patch to die? Do you think that he wakes up in the morning and says to himself, 'I guess I'll do a hurricane today, and a cholera epidemic, and how about a swimming accident?'? You know too much to believe God works that way."

"Actually, I don't believe God killed Patch. But I do believe that if he really exists, he could have stopped it. And he didn't. If he's so great, why didn't he stop it? Patch wasn't killed robbing a store or shooting at a cop. He was a good kid. He believed in God. But when Patch needed him, God couldn't find the time to save his life."

"No, God didn't save his life. I wish I knew why; unfortunately, I don't. But where do you think Patch is now? God didn't save him from drowning, but I know with all the certainty I can have in my soul that he saved Patch—that Patch is alive right now and that you'll see him again someday."

"Save it for Sunday, would you?"

David felt for the edge of the coffee table, picked up his mug, and took a drink. "I'm no expert, Jack. I'm just a sinful man. I'm trying to figure things out like everyone else. I do know this: God doesn't cause evil things to happen. As to why God intervenes sometimes—or doesn't—I have no clue. But Patch is with God now; he's fine, and he's waiting for you. You have to believe that."

Jack rubbed his forehead. "I'm tired," he said. "I've got to get to bed. Where are you staying? I'll give you a lift."

"No, thank you." David rose to his feet. "I'm not going to impose on you for a ride. Just call my cab, if you would. I told him I'd need him to pick me up. Here's his number." David reached into his shirt pocket and pulled out a card.

Jack didn't want to give him a ride, so he took the card, went into the kitchen, and made the call. Then he excused himself for a minute, went upstairs to the bathroom, and threw cold water on his face. Just as he came back down, a horn honked outside. He walked David to the door.

"I've got tickets for the Rangers game Sunday night," David said. "My church sent someone with me, a chaperone for the blind man in the big city. Do you want to go with us? I thought maybe we could talk some more."

"No. Thanks anyway. How long are you in town?"

"As long as it takes. My chaperone's retired and is staying with his daughter in Dallas, so he's in no hurry at all. I'll leave this ticket for you, just in case. One of the few advantages of a disability is that they give you special seats, and good ones." David felt for Jack's hand and placed a ticket in it. "Even if you can't make it for the whole thing, drop by for an inning or two. You always loved baseball. So did I, remember?" Shelly led him through the door and down the walk.

Jack watched until the cab pulled out of sight. He walked back into the family room and over to the coffee table. Picking up the gun, he turned it over in his hands. It was difficult for him to focus on what he had done; it had been so stupid, so crazy. He placed the gun in its box.

Spotting the container of cartridges, he scanned the coffee table for the bullet he'd unloaded. It wasn't there. Perplexed, he opened the box and looked inside. Something didn't seem right. He stared at the gun in the gun box and tried to reconstruct what he'd done with the bullet. The doorbell had rung. He had opened the cylinder. He had intended to remove the bullet. Then the doorbell had rung again.

He snatched the revolver out of the box and flicked open the cylinder. The bullet was in the gun.

He put his hand on the couch behind him and eased himself down onto the cushion. He had pointed a loaded gun at his father's head and pulled the trigger. But why hadn't it fired? Then he remembered. He had spun the cylinder just before the doorbell rang. Instead of playing Russian roulette with his own life, he had played it with his father's.

Jack shook the cartridge out of the chamber and put the empty gun back in the box. He took the gun and cartridges to the closet and stuffed them into the back corner of the shelf under a blanket. After closing the closet door, he held on to the knob for several moments, as if afraid that something—the gun, maybe—might turn the knob from inside and push its way out. He shook his head and crossed the room to the couch. Lying down on his back, he pulled a pillow onto his face and closed his eyes.

chapter 43

Jack licked his lips. It was like dragging sandpaper across pavement. He realized he was on the couch and was puzzled for a moment. Then he remembered the night before, his dad, the gun. He rolled over and groaned.

The phone on the end table jangled.

"Hel—ah hem . . . ah hem." His voice finally fought its way past his tongue. "Hello?"

"Are you sick? You sound terrible."

It was Katie. Jack looked at his watch: eleven-fifteen. He concentrated on stabilizing his voice. "Hi, Kate. Can you hold on just a minute?" He put the phone down and ran on tiptoe into the hall bathroom. He turned on the faucet, shoved his mouth under it, and took several gulps of water. Then he hurried back to the couch and sat down.

"Okay, I'm back."

"Where did you go? Is there somebody with you?"

"Who would be with me? I woke up with some gunk in my throat. I went into the bathroom to drink some water so you wouldn't have to listen to it."

"You sounded strange. Did you just get out of bed?"

"Actually, I did just wake up, yes." His lawyerly instincts took over and put him on the offensive. "Someone dropped by to see me last night and kept me up half the night."

"Who?"

"I think you know who."

"No, Jack, I don't. Why don't you tell me?"

"My dad."

"Oh."

Jack waited for a few moments, but she apparently did not intend to respond any further. "He told me he'd talked to you and Mom."

"That's true, we did talk to him. How did it go?"

"It didn't go at all. He barged in around midnight and I finally had to kick him out so I could get some sleep."

"You mean he just showed up on your doorstep?"

"That's exactly what I mean. It was bizarre."

"Well, I'm sure you were surprised, but you don't have to act like he's some sort of psychopath or something."

"Why not?"

"Oh, please, Jack. What did you talk about?"

"He shared his philosophy on life. The whole thing was surreal." Jack twisted and stretched in his seat as he talked, trying to work out the kinks from his night on the couch.

"I hope you were polite to him. What good does it do to be mean to him now? He's a sick old man."

"You knew he was blind?"

"I just found out. Your mother told me."

"That was a shock. Actually, I was very polite to him. I even made him coffee. I surprised myself, frankly." He felt as if he were looking her in the eye and lying to her. But what was he supposed to do, tell her about the gun?

"Jack, if you would give him a chance, you might find that he's a pretty good guy. Thirty years is a long time to hold a grudge, especially against your own father."

"Butt out, would you, Katie? He's my father and it's my business, not yours." He knew that would draw a response. He braced himself.

"You've got no reason to talk to me like that. Maybe it's time for you to start thinking of somebody other than yourself for a while!"

"Fine. I can only hope to become as perfect as you."

"You'd better talk to Lizzy. I can see this is going nowhere."

"Sure." He heard clicking and clacking on the other end.

"Hi, Daddy. You should see the cat-dog! He never barks. He's real pretty. Mom says he's distinguished looking. He doesn't behave very well, though. Grandma said the neighbors told her he's got an independent streak."

"Well, he sounds like quite a dog, er, cat-dog, sweetie. What did Bandit think of him?" Jack stood and walked to the window. He looked out between the shutters and half expected to see Bandit romping in the yard.

"He didn't like him at all. We tried to take them for a walk together, but they almost got in a fight. We had to put Bandit in the house."

"That must have been wild. Have you made any new friends?"

"Not yet."

"Are the neighborhood kids nice?"

"They're okay," she said. He didn't detect much enthusiasm. "Daddy, when are you gonna come see us?"

"I don't know, honey. We'll have to see. Soon, I hope. You better let me talk to Mom, okay?" Turning away from the window, he sat on the couch again and crossed his feet on the coffee table.

"Okay. Bye. I love you."

"I love you, too, sweetie." More clicking and clacking.

"How did you leave it with your dad?" It was Katie again.

"I didn't leave it any way at all. I called him a cab and he went away. Was something else expected?"

"A cab?" He heard what sounded like an exasperated sigh. "Do you think you could have driven him?"

"I offered to drive him. He insisted on taking the cab. What am I supposed to do, kidnap him and throw him in the trunk?"

"Jack, I hope you're going to give him a chance. He's not going to live forever, you know. Someday you'll wish you'd made the effort."

"Right."

"Okay, forget it. Good-bye, Jack. I love you," she said.

He took his feet off the coffee table and leaned forward. "That was abrupt."

"I don't have anything more to say right now."

"Fine." He pondered whether to say he loved her. "Good-bye."

As he hung up he knew that he had been a jerk and regretted it. He noted that he should have been pleasantly surprised that Katie even called. Reclining on the couch with his arms around an accent pillow, he ran the previous evening through his mind. He tried to quarantine the gun incident in a remote corner of his brain and focus on the things his father had said. Strangely, he was able to picture vividly the entire conversation. He recalled nearly every word.

After fifteen minutes or so he muttered, "Garbage," and got up. He walked upstairs to change. When he began to pull off his rumpled clothes he thought of Patch. His heart sank, as it did each morning when the thought of his son first entered his mind. For some reason, though, the usual blackness, the dread, wasn't quite as dark.

He thought again of what his father had said. He tried hard to picture Patch alive somewhere, maybe on a golden sidewalk, standing with a godlike old man with a white beard. It didn't work. He couldn't see it. Then he realized he was glad he couldn't see it. He liked the darkness better. As he pulled on a clean T-shirt, he vowed to capture his usual emptiness again before the morning was through. He owed Patch that much.

chapter 44

Sunday morning Jack slept until ten o'clock. When he awoke, he was pleased that his first thought was of Patch. He lay in bed for twenty minutes, until his thoughts had reached a depth sufficient to convince him that his grief had not waned. At that point, he rose, pulled on a pair of shorts and a T-shirt, and walked downstairs barefoot. After putting on a pot of coffee, he went out front to get the paper.

The electronically timed lawn sprinklers were running, and the paper, in its plastic delivery bag, was sitting in the middle of the down-pour. After a moment of indecision, he ducked his head and ran into the spray, his feet tossing up tiny splashes. He unwittingly grabbed the wrong end of the bag. As he turned to run back to the house, the whole paper slid out onto the wet grass.

Muttering, he dove back under the sprinklers, scooped up the soaked sections of paper in both hands, and headed for drier ground. By the time he got back to the door, water was dripping off his hair and nose, and his T-shirt was plastered to his chest. Fortunately, the sports section was safe and dry, buried in its usual spot deep within the Sunday edition of the *Dallas Morning News*.

When he got in the front door, he shook himself off, tossed the dripping paper on the entry rug, and bounded up the stairs. He peeled off his wet clothes, tossed them on the bathroom floor, and pulled on his white terry bathrobe. Then he went back downstairs to try it again.

At the kitchen table, he separated the hopelessly soaked portions of the paper from those that were still readable. He opened the sports: "Yankees Blank Rangers 2-0." He sneered and put it down. Picking up the metropolitan section, he scanned the headlines: "Son Held in Woman's Knife Murder," "School Official Indicted," "Boy Scout Offices Vandalized." Grunting, he tossed it aside and picked up the sports again. He hated the Yankees, but at least they weren't killing anyone.

After he finished his coffee, he went upstairs, put on athletic shorts and a running shirt, and headed outside. The air was unusually crisp for April, but the sky was a deep, high blue, the kind of Texas sky that usually didn't appear until late May or June. On the front sidewalk, he bent over and stretched his hamstrings and calves before strolling a few steps and breaking into a jog. He pounded down the sidewalk to the corner. There, he turned and headed down the road that led out of the subdivision and toward Preston Park.

As he passed the neighborhood pond, he noticed three boys fishing. They couldn't have been more than eight or nine years old. He looked around for a parent, but there were no adults in sight. He wanted to yell to the boys, to warn them to get away from the water. Couldn't they see the danger? The back of his neck began to sweat. He swerved off the sidewalk and onto the grass that funneled down to the water. He opened his mouth to shout. Then he caught himself. The boys were all right. They were fishing, that was all. He slowed his gait, moved back onto the sidewalk, and continued toward the park.

Settling into a mechanical rhythm, he allowed his mind to wander.

He supposed that Lizzy had been wondering what was going on. How could she not? Suddenly she was living in a strange house a thousand miles from home. Katie could handle her questions for a while. Whatever Katie's faults, she had a good head on her shoulders. Nevertheless, this couldn't go on forever. Lizzy also had a good head on her shoulders. Sooner or later she would begin to ask questions too hard to fluff over.

As he entered the park, he looked around. It was past noon and there were lots of people—joggers, teenagers playing basketball, little kids shouting and swinging on playground equipment. They looked so happy. Didn't they know how quickly it could all change? Couldn't they see that none of this would last? It was an illusion, a transitory moment of pleasure in a tough, unforgiving world. He shook his head, as if to change the channel. His thoughts were becoming so morbid that he was frightening himself.

"Hi, Jack." The voice jolted him out of his musing. Sally Maples, one of Katie's closest friends, was walking toward him with her youngest son, Daniel, and dog, Pretzel. Daniel was enjoying the walk from the luxury of a cavernous stroller, leisurely turning his head from side to side like a politician riding in the front of a parade.

"Hi, Sally. Nice morning, huh?" As Jack passed her, he pointed at Daniel and added, "He's really growing." She said something, but her voice faded out behind him. He supposed that she knew everything about Katie and him. It made him uncomfortable. He recalled the time, a few years back, when Sally and Katie had performed a soulful rendition of "Heat Wave" at a neighborhood cookout. The mental picture of the two clean-as-a-whistle suburban moms belting out the lyrics with satirically sultry wiggling made him smile. Real hot tamales, as Katie had said afterward.

On the return route, running seemed harder than usual. By the time he hit the home stretch, he was gulping air and had a side ache. When he rounded the corner onto his street, he heard the roar of a lawn mower. Someone in a red T-shirt and shorts was cutting his grass. He squinted to try to make out who it was. As he got closer, he recognized Seth.

"Seth, what are you doing?" he yelled over the din. Seth had his back partially turned and couldn't hear him. Jack tapped him on the shoulder. Seth jumped. When he saw who it was, he turned off the mower.

"Hi, Mr. Parst. I must have been daydreaming."

"Seth, why are you cutting our grass?"

"I just thought I'd do it for you. I've been cutting Mrs. Salantro's yard. She's pretty old, and she doesn't have any family around. I looked over and saw that yours was getting pretty long. I figured you'd probably been busy lately. I hope you don't mind."

"Mind? Are you kidding?" He paused. "You're a great kid, Seth. I'm very proud of you, you know." Jack wanted badly to hug him, just like he used to hug Patch, but he didn't.

Seth put his hands in his pockets. "Well, I'll just finish up, Mr. Parst. I won't be long."

Jack squeezed Seth's arm. "Thank you, Seth." He walked into the house and shut the door behind him. Standing with his back against the door, he closed his eyes. For the first time in nine months, he allowed himself the thought that maybe the world wasn't all bad.

WITH NOTHING ELSE TO DO, Jack spent the afternoon at his office, slogging through a pile of documents. On his way home he impulsively veered his car into a local drive-in. The Beach Boys blared on loudspeakers while high school carhops in ponytails and capillary-constricting red shorts hurried in and out of the glass-encased building. Jack assured himself that when Lizzy got to high school she'd wear shorts like that over his dead body.

As he looked over the menu, he noted that he hadn't eaten a green vegetable in days. He pushed the speaker button. Something sticky tried to prevent him from removing his finger. He started to wipe the finger on his T-shirt, but shifted to his jeans when a quick mental calculation concluded the mysterious goo was less likely to do permanent damage there. A woman's voice came through the box and asked him what he wanted. He ordered a chili pie to go.

As he pulled out of the drive-in, the spicy smell of chili and corn chips wafting from the bag on the seat next to him released a flood of juices in his mouth. As if there were a direct neural connection between his taste buds and his foot, he increased the pressure on the gas pedal and zipped across the five blocks to his neighborhood. When he wheeled into his subdivision the tires squealed, drawing a sharp glare of disapproval from a young mother guiding a stroller next to the pond. He eased his foot off the gas. Neighborhood jaws were surely chewing over his situation already. He didn't want to provide more fodder.

When he got home he grabbed a soda out of the refrigerator and flopped onto the couch. Flicking through the TV channels, he found the Rangers game. He leaned over and tore open the foil bag that protected his dinner. A cloud of steam rushed out, moistening his nose and mouth. He pulled a plastic fork from the bag and dug in. As he ate, he looked around the room. Despite the chatter of the baseball announcers, the emptiness of the house worked on his mind. The thought of helping Lizzy with her homework had never seemed so enticing.

After finishing the chili pie and soda, he rummaged in the freezer.

He found an ice cream bar hidden in the corner behind a bag of vegetables. It was gone in a few bites. He wondered what his doctor would think of him now that he'd stored enough fat in one meal to last through a winter in Yellowstone. Kicking off his shoes, he pulled a pillow under his head and stretched out on the couch to watch the game.

Within a few minutes he was nodding off. Each time he was about to fall completely asleep, though, his mind startled him back to consciousness. He kept seeing snapshots of Friday evening—pictures of himself sitting on the couch, pointing a loaded gun at his father's forehead. He figured that a shrink would have a field day with that one. His stomach rumbled and churned. He knew it was the food and kicked himself for indulging like a school kid.

The things his father had said flashed through his thoughts, then circled back and lingered. Irritated at his inability to erase his father from his mind, he focused on stoking the embers of hatred that had reliably smoldered in his gut for thirty years. He succeeded in fanning the coals to a low glow, but no matter how he tried, he could not make them burn. He began to wonder if he still wanted them to burn.

Then he thought about Seth. *Imagine that: cutting my grass. What a nice thing; what a nice kid. Patch was like that, a nice kid.* Somehow he sensed that it was all connected—his father, Katie, Patch, Seth, but he couldn't decipher how. There had to be an answer. Otherwise, what was the point? Eventually, he sat up and looked at the TV. It was the fifth inning. Glancing at the coffee table, he saw the ticket that his dad had left him. He picked it up and tapped it on the edge of the table. If traffic cooperated, he could still make the last couple of innings.

chapter 45

Jack's loafers tapped out an echoing *click, clack, click* on the floor as he made his way toward the light at the end of the dim concrete tunnel. The closer he came to the brightness, the louder was the happy roar that rushed over and around him from the crowd on the other side. He felt the same exciting sense of anticipation that he'd felt since he was a kid whenever he was around a ballpark.

When he emerged into the glare, he shaded his eyes and squinted into a rustling, colorful sea of people. Fifteen rows below him was the third-base dugout. On the field, the Yankees were batting. The scoreboard showed the Rangers leading four to two. Just to his left, a kid's face was buried in a sticky cloud of pink cotton candy. The warm aroma of roasted peanuts and popcorn was everywhere.

He scanned the crowd until his eyes fell on the special group of seats for the disabled, just off to his right. Sitting at the far end of the row, munching on a hot dog, was his father. He wore khaki shorts and a white American Heart Association T-shirt that had a red jump rope on the front. Perched haphazardly on his gray head was a blue Rangers cap with a red "T" on the front. Along with the hot dog, he was jug-gling a soda and some sort of electronic device that looked like a hand-held video game. Shelly sat on the step next to him, her ears perking with each reaction of the crowd.

Jack fought the urge to smile. His father—dark glasses, guide dog, and all—looked like a twelve-year-old having the time of his life. Jack wondered how in the world he knew what was going on in the game. As he walked down the aisle in back of the section of seats, Jack could hear his father giving it to the Yankee players in the dugout below. "Go back to the Bronx, ya bums," he yelled. The batter in the on-deck circle looked up, saw the dark glasses, shook his head, and chuckled.

Shelly snarled when Jack rounded the corner and moved onto the step next to her. David lifted his head. "What is it, girl?"

"It's me," Jack said. "How did you get here? I thought somebody was going to be with you." Jack squeezed past his dad and sat in the seat next to him. Shelly lay down on the step, but rested her head at an angle so she could keep an eye on Jack.

"I had given up on you. I'm glad you decided to come. How did I get here? Ah, the benefits of the Americans with Disabilities Act," David said. "All I have to do is call and tell them what time I'm arriv-ing. The good people at the ballpark meet Shelly and me and escort us to my seat. My cabdriver listens to the game and pulls up to the gate when it's over. They escort me out. Before you know it I'm back in my hotel room. The cab fare's pretty expensive, but it's not like I do this every day. Under the circumstances, it's the only way to go to a game, don't you think?" He smiled broadly. "To answer your other question, I told my chaperone not to come. I was hoping you'd show up and we'd have a chance to talk."

Jack grudgingly admired his father's gumption. For an instant he thought of Patch. Before he could figure out why, his dad said, "You know, Jack, I'd probably rather be here than any place on earth. You understand that, don't you?"

"Yes, I do." Jack's eyes drifted out toward the field. He wondered if it was possible to be anything other than happy at a baseball game.

"I've always thought that baseball was a little closer to heaven than any other sport," David said. "Anyway, let's talk about you. I suspect you're starting to miss Katie and Lizzy quite a bit by now, aren't you?"

Jack's back stiffened. The old guy didn't beat around the bush. Nevertheless, Jack resolved to control his temper. He had come here because he needed to talk, so he was going to talk. "I miss Lizzy a lot. Katie . . . Well, there are things I miss about her too. There are other things I don't miss."

"Things you miss? You're kidding yourself, son. You miss her more than you'll even admit to yourself."

His fingers digging into the edge of his seat, Jack replied in a clenched voice, "How would you know?"

"Now, don't get upset with me. I'm just stating the obvious. It doesn't take a genius to figure out that you didn't go from loving her to not loving her in the span of a few months. It appears to me that you're running away from something, but it's not from Katie." David put his hand to his ear. The crowd roared. "Whoa! How about that?" The catcher, Esteban Castillo, had picked a runner off first base. "I'll tell you, Jack, I've seen a lot of catchers in my time, Bench, Berra, Campanella, but I wish I could see this Castillo kid throw, just once. From what I can tell there's never been anyone like him."

"He's the best I've ever seen," Jack said. He wasn't interested in talking baseball, though. "Running away from something? Where did you get that?" Just as he had been on Friday night, Jack was taken aback by his dad's directness, his refusal to play the whipping boy.

"It's just an observation. I'm trying to help." David punched some buttons on the gadget he was holding.

"What is that thing?" Jack asked. "And how did you know Castillo had picked off the runner a minute ago?" He craned his neck to see over his dad's shoulder.

"Technology at work. It's an electronic scorecard. See, I've got an earpiece." He turned his head so Jack could see his other ear. "Part of it is a radio. Then I've got scoring buttons in Braille for runs, hits, errors. You punch in the lineup and any substitutions. If I want to know what happened in, say, the top of the fifth, I punch five and the up arrow. Listen."

He put the earpiece close to Jack's ear. A robotic voice narrated, "First batter, Simms, bunts for a hit. Second batter, Daley, hits into a fielder's choice, shortstop to second baseman."

"Okay, that's amazing," Jack said.

"Do you want to try it?"

"No, no thanks. Where did you get it?"

"You'd be surprised at the specialized gadgets they sell for blind people. It's like an underground industry. By the way, it is a fascinating device—but seeing's better, believe me."

Jack had no idea how to respond. "Yes, I'm sure that's true," he said.

The two men sat for a minute as if neither knew how to pick the conversation back up. David took the last few bites of his hot dog.

Jack broke the silence. "You said you think I'm running away from something. That's ridiculous. What would I be running away from?"

"I don't know. Maybe you're not. But there wouldn't be anything wrong if you were. At some point we all run away from life to some extent—and sometimes we run away from God. I did. But you knew that, didn't you?"

Jack didn't like where this appeared to be going. He didn't answer.

"When you were little, you used to crawl up on my lap and I'd tell you Bible stories." David said. "Do you remember that?"

"What does that have to do with anything?"

David took a plastic container out of his pocket. His hands trembled as he shook out a tiny pill and washed it down with Coke.

Jack raised an eyebrow. The feebleness of those hands did not fit with the old man's steady voice. Although he wondered about the pill, Jack said nothing.

David closed the container, put it back in his pocket, and said, "I want to tell you a Bible story."

"Now?" Jack swiveled his head to see who was sitting around them. He lowered his voice. "Of all people, I don't think you're exactly in a position to be telling Bible stories."

"I'm a preacher, Jack. I tell Bible stories for a living. I don't apologize for that. Yes, I'm a sinner too. You may think I'm the biggest one of the bunch. In fact, you could be right. But remember, I didn't write the story, I'm just telling it. It's a story that's helped me. I think it might help you too."

"Well, I'm a grown-up now. I don't have to listen to your stories anymore. I did that once and it didn't get me anywhere." Jack rose from his seat.

David felt for Jack's arm and clutched it. "Wait. I want to say one thing. Please listen. Then you can leave if you'd like."

Jack looked at his father's hand. It was gray and spotted, and it trembled despite the anchor that Jack's forearm provided. He sat back down. "Okay, what is it?"

"I made a huge mistake a long time ago. Because of it I've lost every-thing I care about in this world. I can't change that now. I can, however, try to help you avoid doing the same thing. And you *are* doing the same thing. You're throwing away everything that's important. Not in the same way that I did, but you're throwing it away nonetheless. If you let Katie and Lizzy go, you will regret it for the rest of your life, just as I have. I don't want that to happen to you. I love you too much."

Jack studied the side of his father's face. Deep creases cut across his forehead and down his cheeks, and despite the energy the man drew from these surroundings, Jack thought how much older he appeared than his age. Swiveling his head again to determine whether anyone could hear, Jack said, "Okay, what's your story?"

"I'll make it quick. It's a story from the Old Testament. It's about the prophet Elijah. King Ahab and his wife, Jezebel, were rotten people. They had convinced the Israelites to worship a pagan god named Baal. Elijah refused to sit by and let it happen. So he set up a contest. He got King Ahab and all of the people together on top of a big hill. The priests of Baal were on one side and Elijah was on the other. Whoever could make fire come down from heaven to burn up a bull on an altar would be the winner."

"I know this story," Jack said.

"I know you do. Bear with me. The pagan priests danced around for hours, shouting and yelling and even cutting themselves. Of course, they couldn't get the job done. Nothing but cold bull."

Jack chuckled.

"Thank you," David said, and smiled. "Finally Elijah got up. First, he poured water all over the bull—nice dramatic touch. Then, he looked to heaven and asked the Lord to show everybody who the real God was. He was hardly finished speaking when a fireball came blazing out of the sky and burned up everything: the bull, the wood, the water, even the stones—some show."

The ballpark crowd roared. David put his hand up to his earpiece. "Two runs. Give me just a minute." He punched some buttons on his electronic scorecard.

Jack tapped his fingers impatiently on the side of his seat. He was interested in the story now, and it irritated him that David had stopped just to score the game.

"Sorry," David said. He put the scorecard back in his lap. "Now, where was I? Oh, yes, the fire from heaven made quite an impression, as you might imagine. The people fell on their faces and praised God. A big win for Elijah."

"So what's the point?" Jack said.

"There's more. Jezebel, who wasn't at the contest, got wind of what had happened. She sent a hit squad to get Elijah. Here's where Elijah did something that's hard to figure. Remember, this is a man who has God on his side. After all, he had just called down a lightning strike from heaven in front of the whole country. So what did he do when the queen threatened him? Did he stand firm and trust God to protect him? No, he ran away. He took off into the desert, sat under a tree, and asked God to let him die."

"I don't remember that part of the story. Why would he run away?" Jack said. "Good grief, even I would believe if God sent lightning from heaven any time I asked for it."

"Oh?" David said.

"What I mean is that if good things happened every time you prayed for them, it would be easy to have faith."

"You're making my point for me. If anyone ever had a reason to have faith, it was Elijah. But he still ran away."

"What happened?"

David took the earpiece out of his ear. Both men had lost track of the game. "Elijah ran away across the desert. He came to a cave and went inside. He whined around for a while about his bad luck. The Lord let him vent and even sent a few impressive special effects his way: a thunderstorm, an earthquake, and the like.

"When God spoke to him, though, he didn't roar like an earthquake. He did it in the tiniest whisper. He didn't get mad at him. He didn't scold him. He basically said, 'You've had your chance to blow off steam. Now it's time to get back to work. Here's a list of things I want you to do.' Elijah just got up and headed back across the desert as if nothing had happened. He went back to work."

Jack looked at his dad. "I guess you're trying to tell me it's time to move on. Is that the point?"

David rubbed his earlobe between his thumb and index finger. "Actually, I think there are a couple of points," he said. "First, even somebody as close to God as Elijah got so frustrated, so beaten down by life that he ran away from it all. If he did it, there's hope for the rest of us when things get tough and we feel like we can't take it anymore."

"And point two?" asked Jack.

"If there ever was a person God had a right to be impatient with, it was Elijah. But God never lost his patience. He gave him some rope. He let him vent. Then he said, 'Okay, now that you've gotten that out of your system, let's get on with your life. I've got things that I need you to do.' In answer to your question, yes, I think he's saying that to you, Jack."

Jack leaned forward with his elbows on his knees and studied the ticket that he still held in his hands. He began to tear tiny pieces off the corners, letting each piece flutter to the concrete at his feet.

David tilted his head in Jack's direction but said nothing.

After a few moments, Jack crumpled the remainder of the ticket and tossed it beneath his chair. "I know it's difficult for anyone else to understand, but since Patch died, it's so hard. There is this incredible emptiness. I don't know how I can ever get over it. I loved him so much . . ." His shoulders sagged. "I'm tired; I'm just so tired of it all."

"I know you are, son." David felt for Jack's shoulder and rested his hand on it.

Jack flinched at his father's touch, but he did not remove the hand. Instead, he put his head in his own hands. "What am I going to do?" he said. "My son is dead. Katie and Lizzy are gone. My life is a wreck. How do I get it back?" Jack raised up and looked into his dad's eyes. All that he could see was his own reflection in the dark glasses.

"That's the part I've learned the hard way, Jack. No matter what you've done, God wants you to come back. When you want to come back, you just tell him. He'll show you how."

People started getting up and moving through the aisles all around them. Looking up, Jack saw that the game was over.

"Think about it," David said. "I'll be here to help any time you want to talk." David moved his head around in response to the sound of the crowd filing out around them. "I guess we lost track of things. What was the score?"

"Six to four."

"So the good guys won."

"Yeah, the good guys won. Can I give you a lift home?" Jack said.

"I'd love to, but if I took a ride from you I'd be doing an injustice to the cabdriver. He should be waiting for me at the gate. I would appreciate it if you would grab an usher for me, though."

"Sure, just a second." Jack started to get up.

"Wait. There's one more thing I want to tell you first." David shifted sideways in his seat and leaned close to Jack. "Right when you want to come back to God is precisely when Satan will work the hardest to keep you from getting back."

"Satan? Listen, uh, I don't—"

David held up his hand. "Save the hemming and hawing, please. I'm talking about Satan, not the bogeyman. Believe me, he's real. It's his job to tempt you, trick you, and destroy you. Unfortunately, he's very good at it. So good, in fact, that if we were left on our own, we'd never be able to resist. But that's the beauty of things. We're not on our own. You believe in Jesus, don't you, Jack?"

"Well, on one level . . ."

David slapped Jack's leg. "Don't give me any philosophical drivel about one level or another. I know you believe. You have since you were a kid."

Jack looked at his father, wide eyed. "Then why did you ask?"

"To make you think about it for a change, that's why. It's easy to wander through life and never give a thought to anything that's important. I know, because I did it myself. This is important. If you believe in Jesus, then you believe that the war between good and evil is finished. Satan lost. He can still win battles, but he can't win the war. Eventually he has to run away."

"The point to this military metaphor is?"

"The point is that when you find yourself tempted, don't try to face it alone. That's where I made my mistake. I became so proud that I thought I was above it all, that I could handle it on my own. You don't know how much I wish that I had said, 'Lord, I'm not strong enough, but you are. Help me.' I'm convinced that if I had had the sense to do that, my whole life would have been different."

"Thanks for the advice, but temptation's not my problem right now," Jack answered.

David nodded. "It wasn't my problem either. Just remember what I said." He stood up and gently tugged Shelly's harness. "Well, I would appreciate it if you could find one of the ushers for me. He'll take it from there."

After his dad was gone, Jack remained in his seat, waiting for the traffic to clear before he went to his car. He thought of Katie and Lizzy; he thought of his mother and the way she said she'd forgiven his dad; he thought of Patch. But mostly he puzzled over his own feelings—a jumble of emotions he didn't fully understand—toward the man who had once again shared some baseball and advice with him after so many years.

chapter 46

Katie held onto the banister and felt her way gingerly down the dark staircase. She made a mental note to pick up a night-light at the drugstore. It was Monday morning and she was learning that shuffling downstairs in her slippers for her five-fifteen a.m. devotional time was a bit more precarious in a strange house in the dark. As she turned the corner into the hallway, she noticed a yellow glow coming from the kitchen. When she entered the room she was surprised to see Sarah sitting at the kitchen table, sipping a cup of tea.

"I'm glad you're up," Sarah said. "I woke up in the middle of the night with something on my mind. I couldn't get back to sleep."

"Are you feeling okay?" Katie headed straight for the coffeemaker. She pulled a filter out of the cabinet and began to scoop coffee into it.

"I'm fine. You're going to think I'm crazy, though."

"Why would I think you're crazy?"

"I have this overwhelming feeling that I need to see David."

Katie put the coffee scoop down and turned toward Sarah. "Would you give me a minute to get over the shock?" She made a show of putting her hand over her heart.

"Very funny, but I'm not kidding," Sarah said. She took a sip of her tea.

"Okay, I think it's a great idea, but why?"

"That's the strange part. I don't exactly know. But I feel like I need to see him as quickly as possible."

"So what are you going to do?"

"It's not what I am going to do. It's what *we* are going to do; at least I hope it is. How would you like a trip to Dallas?"

chapter 47

David sat with his hands folded on the small round table. Shelly was lying on the carpeted floor at his side. They were in a tiny conference room at Challenger Airlines' Captain's Club in Dallas/Fort Worth International Airport. It was Tuesday evening, two days after David's visit with Jack at the ballgame. They were waiting for Sarah and Katie to arrive.

"What do you think she'll make of me after all these years, Shelly?" David reached down and stroked the German shepherd's back. "Some of my parts don't work so well, and my chrome doesn't shine the way it used to. I never thought it would be this way." He wiped his forehead with a handkerchief. Breathing was more difficult for him each day, and his shortness of breath sapped his energy.

Shelly whimpered. He patted her side. "I know. You didn't picture it this way, either." His hand trembled as he moved it from Shelly back to the tabletop.

Katie had called the day before. She said that Sarah wanted to know if she could meet him in Dallas. Katie had seemed perplexed, but happy, at Sarah's urgency. With Sarah in a wheelchair, the airport had seemed the most viable location. David had assured her that he would get there, even if he and Shelly had to walk.

He tapped his finger on the table and tried to visualize Sarah's face. He could get the basic features right—the brown hair, the creamy complexion—but somehow could not make the entire picture come together. It was a blur, an outline. Katie, on the other hand, was as clear in his mind as if she were standing right in front of him. He felt guilty and frustrated about it. After all, he had met Katie only once, and he had been married to Sarah for all those years.

He knew that he could not allow himself the hope of touching Sarah's face—her eyelids, her nose, her cheeks—though he would gladly have given everything he owned for the opportunity to see her again, just once, through his fingertips. He remembered how she had reacted the last time he tried to touch her, at her mother's house thirty years earlier. She had recoiled from him, as if he were filthy. And he had been filthy. No, there would be no touching this time. But he would hear her voice, smell her loveliness. That would be enough.

Shelly sat up. Just before the door opened, David stood.

"David?" It was Katie's voice. He remembered it as clearly as her face. He heard the whirring motor of Sarah's wheelchair enter the room first, then Katie's footsteps coming around the wheelchair and across the carpet. To his surprise, Shelly didn't flinch as Katie wrapped her arms around David's neck. She kissed him on the cheek. He held her tight and thought how much he would have liked to have a daughter. Perhaps it would have changed him, made things different.

"I love you," she whispered in his ear.

He was unprepared. It had been so long since he had *felt* love. Tears edged down his cheeks from beneath his dark glasses, and he was not embarrassed; he was glad to cry for this. It was his first real joy in thirty years. He held her tighter yet.

From across the room he heard Sarah sniffle and fumble in her purse.

Katie drew back from him. "Thank you so much for what you're doing," she said softly.

"No, Katie, thank you. You have no idea what you have just done for me." He wiped his sleeve across his cheek.

"Do you think we've forgotten you, Sarah?" Katie said.

"It's all right. I'm not going anywhere," Sarah said.

Katie laughed. "Sarah's MS is acting up, so she's in her go-cart for this trip," she said. "As you probably know, she's not one to feel sorry for herself."

David turned his head in Sarah's direction. "Are you in pain?" he said.

"Oh, no. It just flares up once in a while. I'll be back on my feet in no time."

Katie looked at David. "See what I mean?"

"Yes," David said.

"Let me move you over here closer," Katie said.

"No, no. I can still move this thing around on my own," Sarah said. She pushed a button and the chair began to roll forward.

David heard her approaching. He reached down, found his chair, and sat.

Katie picked his hand up gently and placed it on the arm of Sarah's wheelchair. "I think I'll go outside and call to check on Lizzy," she said. "I'll be back in a few minutes."

David heard Katie's footsteps move away from him. The door closed. He could hear Sarah's breathing and tried again to picture her sitting beside him.

"Well, we make quite a pair after all these years, don't we, David—me in my wheelchair and you with your guide dog," Sarah chuckled.

He smiled. "Life doesn't seem to work out the way young people envision it, does it?"

"No, I suppose not," she said.

"Sarah, I want you to know how sorry I am—"

"No, stop. You've apologized for thirty years. I forgave you long ago. We're too old for that now."

"Thank you."

"There's one thing I would like for you to do, though."

"Anything. Just ask."

"I'd like for you to hold me, just once more."

David couldn't believe what was happening. He squeezed the arm of her wheelchair and tried to compose himself.

After a moment, Sarah said, "Well, what's wrong? Can't you find me?"

"I *have* found you." He rose from his chair, one hand still gripping the arm of the wheelchair. He moved his free hand up to her shoulder. Then he leaned over the wheelchair, slipped his arms under hers and pulled her to him.

She wrapped her arms tightly around his neck and pressed her cheek to his. They held each other for a long time, neither in a hurry to move away. The fragrance of her skin washed over him and a picture began to form in his mind. He pulled one hand from behind her back and tentatively touched her face. She did not pull away. Instead, she placed her hand on his and helped him as he gently sketched her features with his fingertips. Gradually her face appeared clearly in his mind, and he remembered it all. He had never seen anything so beautiful.

chapter 48

Jack pulled hard on the laces of his golf shoes. One snapped off in his hand. "I'll be a . . ." He looked over his shoulder toward the shoe cage in the hope that one of the clubhouse workers would have some extras. No one was there. He bent over the shoe and began the tedious process of unlacing and jerry-rigging it.

It was Thursday afternoon, two weeks since Katie and Lizzy had left. He was standing in the walnut-paneled locker room of the Westwood Country Club. The Parsts had been members of the venerable club for five years, a company perk. Jack had never pictured himself as the country club type, but he did enjoy golf on the few occasions when he could find the time.

He was waiting for his longtime buddy Tom Phipps. Jack and Tom had attended law school together at the University of Illinois and were the only two in their class who took jobs in Dallas. Tom was a partner with the elite law firm of Kendall & Matheson and was one of Challenger Airlines' primary outside lawyers. Jack was muttering and threading the frayed string through an impossibly tiny eyehole when a slap on the back jolted him. He turned around and smiled at his bespectacled friend.

"Hey, buddy! How's the bachelor life?" Tom asked. He was already pulling off his shirt and tie.

"Oh, it's great. I'm a real party animal. Just last night I came home from work, had two bowls of cereal for dinner, and went to bed at nine. I'm a regular rock star. You don't have an extra shoelace, do you?"

"Sorry, fresh out. Do you know very many people who carry extra shoelaces around?"

"Who knows? You could have had one in your bag."

"Now that you mention it, I haven't cleaned out that bag for so long, I'd probably be surprised at what's in it." Tom was already down to his underwear and was hopping around on one foot, pulling on his sock.

A few minutes later Jack said, "Okay, I've got this rigged so it ought to hold. Let's go." He slammed his locker door and the two friends walked out of the locker room. As they wheeled around the corner into the hallway, Jack barreled squarely into the ample figure of Julie Stinson. She staggered back a step. He grabbed her arms.

"Well, hey, Jack Parst," she said, as soon as she gathered herself. She flicked her head back and ran her fingers through her feathered black hair. "What brings you out to the club on a Thursday afternoon?"

Julie's khaki shorts revealed the slightest glimpse of smooth bronze thigh. Over what the men of the club had unanimously concluded were man-made breasts, she wore a pink-and-blue-striped golf shirt. Her makeup was immaculate, as if she were going to the opera, not the first tee. She was carrying a golf visor with the club logo, a crape myrtle tree, on the bill. As they talked, she pulled it on, which funneled Jack's attention toward her deep brown eyes.

Despite Jack's disdain for her fashion-conscious approach to the sport, he couldn't deny that Julie was a knockout—and she obviously knew it. She had the demeanor of a woman who considered it a birthright to be the object of men's attention. More than once Katie had complained to Jack after a club social event that Julie had been a bit overly attentive to him. Jack honestly had never noticed, but he always felt that it was his role to act a bit chastened anyway.

"Excuse me, Julie. I should have been watching where I was going instead of storming around the corner like a klutz. Are you okay?"

"I'm fine. Don't worry about it. Are you two gettin' ready to tee off?"

"Yeah. We're hustling out to hit a few on the practice tee, but I don't know if we're going to make it."

"I must be playin' right behind ya. I'm meetin' a friend from over in Settleton. It's a beautiful day to play, isn't it?"

"Sure is. Couldn't be better."

"I'm sure we'll see ya out there. Hit 'em straight."

"You too," Jack said. He realized that he should have introduced his friend, but it all happened so fast that he didn't think of it. He and Tom continued down the hall toward the back door.

"Who was that?" Tom said. He looked over his shoulder as Julie disappeared into the women's locker room.

"Julie Batton. Wait, it's Stinson. Julie Stinson. She used to be Batton, but she changed her name back to Stinson after she got divorced a year or so ago. Her husband was a big wheel at one of the banks in town. He must have been seventy years old or so, almost twice her age. She supposedly had a thing going with one of the tennis pros out here. Her husband learned of it and threw her out, no questions asked. He was a tough old goat. It was big-time gossip around here for a while."

"One thing's for sure. She's a babe."

Jack did a double take. Tom was happily married and as true-blue as could be. Jack had never heard him comment on any woman other than his wife, Jennifer.

"Cool down, Romeo," Jack said.

"Hey, I was just commenting, not ogling."

"Oh, I see. That's a distinction I'll have to think about for a minute."

"Get outta here."

"Okay, okay. Looks like we're not going to have time to hit any balls. We'd better head for the tee."

The two wound their way through the pro shop's colorful maze of overpriced golf attire and down the steps to their waiting golf cart. They had picked a perfect day to play. The leaves flickered silver-green in the sunlight. Red and white petunias lined the stone path to the tightly manicured first tee.

Jack was not the golfer he used to be, but he was still capable of posting a good score once in a while if everything was clicking. Today it was. By the time they finished the front nine, he was only two over par, despite having missed a three-foot putt on number seven.

As their cart flew by the concession stand halfway between the ninth green and tenth tee, the smell of hot dogs drifted over them. Tom slammed his foot on the brake. They skidded to a stop. Jack's hat flew off his head and out the back of the cart.

"What the . . . !"

"Hungry?" Tom said.

Jack looked around. The course was almost empty, so no one was pressing them from behind. "Great idea."

Before long they were munching dogs at one of the wrought-iron tables on the little patio. As they got up they heard the whir of an electric cart approaching from behind. It was Julie.

"Hey, guys. Mind if I join ya?"

Jack looked around with a puzzled smile. They hadn't seen her behind them all afternoon. "Sure, but where did you come from?"

"I just finished number eight. My friend never showed up. I waited and waited and then decided just to come out and play by myself. When I saw you guys on the green, I decided to skip nine and come ask ya if I could play along. It's really not much fun to play alone. D'ya mind? If you're talkin' business or somethin', just tell me, and I'll go back and play by myself." She batted her eyes.

Jack tried to recall if he'd ever seen a woman older than eighteen bat her eyes. After a few seconds he gave it up. "Sure, come on and join us," he said. "We'd be glad to have you. Julie, this is my good friend Tommy—er, Tom Phipps. I'm the only one who calls him Tommy. I've known him since law school."

"Nice to meet ya, Tom. I'll bet you've got some stories to tell about Jack."

Jack thought Julie's tone suggested considerably more familiarity than actually existed between the two of them. "Actually, I was almost as dull as a child as I am now," he said.

"I don't know about that. I'll bet there's been some partyin' goin' on since you've been batchin' it," she said.

That settled it. Everyone in town must know. "Oh, yeah. It's getting so wild in front of the house that the neighbors are demanding crowd control," he said.

The threesome worked their way through the next few holes. On the thirteenth tee, the muffled sound of a cell phone ringing came from the side pocket of Tommy's golf bag. Tommy snarled at the bag, unzipped it, and pulled the phone to his ear. "Hello?" A long pause. "Has anybody called opposing counsel to ask him to put it off until tomorrow morning?" Another pause. "What about Cynthia? Can't she handle it for them?" he said. "Okay, call Stephen and tell him I'll meet him at Judge Feingold's courtroom at four-forty-five. I guess I'll just have to show up in my golf clothes. Be sure to call opposing counsel and tell him we intend to be there, and we expect him to wait."

Tommy shoved his phone back into the golf bag. "I'm sorry. Some jerk over at Manley & Tate is trying to get a temporary restraining order against one of my clients. He called and said he was going to be at the courthouse at four-thirty. I've got to go. The client won't let anybody else handle it."

"Oooh . . . you must be a real big shot," Jack said. He raised his hands above his head and bowed toward Tom.

"Shove it. Look, I'll take our cart, and you can ride with Julie. There's no sense in your having to quit just because I've got to leave."

Jack stuck his hand in his back pocket. "I don't know, Tom, I hate to—"

"Sounds great to me. We'll knock 'em dead, won't we, Jack?" She tilted her head and raised an eyebrow.

Jack shot Tom a frown.

Tom smiled. "That's the spirit, Julie. You two *will* knock 'em dead, won't you, Jack?"

"Yeah, sure. Don't worry about us. Julie and I will probably par out, won't we, Julie?" he said, halfheartedly.

"Par? We may birdie out," she said, perkily.

Tom moved Jack's bag onto Julie's cart and strapped it in. "Adios." He gave them a backhanded wave and sped off toward the clubhouse.

"Well, let's get goin'. Maybe you can teach me a few things," Julie said.

"I seriously doubt that," Jack said.

Jack was pleasantly surprised to find that Julie was entertaining company. Over the final six holes, he learned about her interest in gardening, her love of golf, and the mathematics retreat her daughter was attending in Austin. She brought up Patch once, while she was talking about her boy. With sympathy in her voice, she asked how Jack was handling it, whether it was getting any easier. She didn't bring up Katie or Lizzy at all.

When Julie's putt gurgled into the hole on the eighteenth green, Jack was prepared to give the obligatory, "Hey, I really enjoyed it. See you later."

Julie preempted him by saying, "How about a drink? I'll buy."

She said it with such assertiveness that Jack was taken aback. "Sure. I'd be glad to," he said.

"I'm going to shower," she said. "Meet you in thirty minutes? Nineteenth Hole?"

"I'll be there," he said. "I'll take care of the cart and our clubs." He took off his cap and scratched the back of his head as he watched her walk toward the locker room. Something told him he should leave. He could make his apologies later. Instead, he pulled the cart around the corner, dropped off their clubs, and headed for the men's locker room.

chapter 49

The windowed back wall of the Nineteenth Hole Grill provided a panoramic view of the final green and fairway. Jack sat at a table directly in front of the big-screen television and waited for Julie. Having tossed his jacket and tie in the car after showering, he was wearing gray slacks and a blue button-down shirt. The six o'clock news was just coming on when Julie walked up to the table.

"Ah, I feel so much better," she said, shaking her still damp hair. She wore a khaki skirt with a cream-colored knit top. "This is my 'vision of beige' look. Do you like it?" She twirled around next to the table.

Jack swallowed. "It's . . . visionary."

"You're a witty one, Mr. Parst."

He stood and helped her with her chair. He noticed that she had lost the made-up, primped-up look of earlier that afternoon. He found her disheveled hair thoroughly intriguing.

She pulled their scorecard from her back pocket and scratched out some figures with a stubby pencil. "You had an eighty-three. I'm impressed!" Julie said. "I had a ninety-two, which is not bad for me either."

"If I'd hit it nearly as well on the back nine as the front, I'd have shot a whole lot better. What do you want? I'll go up to the bar and get it. It looks like the waitress is taking a break." Jack nodded toward the lithe young lady who was leaning against the kitchen door, chatting with one of the assistant tennis pros.

"No, I'm buying."

"Okay. I'll have whatever they've got on tap. A cold beer sounds pretty good right now."

Julie got up and headed for the bar. Before long she was back with four bottles.

"What's this? I only want one, really."

"That's okay," she said. "They had a special on this imported Dutch beer. Neat bottle, huh? I've never heard of it, but it's different. I thought you'd probably like it better than that watery stuff they have on draft. We don't have to drink it all. It's here if we want it."

They chatted about the golf game, about Tom and Jack's law school adventures, about other club members and the current gossip. They went through the four beers, and Jack went to the bar two more times to restock. When they finished those, Jack glanced at the TV to check the Rangers' score. It was already the eighth inning. He looked at his watch. "Wow, how long have we been sitting here? I've really got to go. It's almost ten o'clock."

"Oh, my. I didn't realize it was gettin' so late," Julie said, looking at her own watch.

The two stood up. Julie swooned and grabbed the arm of her chair. "Oh, my! I haven't had this many beers at a sittin' for a while. I'm a little tipsy, I think. I don't know if I ought to be drivin'. I think I'll ask them to call a cab for me. I can come back and get my car tomorrow."

"There's no need for that. I'll drop you by your house."

"Oh, that's sweet of ya, Jack, but it's too much trouble." She slumped back into the chair and put her hand to her forehead.

"No. It's no trouble, really," Jack answered. With the help of the beer, he was feeling something he hadn't felt for a long time—at least with a woman other than Katie. He really wasn't seriously contemplating acting on it, but it was exciting enough that he wasn't ready to be done with it either. "As I recall, you live over on Myrtle Drive, don't you?"

"Not anymore. Now I live on Whitehaven, over by Terrence Hall High School."

"That's even better. That's barely out of my way at all. Let's go."

"I really appreciate it, Jack. I'm embarrassed that I've put myself in this situation. I hope you won't think badly of me." She placed her hand lightly on his arm.

"Don't be silly. I admire you for having the good sense not to drive if you think you've had too much," he said, with the over-the-edge sincerity of a man who's had too much to drink.

When they got to the car, Jack opened the door for her. Her breast brushed his arm as she slid by him into the seat. On the way to her house, they made small talk until they were within a few blocks. She curled her legs up on the seat and leaned closer to him. "Jack, I feel so bad that you went out of your way to give me a ride. Why don't ya let me make it up to ya? When we get to my house, come on in and let me fix ya some scrambled eggs and bacon. I'm just starvin', and I always have loved eatin' breakfast at night. It makes me feel like a kid."

Perhaps because of the sun that day, her cheeks appeared flushed, even in the low light that filtered through the windows into the dark interior of the car. The responsible side of his brain urged caution. "What about your daughter? Won't she be getting ready for bed?"

"She's in Austin this week, remember?"

"Of course. Scrambled eggs, though? At nine-thirty? I will say, however, that when it comes to scrambled eggs, nobody makes them like Jack Parst." He focused on the road and wondered if what he had said sounded as stupid to her as it had to him. He reminded himself of a high school kid trying to impress a cheerleader. Glancing over again, he noticed that her left hand rested on the side of his seat, within inches of his hair. If he went in her house, he knew she would expect him to stay until morning.

"It's that one over there on the right," she said.

Jack pulled up to the curb in front of an ivy-shrouded colonial. When he slipped the car into park, Julie slid as close to him as the bucket seat would allow and leaned her face within breathing distance of his. He could feel the warmth radiating across the sliver of space between them. He clenched the knob of the stick shift.

She eased her hand over to his and gently traced the back of his wrist with her fingertips. "Won't ya let me fix ya breakfast, Jack? It's the least I can do to pay ya back for the ride."

He noticed that her lipstick seemed to be virtually gone, but where? In its place were moist, natural lips, and they were within inches of his. There was something about the way she smelled—flowers, or something else from a garden, maybe. She must have put it on in the locker room. She moved her hand from his and placed it lightly on his knee, sending a guilty, but irresistible, shudder through him.

She raised her free hand, twisted her fingers gently in the hair on the back of his head, and let her nails glide slowly behind his ear and down his neck to his collar, sending chills down his shoulders and back. After slipping her nails lightly side to side just beneath his collar, she let her fingers meander back up through his hair again. Gently nudging his face toward hers, she closed her eyes and parted her lips as she raised them toward his. Any thought Jack had of resisting had evaporated when her nails began to slither down his neck. He leaned forward and turned his head to meet her.

Just as he felt the brush of her lips against his, an image of Katie and Lizzy flashed through his mind. *What am I doing? I'm not strong enough. Help me.* Every muscle in his body tensed. Julie pulled back with a puzzled expression.

"No . . . No. I'm sorry, Julie, I can't come in. It's late. I've got to get home." He leaned back in his seat. Her demeanor changed in a way that shocked him. The look on her face wasn't anger or embarrassment; it was abject loneliness and rejection. He felt sorry for her, but afraid of her at the same time. She opened the door and got out without a word.

Jack pulled away from the curb and waited for the rush of guilt that he deserved to feel. It never arrived. Instead, he was strangely exhilarated, as if he had won a big game or a successful verdict. Initially he was perplexed, but then it came to him. He *had* won. He knew that he was a lot of things, many of which lately he didn't like at all, but he wasn't a cheater; he wasn't an adulterer. God had helped him when he was too weak to help himself. He was married to Katie and he loved her. Realizing that, he had never felt so free.

WHEN HE GOT BACK TO THE HOUSE, Jack went straight to the kitchen telephone to call Katie. The voice mail signal was beeping when he picked up the phone. He dialed the number to check his messages. A man's voice came on the line and said, "Mr. Parst. This is Bill Coniglia at Parkway Hospital. Please call me as soon as you get this message. It's an emergency. Thank you."

Jack thought of Katie and Lizzy. His stomach churned. But they were in Chicago. Parkway Hospital was in Dallas. He listened to the message again, wrote down the number, and dialed it. "May I speak to Bill Coniglia, please?"

"One moment."

Jack sat down at the kitchen table. "Bill Coniglia," a man's voice answered.

"This is Jack Parst. I'm returning your call."

"Oh, yes, Mr. Parst. Are you related to David Allen Parst?"

Jack's shoulders slumped. "I'm his son."

"Mr. Parst, I've got some bad news. Your father was brought in about seven-thirty this evening. He had suffered a massive heart attack. The paramedics did everything they could do, but they couldn't save him. I'm sorry."

chapter 50

Katie sat in a cotton nightgown and pointed the remote at the late-night comedy host's gap-toothed smile. The volume on the family room television was set so low that she could barely hear him say, "Well, I can honestly say that I've never seen a chicken do that before!" She flicked him into oblivion. Dropping the remote onto the chair beside her, she stretched her arms and yawned. She looked at Bandit, who was sprawled on the ottoman next to her feet. "C'mon, Bandit, it's time for bed." She gently swatted him on the rump.

Bandit dragged himself up and stretched. After one all-over shake, he hopped down from the ottoman and trotted toward the stairs.

As Katie rose and reached for the lamp, the phone on the end table rang. Bandit looked over his shoulder. Katie picked up the handset while glancing at the ceiling beneath Sarah's bedroom. In a voice just above a whisper, she said, "Hello?"

"Katie, it's me."

Surprised, she blurted, "Jack?" She quickly lowered her voice again. "Is something wrong?"

"Is Mom asleep? I thought about waiting until morning, but I decided I had to call tonight."

"Yes, she's asleep. Are you all right?"

"I'm fine. It's my father. He's dead."

Katie let herself down into the chair. "Dead?"

"He had a heart attack. I just came home and there was a message from Parkway Hospital. That's where they took him."

"You just came home? Where were you?"

There was a pause on the other end of the line. "I played golf with Tommy late this afternoon. I stayed at the club for a while."

"Was he alone?"

Another pause. "Was who alone?"

"Your father. Who else would I be asking about?"

"I thought you might have meant Tommy."

"Tommy? Jack, what's wrong with you? You told me your father was dead. Why would I be asking about Tommy?"

"I'm sorry. I misunderstood. He was in his motel room when he had the heart attack. He apparently fell and dragged a lamp off a table. A man in the room next door heard the crash. When dad's dog started barking, the man called the front desk."

Katie felt tears rising in her eyes.

"He made it to the hospital," Jack continued. "They couldn't save him."

"So he died in the hospital all alone?"

"Yes, I guess so. Nobody should have to die alone."

Katie thought of Patch and gave up any hope of holding the tears back. She knew that Jack must be thinking of Patch too. "How are you doing?" she said.

"I'm all right. I haven't had time to think much yet. I suppose that's good. Listen, Katie," he said, "I was getting ready to call you just before I got the message from the hospital. I need to talk to you about something, but obviously now's not the time. Will you wake up Mom?"

"I hate to get her up in the middle of the night to give her this sort of news. Maybe we should wait until morning." Katie wiped her eyes with the sleeve of her nightgown.

"She'll be mad that we didn't get her up. You know my mother. She wouldn't appreciate our playing nursemaid to her."

"You're right. I was probably trying to put it off more for my sake. This is going to be gut-wrenching. I'll go upstairs and get her. We'll call you back from the phone in her room."

JACK PACED THE KITCHEN FLOOR. He looked at his watch. *What is taking them so long? Katie must be telling her. That's it. She couldn't just wake her up without explaining.*

He pulled out a chair from the kitchen table. Turning it around backward, he sat straddling it. He wondered how his mom would react. Would she even care? *Of course she'll care. After all, they had some good years. She won't discount their entire marriage.*

He wrapped his arms around the back of the chair and stared at the phone. *Please ring. Don't make me sit here and think.* He tried to keep his mind blank. He pictured an empty blackboard. Before long, though, Patch appeared with chalk in his hand and began to draw. Jack shook his head to erase the image. He couldn't allow it. He couldn't stand that pain now.

He forced himself to think of his father. He knew that he ought to feel something—he wanted to feel something. He tried to focus on the old days, the days in O'Fallon. The only picture that came to mind, though, had nothing to do with O'Fallon. It was the old man in the family room with Shelly. He turned his head and looked past the breakfast bar into the family room. There was the chair where his father had sat. *Why did he come? Why now?*

The phone jangled. Relieved, he picked it up and hit the button. "Mom?"

"It's Katie."

"Where's Mom?"

"She's here. She's taking it hard, very hard. I don't think she's going to be in any condition to talk to you tonight."

"What's wrong? What did you tell her?" He pushed the chair away and stood up.

She lowered her voice to a whisper. "What do you mean, what's wrong? Her husband just died—and your father. Don't you have any feelings?"

He put his hand in his back pocket. "Of course I do. Please, Katie, give me the benefit of the doubt. I just didn't expect her to react so emotionally."

"Wait," she said.

Jack could hear muffled voices, as if Katie had her hand over the phone.

She came back on the line. "Just a minute, Jack. She wants to talk to you."

"Jack? Are you okay?" Sarah asked, in a hoarse voice.

He had never heard his mother sound so broken. "Yes. The question is, are *you* okay?"

"No, I'm not. Right now, I'm more interested in you, though."

"I'm fine, really. Don't worry about me."

"He loved us so much, Jack." Her voice cracked and she sobbed.

After a moment, she said, "I keep thinking of the things I could have done differently . . ."

Jack pulled the phone from his ear and stared at it. He put it back to his ear. "The things *you* could have done differently?"

"I'm sorry, Jack. I can't talk. I'll have to call you tomorrow morning."

He heard her sobbing again. "That's fine, Mom. Whenever you're feeling better. Try to get some sleep."

Katie came on the line. She whispered, "I need to get her back to bed."

"Do you have any sleeping pills she could take?"

"You know your mother. She won't even take an aspirin. If you want to try to convince her, feel free."

"No, you're right. Will you call me after you get her settled?"

"Can it wait until tomorrow?"

"I'd rather talk tonight if we can."

"It might be a while."

"Whenever you can. I'll be up." He carried the phone into the family room and lay on the couch. Closing his eyes, he strained once more to picture the empty blackboard.

JACK WAS SLEEPING WITH ONE ARM dangling off the couch when the phone rang. He sat up and grabbed the handset. "Katie?"

"Yes. She's finally asleep."

He looked at his watch. "My gosh, it's three o'clock." Brushing a hand through his hair, he stood and walked to the kitchen sink.

"You said to call no matter what time. I'm really worried about her, Jack. She's devastated."

"Never in my life have I heard Mom like that. In fact, I've hardly ever seen her cry at all. I'm stunned. My gosh, she hadn't seen him for thirty years." He filled a glass with water and lifted it toward his mouth.

"Actually, she saw him Tuesday."

The glass stopped before reaching his lips. "This Tuesday?"

"Yes. She met him at the airport."

"How did he get to Chicago?"

"Not the Chicago airport, the Dallas airport."

"Mom was in Dallas Tuesday?" He set the glass on the counter.

"Yes. So was I."

"Why?"

"I think she had a premonition. On Monday she decided she needed to see your father. She made it clear there was no time to waste. We called him and flew down Tuesday evening. We took the last flight back out the same night."

"Why didn't you tell me you were coming?"

"We talked about calling you, even about coming by to see you."

"Well, why didn't you?"

"The timing didn't seem right. We were afraid we might mess things up between you and your dad, and, frankly, I didn't know if I was ready to see you. Listen, we didn't know if we were doing the right thing. I guess we should have—"

"It's okay. Believe it or not, I can understand your thinking. I'm glad she got to see him. Do you think she knew he was going to die?"

"I don't know. She was adamant, though. She said it couldn't wait. Strange that after thirty years she would pick this week, huh?"

"Yeah, in fact, it's eerie," he said.

"It was a beautiful thing. As crazy as it sounds, they really loved each other. I hope it gave him peace."

Jack opened his mouth, but closed it again without speaking. He rubbed his hand back and forth across the back of his neck.

"Do you think your mom will be all right?" Katie said.

"She's as tough as they come. She'll be okay."

"I hope you're right. I called your Aunt Becky in St. Louis. She handled it pretty well. She said she wants to have David flown up there for burial. Is that okay with you?"

"Of course. I guess I'm in the best position to help with that, since I'm down here. I'll call her in the morning."

"I'm sure she'll appreciate that."

"How is Lizzy?"

"She slept through the whole thing."

"Good." He leaned back against the counter. "Katie, remember that I told you I was about to call you when I got the message from the hospital?"

"No. When did you say that?"

"When I first called."

"I'm sorry. It must not have registered. What did you need to talk about?"

"About us."

"Oh."

"I've been doing a lot of thinking. I talked to my dad a couple of times—before. I wouldn't say that we exactly became best friends, but he raised some issues that were worth thinking about. He helped me understand some things. There's one thing on which I agree with him completely. I love you and I've treated you very badly. You and Lizzy are the most important things in the world to me. I'm sorry."

"This isn't the best night to have this discussion."

"I know that. I just didn't want to wait another day without telling you how I feel, and how sorry I am."

"I appreciate what you're saying, Jack. Remember, though, you've said the same thing before."

"I know. That's what makes this so difficult. I don't know how to convince you that I mean it. I'll change. I already have changed. I want you to come back. I—"

"Wait. We should talk about this tomorrow. It's late."

"You're right. I'll wait. Will you look in on Mom before you go to bed?"

"What did you think, that I was going to forget all about her?"

"Please, Katie, I'm really trying."

"I'm sorry. That wasn't fair. It's the stress of all of this."

"I'll call in the morning. If anything happens tonight, call me, no matter what time it is."

"I will. Good night."

Jack pushed the button on the phone. As he walked up the stairs, he wondered how he would ever get to sleep. He shook his head. It was not a night for sleep anyway. As frightened as he was of his thoughts, he knew that he could not run away from them anymore. His father had been right about that. It was time to come back. He had to think; he had to pray.

chapter 51

Katie put her car keys in her mouth and juggled a cup of coffee and a *Chicago Tribune* as she reached up to push the garage door button. Sliding the paper under her arm, she twisted the doorknob and stepped into the back hallway that opened onto the kitchen. The coffee cup tilted. A trickle of hot coffee spilled onto the leg of her jeans. She hurried into the kitchen. Dropping the paper and her keys on the table, she brushed at her jeans. "Yeow!"

Sarah was standing next to the kitchen table, talking on the phone. "She's just coming in," she said into the phone. She whispered in Katie's direction, "Are you all right?"

Katie nodded.

Sarah turned her attention back to the telephone. "Yes, I'll be fine. You'll call me about the flights?" She paused. "All right. Thank you for going, Jack. Here's Katie."

Katie took the phone from Sarah. "Hi. I just ran out to Starbucks." She lowered her voice and walked into the back hall. "I needed to get out of the house for a while."

"Yeah, I understand," Jack said. "Did you get any sleep?"

"A few hours. Lizzy got me up at eight. How about you?" She took a sip of her coffee and walked into the laundry room off the hall. She closed the door behind her.

"None."

"None at all?"

"No. What time is it? Eleven? I figure I'll probably crash by two o'clock or so. How's Mom?"

"She's an amazing woman. This morning she was up before anyone. She seems steady as a rock now."

"She *is* a rock. I told you. And Lizzy?"

"She's fine. She'd never even met your father, so it doesn't really register with her. In a little while she's going over to a friend's house to play. Did I hear Sarah say something about flights when I came in?"

"I'm meeting her in St. Louis for the funeral."

"That's good. I'm glad you're going." Katie leaned back against the washing machine.

"She said that you're not going."

"I don't see how I could. What would I do with Lizzy? It was hard enough finding someone for her to spend the night with when we went to Dallas for one evening. She doesn't know very many kids up here yet."

"I'll miss seeing you. I've had a chance to think about a lot of things. I've done some praying too."

"I'm very happy to hear that."

"You know, it was an interesting thing. It's kind of like riding a bike, I guess. The hardest part was remembering how to start and stop, but it all came back to me. The rest was pretty easy."

She smiled. "Well, I'm glad you got the mechanics down. Somehow I think the substance might be the more important part, though."

"I was at it for two hours. Don't worry, there was plenty of substance. I'm really sorry about everything, honey. I want you to come home. I can come get you after the funeral."

"Whoa." She put her hand in the pocket of her jeans. "I appreciate what you're saying. It's a little bit early to talk about that, though."

"I don't know what you mean by early. Is there some sort of time parameter? You've been gone for weeks."

She pulled her hand from her pocket and put it on her hip. "And we left for a reason, remember?"

"You're right. I was getting ahead of myself. I'm just eager to get you both home. Whatever your timetable to get comfortable, though, it's okay with me."

"That's just it. I'm not comfortable talking about this now. Your father died last night. It seems that we should wait until after the funeral to have this conversation. At a minimum, our heads will be clearer."

"Like I said, I'm okay with your timetable, but there is one thing I know for certain. My father would have wanted us to have this talk right now. There was nothing more important to him than getting us back together."

"Actually, there was one thing more important to him."

"What?"

"Your attitude toward God. He believed that he had driven you away. It tortured him."

"How do you know that?"

"He told me, that night at the hospital when you hurt your knee."

Katie braced her hand on the washing machine and waited for a response. There was silence on the other end of the line. "He told me to forget about him, to forget about everything," she continued. "He just wanted me to convince you somehow to come back to your faith. He cared about that more than anything."

"He always had a way with words. You have to be careful, though. He meant some of those words more than others. I learned that the hard way."

Katie knitted her brow. "I'm surprised to hear you react that way. I got the impression that you had come to grips with your feelings toward your dad."

"I thought I was getting there too. Old habits die hard, I guess."

"Well, you'll have time to think about it in St. Louis. Maybe attending the funeral will help."

"I'd like to come to Chicago after the funeral."

She chewed her lip. "Okay. That would be good. We can talk then. No promises, though."

"Fair enough. No promises."

"I've got to get Lizzy going, so I'm going to have to run."

"Can I call you later tonight?"

"Yes."

"Katie? Thank you—for giving me a chance."

"This might surprise you, you knucklehead, but I love you."

"I'm so glad you said that."

She laughed.

"Not the knucklehead part, the 'I love you' part. I'll call you tonight."

"Make it after nine. Lizzy will be in bed. See you." Katie clicked the phone off and stood staring at a bottle of glass cleaner on the shelf in front of her. It occurred to her that life was strange. As sad as she was about David's death, she had a pleasant feeling that he was looking down at her and smiling. After all, it was the first time in months that she had felt real hope for her family.

chapter 52

Jack slouched in the driver's seat of the rented Ford, his elbow propped in the open window, his head resting in his hand. The weather was clear, unusually cool and dry for a June afternoon in St. Louis. The wind rushing through the window flipped and snapped his hair against his fingers. He was gloomy, and the beautiful weather only made things worse.

With one hand, he steered the car up the exit ramp off of I-70. It would be only a few minutes now. He and Sarah hadn't said much since they'd gotten into the car after leaving the graveside. The service had been poorly attended and sad. He had tried hard to concentrate on the preacher's words, but his mind had repeatedly wandered to what they were going to do afterward, what they were doing now.

After his mother's reaction over the telephone on the night his father died, Jack had been taken aback at how little emotion she had shown during their stay in St. Louis. She had behaved more like a close family friend than the wife of the deceased. Becky and Sarah had maintained a cordial relationship over the years. Since their arrival Sarah had seemed more intent on tending to Becky's feelings than to her own. As Jack watched Sarah function under the awkward circumstances, he noted for the thousandth time in his life how much he admired her.

It was on their way to the service that his mom had surprised him by suggesting they drive by the old church after the funeral. She said she just wanted to see the place. He had reluctantly agreed because he wasn't sure how to say no under the circumstances. Clearly, though, something inside of him was fascinated by the idea—in the same way that a child feels irresistibly drawn to a hot stove despite his parents' warnings. Now he had no idea what to expect as they approached the neighborhood.

He thought of Katie and his countenance brightened. Despite her initial reluctance, they had talked about their marriage several times during the few days since his father died. Her resistance had gradually softened. Cautiously hopeful, he was eager to get to Chicago.

He eased the car to a stop sign, then turned onto the familiar narrow street where he had grown up. Steering tentatively between the cars parked on each side, Jack was surprised at how little things had changed. Two narrow brick townhouses efficiently occupied the vacant lot where he had spent so many hours playing catch with his dad. Other than that, the street looked pretty much the same, even better in some respects. The lawns were well groomed. Flowerbeds full of petunias and marigolds quaintly framed the front stoops in red, white, and yellow.

They pulled into the driveway that funneled them to the parking lot between the parsonage and the church. The old black asphalt had been covered over with cream-colored concrete, and decorative pavers lined the crosswalks. It gave the place a lighter, less forbidding feel than he had remembered. He parked facing the side door of the church, the door through which they had walked so many times when he was a boy. He turned the key off and they sat.

As he looked around the church grounds, Jack's mind played back images from his childhood as crisply as if he were watching a home video. He saw himself walking with his mom across the parking lot to the side door, talking about their day. He saw himself playing three-way catch with Wally and Phillip on a muggy summer evening. Between throws they would jump and swat at lightning bugs that flew close enough to tease them. Somehow the fading sunlight always seemed to hold on gamely, just long enough for them to toss it around one more time. And he saw his dad: sharing a corny joke with Don and Betty Franklin in the vestibule, grabbing his coat and rushing out the door the night Bill Caldin lost an arm in an accident at the train yard, tossing the ball and catching it, tossing it again.

"Well, it hasn't changed much, has it?" his mom asked, startling him.

"No, not much."

"Let's go in." She opened the door and struggled out onto her cane.

"What? Why?" She was already hobbling down the sidewalk. "Mom! We can't go in there. It's probably locked. We'll get arrested." He jumped out of the car and hustled to catch up with her as she made her way toward the front of the building.

"Arrested? It's a church, Jack."

"On Sunday. This is Saturday."

She rolled her eyes. "I'll tell you what, let's live on the edge and give it a try anyway."

"Okay, but don't blame me if this time next year you're breaking rocks on the chain gang with your cane. Like I said, it's probably locked anyway."

They paused at the spot near the front steps where Ted Balik's body had sprawled. Sarah looked at Jack. He frowned but said nothing. She turned and worked her way up the stairs, leaning alternately on her cane and the railing. She grabbed the door handle and rattled it. It didn't budge.

"You can always wrap a towel around your fist and pop a window," Jack said. He smiled smugly at her from the bottom of the stairs.

"I don't recall your having been this clever as a child," she said. She shaded her eyes with her hand and peered through the narrow window next to the door.

"You've just forgotten. You should visit more often."

"Let's try the side door." In a moment she was down the stairs and off again with Jack in pursuit.

"Mom, the side door is not going to be open if the front door is locked," he said, as he trotted to catch up. "Let's just leave."

"I've lived long enough to know that sometimes things don't work the way you would think. Let's try it and see."

"If you must."

She struggled up the short stoop to the side door, grabbed the knob, turned it, and pushed the door wide open. She leaned her back against the door and with a flourish swept her hand through the open-ing to invite Jack in. He gave her a good-natured scowl and walked through the door.

They turned to the right, stepped into the sanctuary, and stopped. Against the dim backdrop of the unlit sanctuary, the prisms of the stained glass windows projected a three-dimensional ballet of colored lights and shadows onto the floor and pews and ceiling. The effect on Jack was dizzying. If it had the same effect on his mom, she got over it quickly. Within a few seconds she was moving up the outside aisle and sliding, haltingly, into her usual spot on the second row. Once he recovered his bearings, Jack slid in beside her.

Instinctively he looked up at the pulpit, which had always seemed so huge and imposing when his dad was behind it. What he saw now was only a smallish wooden stand, painted white to match the other furniture. He wondered if the orange crate was still there, if there was a song leader small enough to need it. He pictured Ginger Halley, with her bubbly southern twang, and he smiled.

There were other pleasant memories, too, of Christmas plays and youth group outings and older people who greeted him with smiles and friendly questions about school. Before long, though, the memories of the awful night began to seep over and around the decades of barriers his mind had erected.

At first his memory presented the events clinically, focusing precisely on what happened and in what order. But then the old deep gashes came back and began to fester: the pain, the humiliation, most of all the rejection. He remembered in great detail the events that occurred inside the church. Strangely, though, it was difficult for him to picture the scene outside the church. He remembered generally that the body was contorted, the face gruesome, but his mind could not conjure details. It seemed odd that that part of the picture had faded so dramatically over the years. He had once assumed that he would never forget it.

Eventually all of the questions returned, the questions that to this day remained unanswered: *How could he have done it? Were we really that bad, that much of a burden to him?* As his thoughts turned darker, the muscles in his jaw tightened and began to squeeze out any mushy sentiments that had recently oozed into his head.

When he couldn't stand it any longer he broke the silence in a clenched voice. "I can picture the whole thing, can't you? The pathetic, cheating—" He turned toward his mother and stopped. She was crying and gently rocking, her arms folded across her chest, just as he recalled from thirty years before. He reached over and closed his hand over hers. "Are you okay, Mom? Let's get out of here. There's no need for you to go through this. He'll never hurt us again."

She stopped rocking and looked at him, her moist eyes wide. "You still don't understand, do you? I'm not crying because of what he did. I'm crying because I loved him. When I sit here I don't think of that night. I think of when we were young, of the things we did together, of how much we loved each other."

Jack shook his head. "Mom, how can you say that? This is where it happened. This is where he did it to us. How can you cry for him after that?"

"It was thirty years ago, Jack. I forgave him. I've told you that over and over. Why can't you believe me?"

He pulled his hand away from hers. "You say you forgave him, but you never let him come back." As soon as he said it, he wished he hadn't. "I'm sorry, I—"

Sarah held up her hand. "Stop. There's a difference between forgiving him and sharing my home and, frankly, my bed with him. I know that I forgave him. I just didn't feel that I could let him come back after he had been with someone else. He was no longer mine. That may not make sense to you. I'm not sure it makes sense to me anymore." She shook her head. "For that matter, I'm not even sure I've been honest with myself about it."

"You're a better person than I am," he said. "I've tried, but I can't see how I can forgive him."

She looked into his eyes. "He told me that once too. He said I was better than he was. He was wrong. In many ways he was the one who was better. I don't know why I couldn't make myself take him back.

Maybe I was afraid he would reject me again. I don't know." She looked down and rubbed her thumb over an age spot on her hand, as if trying to scrub it away. "If the tables had been turned, I know that he would have taken me back."

Jack shook his head. "No, Mom."

"It's true," she said. "And you're so like him, Jack."

"Thanks a million."

"That's a compliment. There is something I wish you could have learned from him. Yes, he had faults. But he could never have hated anyone. You really hate him, don't you?"

Jack flinched. "I don't know. I did for so long. I'm not sure now. When he came back he was different from what I expected, from what I had imagined. He did seem to want to help. I'll give him credit for that. But how can I forgive him when I know what he did? Forget about me for a minute. What about what he did to you?"

She closed her eyes. "Do you really think that you help me somehow by hating your father?" She opened her eyes and looked at him. "Don't you know how long I've prayed for you to get over it, to forgive him?"

"I said I don't know if I hate him."

"He was not a bad man, Jack. He was a good man who made a horrible choice, and he paid for it dearly. If you think it didn't matter to him that he lost us, if you think he didn't care that Ted Balik died, then you didn't know him at all. He suffered greatly. Most of all he suffered over losing you."

"He got what he deserved. Don't ask me to feel sorry for him."

"I'm not, and neither would he. But what about the rest of us? I think most people can look back in life and find situations in which they were tempted, and I mean really tempted. I know I can. Sometimes we're strong enough to choose the right thing, sometimes we're not. Sometimes something intervenes, luck or God's mercy, or something else, and saves us from ourselves. Can't you look back and see things like that in your own life, Jack? Haven't you ever been within an inch of a disastrous choice but somehow avoided it?"

He sat back in the pew. Not only could he look back and see it, but he had to look back only a few days. He had been closer than an inch from a choice that would have ruined his life—and he knew whose advice had saved him.

"People don't earn forgiveness," Sarah said. "It's a gift that someone else has to give them. Do you believe that God has forgiven your dad?"

Jack thought for a moment. "I don't know. That's between God and him, I guess."

"Well, do you know whether he asked God to forgive him?"

Jack shifted his weight on the pew. "I don't know that either."

"What do you think God would have done if your dad had asked him to forgive him?"

"He'd have forgiven him, I suppose. That's his job, to forgive."

"You're right. It is his job. Praise the Lord for that. Where would we all be if it weren't? I can tell you, Jack, I'm certain that God has forgiven your dad. I know that your father is in a place where the sins and slights that seem so important to us now are erased from memory. We'll be there with him someday and it will last forever. If God can forgive him and take him to a place like that, don't you think it's time that you forgave him too?"

Jack could feel his resistance weakening, but his lawyerly instincts wouldn't let him quit the argument. "There's one big difference, Mom. Dad never asked me to forgive him. He never even had the decency— or the guts—to ask."

"How do you know?"

"What do you mean, how do I know? He never asked. Even when he came back at the end, he never asked."

"What about the letter, Jack? You remember the letter he sent us, back in the beginning. I begged you to read it, but you wouldn't. He tried. You wouldn't even talk to him. Finally he quit trying. He asked. You didn't listen. Finally, when he knew he was dying . . ." She looked down at her hands again.

"What do you mean, when he knew he was dying? The hospital said he had a massive heart attack."

"He did. He had had several before. There were things he could have done, even open-heart surgery, but he refused. He was ready to go, ready except for one thing. He wasn't willing to go without trying one more time. He was afraid because he didn't want to hurt you any more than he already had. But when I told him about you and Katie, I think he made up his mind that he had to try. He wanted to help you. That's why he came back."

"Why didn't you tell me this?"

"He made me promise not to. Besides, you wouldn't have listened. I had given up on that long ago."

"Where is the letter? Do you still have it?"

"Yes, I've got it. I hope you'll look at it now. Maybe it will change the way you feel."

"I'd like to see it."

"There's something else, Jack. I don't know how to say this, but I think it's important that we talk about it."

"What is that?"

"Patch."

Jack crossed his leg. "What about Patch?"

"You obviously have had a difficult time getting on with your life, and I can understand that. I know how hard it was on me. I can't imagine what you've gone through. But at some point you have to go on. You haven't been able to do that. I see what it's done to your family, and it breaks my heart."

Jack grabbed a pew card from the back of the pew in front of him and rolled it up in his hands. "Do you think I want my life to be this way, Mom? Don't you think I want to go on? It's so hard."

"I know it is. But you've got to wake up each day and focus just on that day. Time will continue to pass and each day will get a little easier."

"Do you know that? Have you ever lost a child?"

She placed her hands in her lap. "No, I've obviously not lost a child. But I lost a husband and a father. I think I know something about going on."

"This is different. Every day I think about the million ways that things could have come out differently, so Patch would still be alive. If the fishing line hadn't been there, if the kids hadn't stopped to help the girl. If I had just been there to help him . . ." Jack rolled the pew card tighter and tighter in his hands. "He was all alone, and he must have been so afraid. That's what I can't get out of my mind. He was under the water and afraid, and alone. I'm his dad, and I wasn't there." Tears filled his eyes.

Sarah touched his face with her hand. "But, Jack, how could you have been there? It was a freak accident. There's no way—"

"Deep inside I know it's irrational, but it eats at me every day. When I was a kid, Dad saved me from drowning in the creek. There was no reason for him to have been there either. Why couldn't I save Patch? I should have been there somehow. Excuses don't bring him back. I was about to die and my dad found a way to be there when I needed him. Patch was about to die and I wasn't there. So he died there under the water, in the dark, alone." He lowered his head into his hands. His shoulders heaved and his breathing lurched. He'd never talked to anyone about the way he felt. In fact, he had barely even acknowledged it to himself.

Sarah put her hand gently on his shoulder. After a few minutes his labored breathing slowed.

"Jack, there was no way you could have saved Patch," Sarah said. She took his hands in hers. "You weren't there, and there was no reason for you to have been there. He was a boy walking home from school. He had a terrible accident. Your father saw you jump into the creek. That's the only reason he was there. You didn't save Patch and you couldn't have. But you never let him down either. Your dad saved you from the creek, but he let you down terribly. You took care of the things you could control. You were a great dad. That's all you could do. Maybe it's time you forgave yourself as well as your dad."

Jack lifted his head and wiped his eyes with his sleeve. "I guess forgiveness hasn't exactly been my thing—for the past thirty years or so." He smiled. "You know, it's funny. The last thing Dad told me was that I needed to move on. He said God might be telling me it's time to get on with my life. Now you're telling me too. I guess with all three of you telling me the same thing, maybe it's time for me to listen." He leaned over and kissed her on the cheek. "You're an angel. You know that, don't you?"

She leaned her head on his shoulder. "I'm no angel, Jack. I'm your mom."

chapter 53

Late on the afternoon after the funeral, Sarah and Jack arrived at Sarah's house in an airport taxi. When they pulled up to the curb, Katie, Lizzy, and Bandit were standing beneath the oak tree in the front yard. Jack helped Sarah out of the cab and paid the driver.

While Jack gathered their luggage, Sarah made her way up the walk. She stopped and whispered something to Katie. Then she kissed Lizzy on the cheek and headed into the house.

Before the cabdriver could hoist their luggage to the curb, Lizzy flew down the walk and into Jack's arms. "Daddy! We missed you!"

"I missed you, too, honey," he said. She wrapped her skinny arms around his waist. He picked her up, hugged her tightly, and noticed the sweet, grassy smell of a little girl who had spent the day playing outside. It was a smell he never wanted to be away from again.

Katie waited under the tree with Bandit's leash wrapped around her wrist. Bandit hopped around so excitedly that he practically turned a backflip as Lizzy and Jack came up the walk. Jack had one bag slung over his shoulder and was wheeling a suitcase behind him.

He had played out the scene in his imagination a hundred times during the flight. Would she cry? Would they kiss? Would they both be so uncomfortable that they couldn't think of anything to say? He had never dreamed, though, of the scene that actually unfolded.

As soon as he reached Katie, she threw her arms around his chest and hugged him, knocking him back a step and giving Bandit's leash an unintended yank. Bandit yelped and hopped sideways, landing right beneath Jack's feet. Twisting to avoid the dog, Jack tripped over the leash. He fell face down on the freshly cut grass, with luggage tumbling to both sides.

Katie threw her head back and laughed. She dropped the leash and helped him up. With grass clippings clinging to his shirt and pants, he looked like an upscale scarecrow. Katie brushed him off and hugged him again. He seized the opportunity to return some romance to the moment. Leaning forward, he gently whispered in her ear, "I love you so much. Can you ever forgive me for being such a jerk?"

Katie moved her mouth near his ear and lowered her voice. "No, actually I can't."

He pulled away and looked at her. She laughed and gave him a long, welcoming kiss.

THEY SPENT THE EVENING playing board games. Lizzy provided a particularly humorous narrative of a recent trip to the Oak Brook zoo, where an ambitious bird stole half of Katie's hot dog and drank from her Pepsi cup. Around ten-thirty, Lizzy wore down. She asked Jack to carry her in to bed. He gladly obliged. When he came back, Sarah excused herself, leaving Jack and Katie alone on the couch.

They discussed the funeral and the visit to the church in O'Fallon. He provided more details about his talks with his father.

He decided that telling her about Julie Stinson would do more harm than good. Perhaps there would be an appropriate time for that, but this wasn't it.

When Katie suggested that it was time for bed, he told her that he was going to stay up for a while. He explained that he wanted to read his father's letter. Without a word, she kissed him on the cheek and got up.

Jack went into the study without turning on the overhead light. He sat in the dark behind the antique writing desk that had belonged to his grandfather. He could recall having been in the study only once before. When Jack was nine, his grandfather had taken him into the room to show him one of his prized possessions: a baseball bat autographed by Mickey Mantle. Jack could recall having been reasonably interested in the bat. The thing that had really impressed him, though, was the toasted syrup smell of his grandfather's pipe, a smell that seemed to have soaked into every element of the room, from the overstuffed couch to the heavy drapes. Jack had felt as if he had been granted a preview admission to a forbidden, manly world of wood paneling, leather, and tobacco.

He flipped on the reading lamp. The house was quiet, save for an occasional creak or groan emitted in complaint of a gust of wind. He turned and looked behind the desk at the wall where the Mantle bat had hung. It was gone. He wondered what had happened to it.

He jiggled open the top drawer and found a manila envelope in the back left corner, just as Sarah had described. Inside was a brittle, letter-sized envelope that had been carefully slit open along the top. Even in the dim light, Jack immediately recognized his dad's precise penmanship. He marveled that there were some things a person never forgot, such as the nuances of his parents' handwriting. In blue ink, the envelope bore the address:

Sarah and Jack Parst
2043 Hampstead Drive
Scudder's Ridge, IL 05156

Jack looked at the envelope for a few seconds. Resolving that he was not going to overdramatize the situation, he carefully pulled out the two sheets of age-stained paper and began to read.

Dear Sarah and Jack,

For the past six weeks, I've thought every day about writing this letter. Each time I sat down to write, though, I stopped, because I knew that I had no right. I still have no right, but I know that if I don't put my feelings down on paper, I will not be able to allow myself to continue to live.

Is it possible for a man to make a choice that is so awful, so hurtful, that it should place him beyond the reach of forgiveness? I believe that the Lord forgives us. And I believe that there is no sin so bad that he won't forgive it. I believe all of that somewhere in the back corner of my soul. But I also know that I have killed a man and cheated on my wife and son. When I think of the enormity of that, I can't believe in my conscious mind that God could ever forgive me—or that he should.

Sarah, you stuck with me through everything; the baseball, the seminary, the church. Through good times and bad, you not only supported me with your love, you sacrificed all of the material things that could have made your life more comfortable. For that I repaid you with selfishness, deceit, and betrayal. I am sorry. So sorry that if I could do or give anything, including my worthless life, to make it right, I would. Please believe that. I am praying—yes, I still have the audacity to pray—that you will find a way to forgive me, not for my benefit, but so that bitterness toward me will not cause another moment of pain and misery for you. I know your kind heart. It is so kind that you may have already found a way to forgive me. That thought tortures me even more, because it reminds me that I never deserved you in the first place. So, in foolishly throwing you away, I was throwing away a gift, a blessing straight from God, not something I had earned. I love you. I will always love you. You have no reason ever to believe me again, but please find a way to believe that.

Jack, my son. Because I made a sinful choice, I am separated from you and your mother. I hope that, in time, you will let me back into your life. I can't bear the thought that I may not see you grow to be a man. But if I never see you again, I have no right to complain. It would be a just punishment. It would also be terrible punishment, though, the most terrible that I could ever imagine. I sometimes think that I would gladly give up my soul to hell for the opportunity to be your dad again. But I can't. I know that my only hope of seeing you again and erasing the awful thing that I've done is to rely on the Lord's grace. I pray that somehow, in this life or the next, your memory of my sin will be erased and all will be forgotten, that I'll be your dad again, that we'll play catch and laugh and fish again. I don't know how that can be, but I know that what is impossible for man even to imagine is possible for God to do. You will have a family of your own someday. Please always remember my mistake and the terrible consequences of it. Don't ever do what I have done.

Please forgive me, Jack. Please forgive me, Sarah.

I love you both,
Dad

Jack sat slumped at the table for a long time after he folded the letter and put it back in the envelope. He was weeping and praying . . . for his dad.

chapter 54

Jack lay with his hands behind his head and listened to the rhythm of Katie's breathing. They had finally gotten home that evening. Having Katie and Lizzy back made everything else in life seem trivial. The drive from Chicago had been hard, but fun. They had stopped to see some sights along the way and had generally made a little vacation out of it.

Jack's mind began to wander sleepily. *Maybe I'll cut back on my work schedule for a while. Need to spend more time . . . That Lizzy, she's a smart one . . . Great to have Katie back . . . Glad it's over . . .* His mind was still racing when he fell asleep and began to dream.

Jack walked down a dimly lit hallway that ended at a cream-colored door. He reached for the knob and swung it open. In front of him, at a considerable distance, was a park. He could see lots of activity, but couldn't make out any of the details. A wood-chip path in front of him seemed to lead into the heart of the park, so he took it. As he got closer, he saw people of all sorts. They were smiling and laughing. Their clothes were brightly colored, as if everyone had on something brand new. Some of them picnicked on the vibrantly green grass; others walked dogs or sailed boats in a crystal-clear lake. And there were kids; they were everywhere. He'd never seen so many kids in one place. They were shouting and giggling and running all over.

He looked up. The sky was deep blue, the bluest he'd ever seen. There was not a cloud in sight. He scanned the sky and puzzled that something seemed out of sorts. Then he realized what it was. There was no sun. The day was incredibly bright, but there was no sun anywhere.

He inhaled deeply. The air was so fresh and full of life that the simple breathing of it, like sucking in pure oxygen, seemed to energize his steps. He continued down a small hill onto a field that sloped gently toward the lake. On a concrete court to his right, some teenage boys played basketball with their shirts off. They glided and bounded effortlessly around the court as another group waited for the next game.

About thirty yards from the lake, he came to a copper-roofed pavilion, framed by a waist-high stone wall and filled with picnic tables. A large group of people—a family, he supposed—was enjoying what seemed to be a reunion. Dishes and trays containing food of all sorts covered two green picnic tables. The smell of fried chicken filled the air. Everyone was laughing and eating.

Some of the older folks held youngsters on their laps and their knees. One cheerful elderly man with a shiny bald head was sitting on a picnic bench and playing with a little girl, about three years old. He held her hands while she faced him from her perch on the shin of his crossed leg. By bouncing his leg up and down at the knee, he was giving her a bumping pony ride. She threw her curly blonde head back and laughed with delight, shouting, "More, Grandpa, more!" Jack smiled at the sheer happiness that radiated from the scene.

As he rounded the corner of the pavilion, he looked to his left and saw an older gentleman standing in the grass about fifty yards away. His back was partially turned. The man had gray hair that splayed haphazardly from beneath the edges of his tan ball cap. He wore a rumpled blue flannel shirt. Jack thought he recognized him. He took a few steps toward the man, straining to get a better look.

The man turned, flashed a big smile, and waved. "Hey, Jack! Come on over!" It was his dad.

Jack began to run. His dad was alive, but how could it be? Jack had so much to say to him, so much time to make up. As he approached, he slowed to a trot. He wondered what had happened to Shelly and the dark glasses. He was close enough now to recognize the ball cap that his dad was wearing: the Savannah Sand Gnats. Just like Patch's cap. Jack had just opened his mouth to ask where he'd gotten the cap when, from just around the corner of the pavilion, he heard a young voice.

"Hey, Dad, grab a glove! Let's play some catch!"

Jack froze. Not twenty feet away, Patch was standing, banging his fist in his glove. He looked exactly the way Jack remembered him: T-shirt, ball cap, and shorts; happy, smiling, and bursting with life. Jack's whole body began to tremble. He searched for words. The only thing he could say was, "Patch?"

"Who did you think?" Patch said. "C'mon, let's play!"

Jack's dad walked over and handed him a limp, ragged old ball glove. Jack turned it over in his hands. He remembered the glove, his dad's glove. "Can you still use this thing?" his dad said. "I've got another one. Be careful, though. He's throwing so hard that I had to stop. My hand can't take it the way it used to."

"Grandpa, you're not old. You just need a new glove!" yelled Patch.

Jack looked at his dad. "You're alive? And Patch too?"

"Yes, and Patch too. He's fine, and we're together. You don't have to worry about him anymore. We'll be here when you're ready—and Sarah

and Katie and Lizzy. It's a wonderful place, Jack. More wonderful than you could ever imagine. And wait until you see the Light. You can't see him yet, but you will someday."

Without even thinking about it, Jack sensed that hugging Patch or his dad was impossible for him here. Strangely, it didn't matter. They were already hugging, although in a way that Jack could not have described. He felt it, and it was just as real as if he were wrapping them both up in his arms, or tucking Patch into bed, or doing any of the thousand other things that they used to do together as son and father, and father and son. They were sharing a lifetime of hugging and roughhousing and fishing and story reading and growing older together, all in that moment. His son was happy, perfectly happy—that was obvious. He was safe with his grandpa. Jack knew the wait wouldn't be long. In this wonderful place, it was just a split second.

Jack slipped the glove onto his hand. Patch tossed him the ball. Before Jack had even caught it, Patch began running away from him, looking over his shoulder. "Throw it over my head, Dad! Watch what I can do!"

Jack tossed the ball in a long, looping arc. Patch turned his back on the ball and ran full speed. Just before the ball reached him, he turned and looked over his shoulder. As the ball passed over his head, he reached out and plucked it effortlessly from the air. He spun and threw a strike back to Jack.

"Not bad, huh, Dad?" Patch yelled. "I've been practicing with Grandpa. I did just what you said. I had faith, and the ball was there."

Jack's dad put on a glove that was lying in the grass. They began a game of three-way catch. Patch threw to Jack, Jack threw to his dad, and his dad threw to Patch, completing the triangle. As they continued their game, for the first time in his life Jack felt perfect happiness. Patch was alive and so was his dad; Jack knew he would be seeing them again soon.

chapter 55

Katie rolled over and focused all of her mental strength on opening one eye to squint at the bright green numbers of the alarm clock: 5:55. The first rays of hazy morning light were swirling through the slats of the plantation shutters. She closed her eye, rolled over, and stretched out her arm to wrap it around Jack. Her hand searched up, down, and across the sheet and pillow, but there was no Jack.

She heard an intermittent tapping from the other end of the room. Peering across the end of the bed, she made out the trim, ethereal figure of Jack against the filtered light. He was standing in his boxer shorts, lightly patting his fist into the pocket of Patch's ball glove, which he had removed from its usual place on the dresser.

She frowned and propped herself on an elbow. He had seemed so much better. Could it be starting again so soon? Her concern disappeared when she caught a clear view of his face. He was smiling knowingly, as if enjoying a satisfying secret.

He still hadn't noticed she was awake, so she continued to watch him. Reaching down to the dresser, he picked up something that looked like a faded, letter-sized envelope, placed it in the pocket of the glove, and closed the glove over it. Then, still holding the glove, he got down on his knees and bowed his head. After a few moments he rose, opened the bottom drawer, gently placed the glove and envelope into the back corner, and closed it again. He was still smiling when he turned and looked into her eyes.